# PRAISE FOR
# *GOING OVER THE FALLS*

"Waeschle's writing is so vivid you can feel the salt spray on your skin and the wind in your hair. This story of surfing, loss and forgiveness is one to savor."

—**Megan Chance,** *Bone River* **and** *A Drop of Ink*

"Reading *Going Over The Falls* is like sitting in the lineup, watching that perfect wave come at you—it builds with speed and strength and then gives you the ride you've been waiting for. Amy Waeschle has crafted a novel with beautiful prose, characters that stay with you, and a story that is as unpredictable as the ocean itself. Catch this wave."

—**Jeff Shelby,** *Killer Swell* **and** *Thread of Hope*

"A thrilling surf adventure, a family drama, a love story, and memorable, complex characters—Waeschle manages all of this in *Going Over the Falls*. Full of suspense, heartbreak, redemption, and unexpected twists and turns, *Going Over the Falls* is a joy to read."

—**Brett Hodus, President,** *Full Tilt Books*

"I love Amy Waeschle's work. She carves a truly unique line as a writer, combining hard-won knowledge of the ocean and surfing with tales of young women on the road that nobody else could tell. *Going Over The Falls* brings all that together with the intricate plotting and rich character development of a strong and fully realized novel. It's Waeschle's best book yet."

*side, A Surfer's*
*alifornia Coast*

"Amy Waeschle is back with another epic surf tale that will take your breath away. Waeschle writes with detail and urgency, her characterization of the sea conveying every mood and nuance. The surfing descriptions read like thriller poetry; your heart races, your fists clench, and you marvel at how an author can capture the distinct personality of every wave in words. *Going over the Falls* is a great read for those who like surfing, like a good love story, like strong female characters—and don't mind getting salty, wet, and gripped from the comfort of their own armchair."

—**Janna Cawrse Esarey,** *The Motion of the Ocean*

"*Going Over the Falls* is a novel about longing, love, and letting yourself trust in something that could crush you or carry you into a dazzling future. Amy Waeschle's characters are achingly human, and her descriptions are immersive, verging on poetic. A great choice for readers craving distant shores."

—**Jennifer Skogen,** *The Haunting of Grey Hills* **series**

"Amy Waeschle knows how to keep the reader interested with keen perceptions into not-so-perfect relationships. This addictive page-turner romance is ripe with seduction and charm, as well as rich and complex characters."

—**Susan Friedmann, CSP, international best-selling author of** *Riches in Niches: How to Make it BIG in a small Market*

"Once again, Amy Waeschle takes you on a memorable journey around the globe with an incredible story of travel meets surf and passion. *Going Over the Falls* will make you want to jump on a plane, ride your first wave, explore a new country, and fall in love all over again. I loved this book!"

—**Mary Osborne, Professional surfer and co-author of** *Sister Surfer: A Woman's Guide to Surfing with Bliss and Courage*

# GOING OVER THE
# FALLS

A NOVEL

AVIVA
PUBLISHING

# AMY WAESCHLE

*Going Over the Falls*
Copyright © 2017 by Amy Waeschle. All rights reserved.

Published by Aviva Publishing
Lake Placid, NY
(518) 523-1320
www.avivapubs.com

Genre: Adult fiction.

Address all inquiries to:
Amy Waeschle, telephone: 360-630-3609
web: www.amywaeschle.com, www.goingoverthefalls.com.

ISBN: 978-1-944335-72-4

Editor: Melanie Austin
Cover Photograph: Karl Lundstrom
Cover & Interior Design: Fusion Creative Works, fusioncw.com
Author Photo: Jeff Schmidt

Printed in the United States of America

First Edition 4 6 8 10 12 14

For my daughters; long may we ride

# PROLOGUE

September 2004

Michoacán, Mexico

Only an hour ago, Lorna had been aboard the *Pearl Shadow*, piloting the big boat home in a menacing storm. Now, she was in the back of a jeep, being driven up the side of a mountain by a stranger. The man behind the wheel snuck another anxious glance at her through the rearview mirror.

*He knows about what happened out there,* Lorna realized, hugging herself tighter.

They entered a small village, and the driver stopped the jeep across the square from the only lit building, a church. The stormy winds outside tore at the banana trees, their shiny leaves flashing wildly in the dim streetlights. Rain like gravel pounded on the roof.

"*Vete!*" the driver said through clenched teeth.

Lorna did not need to use her combat Spanish to understand that he wanted her gone. Stepping into the maelstrom, her bare feet slid into cold mud. Hard rain pelted her skin and soaked through her salty curls. Shivering in her board shorts and T-shirt, Lorna squinted through the blasting grit and rain. The church's six rectangular windows glowed pale in the darkness. "There?" she yelled at the driver, but the jeep sped off, its tires spinning in the muck.

When something large crashed down nearby, Lorna forced her legs to move towards the church. She leaped onto the ancient cobblestone square and splashed through a lake of storm water. At the church door, she paused, breathing hard. What was waiting for her inside? An irrational image flashed into her mind of WANTED posters and a posse of vigilantes waiting to take her away. She thought of the driver's fierce stare.

Before she could make a plan, the door opened and a hunched figure beckoned her inside. He draped a scratchy blanket over her wet shoulders, and then a woman with tired eyes pressed a Styrofoam cup into her shaking hands. Lorna shuffled through the dark entryway to the church. Looking around the room she saw there were no posters; there was no posse. The storm must have created bigger problems than finding a murderer.

But they would come for her eventually.

Through the dim candlelight Lorna noticed the others: people sleeping on the pews, a couple praying at the altar, a young woman huddled on a cot with an infant and several small children. Had someone they loved died, too? At least they had a home to return to—wrecked perhaps, but a home they could rebuild, together. Lorna tried to remember the last time she'd had a home, but her mind went blank. Was that the reason she had come at all, to find a home? And now that dream was gone.

A clap of thunder made her start. Spears of rain smacked the stained glass windows. Her head throbbed and her salty eyelids itched. She lifted the warm cup to her lips, but the sweetness of the liquid made her gag. Swiftly, she dropped the cup into a trashcan and moved to a row of cots. Lorna lowered into one, but the unnerving swaying sensation of being on the boat persisted.

*The boat. Alex.*

A rush of heat flooded her skin, and her mouth parted wide for a scream. When she opened her eyes, she couldn't be sure the sound was her own or the screeching wind's. How had everything gone so wrong?

Lorna didn't feel lucky to be alive; she felt cursed. She would be on the run now, forever.

# PART I

# ONE

May 17, 2004
Vunde Bay Surf Hostel, Fiji

Lorna stepped down from the bus, retrieved her board bag from the undercarriage, and set off down the winding road, the crushed shells grinding beneath her sneakers. Her skin tingled with anticipation. *I've waited so long for this*, she thought.

As she walked, listening to the birds call and chatter from their hidden perches, she packed away the memories of her best friend Miles' wedding on beautiful Taveuni. She recalled the white-sand beach where she had reconnected with old friends—those who weren't deployed—and made her nerve-racking speech to Miles and his bride. And the food! An endless bounty of exotic, fresh fruit, with fish and meat roasted to perfection, *lovo* style, and of course Miles's favorite treats: chocolate-covered bridge mix, pickles, and tart, yellow oranges. Some of the details of her days were lost in the jet-lagged fog she had tried to out-drink, but now she was going to spend every last minute of her remaining week off doing what she loved: surfing.

A long bend in the road ended at a large thatched-roof building. She stepped through a screened entryway, and her eyes adjusted to the low light in the L-shaped room. Halfway along the left wall, a man stood typing at an ancient computer behind a bar made of plywood and fake hula grass. Past him, the view through the glass doors at the end of the large room took her breath away. Turquoise water lapped a white-sand beach crisscrossed by lanky palm tree shadows.

"*Bula!*" the man said with a wide grin. He had large, yellowish eyes and skin like melted chocolate. He wore an oversized, sun-faded polo shirt, and his thin, nimble fingers quivered as if still typing. Lorna noticed that they were the only two people in the room.

After three days on Taveuni, the Fijian greeting came easily to her. "Bula," she replied, and introduced herself. Covering the wall behind him were photographs of surfers riding big, beautiful waves so pure blue they could have been poured from the sky. Lorna automatically searched for someone she used to know in the photos. People used to say Lorna looked like her, but no one had said that in a long time.

The faint whine of an outboard motor caught her ears. Lorna looked toward the water where a small boat entered the bay. Her heart hummed with excitement.

"Is that the surf boat?" she asked the man at the desk, who was dangling her room key from his long fingers. She knew from studying the layout of Vunde Bay that the reefs where the waves broke could only be accessed by boat. She also knew that this boat could be the only one going to the reef that day, due to the tides.

"Yesss," the man hissed.

Lorna stopped herself from whooping out loud.

"*Bure* two," the man said, pointing to a small square on a map.

"Thanks!" Lorna plucked the key from his grasp, remembering that the word *bure* meant *house*.

She sprinted to her bure, a one-room bungalow, and threw on her bikini and board shorts, then popped her fins into her surfboard, and packed her knapsack. Three minutes later she was the last to board the boat, which bobbed in the chop while the dozen other surfers—guys in baggy board shorts and limp T-shirts—stowed their gear and crowded onto the bench seats lining each side. The man at the wheel, a Fijian wearing faded board shorts and a Rip Curl T-shirt stood stoic, his weathered and cracked bare feet planted wide, like tree trunks. Lorna placed her surfboard with the others in the middle of the floor, and looked for a seat.

A few of the surfers were staring at her.

"Well, hello there," one of them said, eyeing her like a hawk.

All heads swiveled her way.

"Here's a spot," another surfer said, sliding sideways to open a space for her.

"Come sit on my lap and we'll see what pops up," a redheaded surfer said in an Australian accent, followed by snickering.

Lorna took an open seat on the bench, hoping they couldn't see her flustered expression. She thought up a few witty replies, but in her head they all sounded lame.

"Let's go surfing!" someone cried, and the Fijian at the wheel pulled the boat away from the dock. Soon they were skimming past beaches of bright-white sand, the palm trees a blur of green, and the only sound the high-pitched whine of the engine. The surfers seemed to refocus on the ride, and Lorna relaxed.

She turned her face to the wind, breathing in the fresh salt, ready for the ocean and riding waves to push everything away. She had often been asked to explain her love for surfing. She knew part of it was the anticipation of challenges that would be solely hers. But it was the way surfing washed her clean that she needed now. No more wedding speeches, tight, itchy dress, or nightmares from her job in the E.R. Nowhere else did she feel this safe, confident, so truly herself.

The boat driver pulled up to a plastic milk-jug buoy floating in the deep, safe channel surrounding the shallow reef. Lorna squinted at a distant mound of white fluff and heard a low rumble. While the driver, whom the others called Veda, anchored the boat, the surfers grabbed their boards and jumped over the side. Lorna was right with them as they paddled in a pack towards the take-off zone.

The water was so warm it felt like a bath, but the afternoon breeze gave her goose bumps. A wave exploded against the reef, the detonating lip sending a plume of white spray into the pale blue sky. A nervous tingle feathered her insides.

One of the surfers paddled up next to her. "Hey," he said with a shy grin. There was something vaguely familiar about him, Lorna noticed. Was it his eyes? They were a sparkly, crisp blue framed by thick dark lashes. Eyes too pretty for a guy, she decided.

"Sorry about earlier," he added, looking sheepish. "That got out of hand."

Lorna shrugged. "Where are we headed?" she asked.

"Vunde's," he said.

"Left? Right?"

"Left. It's been a little choppy in the afternoon." He shrugged. "But still fun."

Lorna nodded. For the past few years, surfing Washington's cold coast had been the only way to get her fix. The waves were good, sometimes even incredible, but it was freezing cold, dark, and sometimes spooky. Vunde's broke from left to right, meaning that she would be riding backside, which some might call a disadvantage, but she was used to it. Her favorite Northwest waves were also lefts.

"I'm Joe," he said.

"Lorna," she replied, keeping pace with him.

"How long are you here?" he asked.

"Four days."

"Wow. Quick trip. Better get busy," he added with a grin before paddling ahead.

Lorna laughed. "Planning on it," she said.

Another surfer paddled near and said, "You ever surfed waves like these before, cupcake?"

It was the redhead, accompanied by a cameraman kicking by in his fins and towing a blocky waterproof camera. *Cupcake?* "Uh, probably," she stammered.

He gave her a shrewd look and paddled off.

She watched him for a moment longer. He had his own photographer? The only people with photographers were professional surfers, and the redhead didn't look familiar. She tried to put his mild threat out of her mind. There were plenty of waves to go around.

At the takeoff, the surfers bobbed in a tight pack, and Lorna settled among them to wait her turn. The first surfer in line paddled for a wave then disappeared behind the wall as the exploding bits of seawater stung her face like a blast of cold sand. She shut her eyes until it passed, her pulse thumping into her throat.

The next surfer dropped in, and the next. Finally, her turn came and she spun for the approaching peak. Watching it rise behind her, she began paddling. *Go.* She burst forward as the speeding rush of water lifted her up. Down towards the trough she flew, her bare feet connecting with fiberglass. The pale blue wall jacked up, towering higher by the second. Adrenaline poured into her veins. She raced forward, carving up then down the face, linking long turns all the way to the wave's frothy end, and soared over the lip as it clamped shut in a roar. She arrived back at the lineup, shaky and breathless, a wide grin stretching her cheeks. *Yes!* she thought. *It's just as incredible as I imagined.* So she did it again and again.

The group traded waves until the tide dropped, and Veda beckoned them in from the boat. Surfers began taking their last waves. Lorna's turn came and she dug hard into the drop, but the sight that greeted her—not a blank wall of blue water but the backside of another surfer—sent a bolt of panic through her brain. Immediately she searched the lip above her for a way out, but it teetered, broken where the surfer ahead of her had dropped in. Could she get around the section? The split second she had to be afraid came too late, and the ocean simply collapsed.

The raw power of the exploding wave made resistance impossible. The ocean slammed her down then bounced her over the reef as if she were a toy. Fighting an increasing sense of panic, Lorna tried to curl up, tried to protect her head, but the current was too strong.

After what seemed like an eternity, the weight of water eased, and she swam towards the light. She broke through the foamy surface with a gasp and lunged for her board floating nearby. Adrenaline fizzed through her veins as she paddled furiously to escape the impact zone.

The next wave loomed, and another surfer paddled into it, above her at ten o'clock. She dug harder with arms already on fire, knowing that if she didn't clear the lip, she risked the safety of the surfer now soaring down the face. Each stroke took her closer to the top, but could she make it? The surfer passed below her like a whisper as she dug the last stroke to the lip and flew over. It collapsed with a boom behind her.

*That was close*, she thought as she cleared the impact zone. Her tired arms felt like noodles. Her ragged breaths echoed inside her head.

Another surfer came alongside her. She turned to see a tanned face with intense blue eyes. Joe.

"Sorry. That was my fault," he said as they continued paddling. "I really didn't think you'd drop into that wave. You were too deep."

Lorna glanced at the handful of remaining surfers hunched together at the takeoff like a pack of oversized birds. When one of them dropped in, the spray from their acceleration fanned out like tail feathers. She stole a glance at the surfer next to her but couldn't read him. Her position on that wave had been perfect.

"You okay?" he asked. "Marty says you went over the falls."

Lorna wondered if Marty had been the surfer she had tried to avoid colliding with. *Going over the falls is a rookie move*, she thought, frowning. "I'm all right," she said, shaking off a shiver.

She and Joe paddled in silence for a moment. "It's cool," she said, "about you dropping in on me." There was something about his voice, soothing and gentle, but strong, too. "Just don't let it happen again," she added with a grin.

"Don't try that at Bukuya," he said. "It's even shallower. Some guy died there last year. Hit his head on the reef."

She had meant to joke with him, and now he was patronizing her? "Okay," she said, feeling awkward.

Lorna rejoined the lineup, hoping to catch one more wave that didn't end in disaster. The cameraman lurking inside the impact zone had focused on Garth—the redhead—all afternoon. Garth took his last wave, then the last two surfers followed, each reappearing in the channel and paddling leisurely for the boat. She moved to the takeoff for an incoming wave but was too late, and it zoomed toward the reef without her. One more try and she would have to follow the rest of the group.

The last few surfers were nearly to the boat before she spotted her last chance. She paddled hard into the steepening wave and jumped to her feet, grabbing her outside rail for stability. Spray peppered her face, blinding her for a thrilling second.

The wave came to life underneath her. She accelerated into it, dropping low into the bowl. As she carved up the wave's face, the feathering lip pitched outward. She ducked beneath it, and the wave exploded against the reef below. She aimed for the oval eye of pale daylight wobbling at the other end of the pipeline. The possibility of getting trapped made her blood race.

*Go.* She knew the safest place on such a wave was inside, even as the walls narrowed. It was so beautiful inside, and still. Her mind emptied, and in its place came a sudden and satisfying quiet.

The wave pulled back, and she flew into the hazy sunshine, blinking away the salt. Once she reached the safety of the deep channel, she noticed several surfers stood watching her from the boat. Joe was one of them, his pretty eyes smiling.

# TWO

Late Afternoon

Vunde Bay Surf Hostel, Fiji

Fixing the dings in her board took less than half an hour, but her trunks, the left hip turned to Swiss cheese by the reef, needed creative patching aided by blobs of seam grip. Dusk had begun its slow creep when Lorna finished her chores, the shadows long and the breeze soft and cool against her cheek.

By the time Lorna made it to the main *bure* for dinner, some of the surfers were leaving with ice cream bars or the remains of an apple or a wedge of ripe melon. Their vibe felt different, warmer, more relaxed. Secretly, she would be thrilled to become part of the group. In medical school, she had so wanted to belong that she had joined the ultimate Frisbee team, meeting for beer and pizza after the games even though she felt guilty about not studying, and eating pizza gave her a stomachache. Though they included her, they treated her as something of an oddity, what with her navy father's political leanings and her eagerness to take on any task, any patient (she had an odd talent for taking down tweakers and a soft spot for old ladies with chest pain), her habit of wearing flip flops into November, and her wild, wavy hair she sometimes clipped with pastel baby barrettes because they were easily replaced and held more hair than one would expect. They had no understanding of her surfing mid-winter and made fun of her obsession with tracking storms, not knowing that surfing was her lifeline, that storms filled her with hope, something that seemed to be in short supply everywhere else she looked. Some thought her an overachiever, an exhausting behavior that Lorna wished she knew how to quit.

Lorna joined the only inhabited table and listened to an older couple's stories of their two-week sailing tour of the outer islands. Lorna had noticed their sailboat anchored at the edge of the bay when they had returned from surfing Vunde's. The couple swam with turtles, ate fresh Wahoo, and helped a village build a water filtration system. They were shiny faced and humble, and their radiating sense of accomplishment filled her with envy.

When Lorna stepped out of the main bure, Garth was there. "Not bad, cupcake," he said, giving her a sideways look.

Lorna had noticed his surfing, too, and was impressed. He seemed to go after only the biggest waves and rode them with an aggressive style, all power. His approval made her feel weird; she repressed the sudden need to chew a fingernail.

His expression changed from mild amusement to scrutiny. "I feel like we've met before."

Was he actually trying to pick her up, or was he still messing with her? "I don't think so," she said, and continued down the steps.

She headed for her bure, but a group of surfers were gathered down at the beach. Some had already claimed the hammocks, and the sand was decorated with empty Fiji Bitters. One of the surfers, Joe, was playing a guitar, and a few other surfers were lounging in lawn chairs or perched on the edge of where the stubby grass met the sand.

She was about to pass them when Joe's blonde friend Marty called out, "Lorna!" He opened a beer with an opener hidden in the bottom of his flip flop, and handed it to her. "The guest of honor's here," he said, grinning.

As if this was some kind of cue, Joe said, "Hey, Lorna!" and the other surfers greeted their hellos too, as if they were all old friends.

"Hey," she replied, feeling the blush rise up her neck. She accepted the beer and settled onto the grassy ledge at the edge of the sand.

"That was awesome, seeing you drop in on those bombs today," Marty said. His nose was pitted with bright red patches of new skin after a recent peel and his blonde hair had that scruffy surfer look. He wore a gray wife-beater T-shirt with "I'm in Heat," written in bold letters across the front.

"You caught some nice ones, yourself," she replied, sipping her beer. She noticed some oozy, red gashes on Marty's foot. Reef cuts.

"Yikes. Where'd that happen?" she asked, pointing to the cuts.

"Bukuya."

Lorna remembered Joe's comment: *don't try that at Bukuya.* "Want me to take a look?" she asked.

"Nah," Marty replied. "Thanks, though."

"So, what's Bukuya?" she asked. "Everyone keeps talking about it."

"You saw those pictures behind the check-in desk?"

Lorna nodded, remembering the pale blue barrels spinning over the surfers tucked inside. She also remembered looking for her mother, Alex, in the pictures, even though she would never surf a place so . . . discovered. Alex had been gone for six years, on a quest for unknown, far-off waves. Searching for her version of paradise.

"That's Bukuya. There's a boat going tomorrow."

Lorna's pulse jumped at the thought of riding waves at such a spot. "What's the swell—?" A loud whistle coming from the direction of the main bure cut her off. She could just make out Garth's silhouette and the glowing end of his cigarette. "Is he some kind of pro or something?" she asked Marty.

Marty opened a beer for someone. "Yeah, from West Australia."

"Ah," Lorna said, putting Garth's profile together in her head: the bone-crushing, sharky surf would make him especially ballsy, the blue-collar, backwoods town he crawled out of would make him crass and chauvinistic. She dropped his "I feel like we've met" comment into her mental file folder for cheesy pickup lines.

Three surfers were heading up the lawn toward him. *He whistles for them and they come like dogs?* "Where're they off to?" she asked.

"Most likely the Hostile Nautilus," Marty replied.

"The what?" Lorna asked.

"It's down the beach a ways," Marty said, nodding to the east. "It's called The Nautilus but it's more like a hostel, and, well, it's mainly girls there . . . "

"And they're hostile?" Lorna asked, still confused.

"No," Marty replied, blushing, "they're not hostile."

"Oh," Lorna said, making the connection. She wondered if she had misjudged their welcoming vibe. Maybe they were still waiting for her to do lap dances or jump out of a cake.

"It's not what you think," Joe said from the hammock, still strumming. "It's just a cheap place and a lot of Aussie kids stay there."

Lorna looked away.

Chords and soft singing floated from the direction of the hammock, and it stirred up the few good childhood memories she had put behind her, of beach barbeques with music and friends and warm nights filled with stars. An image of her mother, Alex, her blonde hair shining in the firelight, filled her thoughts. Lorna pushed the image away. Alex was out of her life, and Lorna was better off if it stayed that way.

"So how'd you end up here, Lorna?" Joe asked, pulling her out of her thoughts.

Lorna paused. She still wasn't sure what to think about the surfer who had dropped in on her then scolded her like a child. "I had a week off, and wanted to surf."

"And?" Joe's dark hair had fallen over his forehead, and the sideways look he was giving her from the hammock made her feel like they were sharing some sort of secret.

Lorna wasn't sure what he meant. "And I . . . What do you mean?"

"This is a long way to come for just a week." His muscular arms flexed as he changed chords.

Yes, it was a long way. And incredibly expensive. She'd scrimped for a year and a half to afford it. But Miles had asked her to be his best man, and there was no way she could turn him down. "I was in a wedding."

"Not yours, I take it?" Marty teased, tipping back his beer.

Lorna laughed. "No. A friend's. At a resort on Taveuni." Lorna thought back to the endless white sand beach, the blooming flowers, the resort's fancy details. Nice, romantic, and totally not her style. And no waves. "And then I came here."

"Where you from?"

"Hawaii, Bremerton, Sicily, Seattle." She sipped her beer.

"Navy," Joe said in a knowing voice.

Lorna wondered how he knew; most people thought her parents were gypsies. Or spies. She was especially thankful that he hadn't called her a navy "brat," a term she loathed.

"Is there surf in Sicily?" Marty asked, raising an eyebrow.

Lorna scooped her feet through the cool sand, the grains tumbling through her toes. Her memory flashed to one session at Agnone, a steep beach break sheltered from south winds. The overhead swell detonated on the sand bars, and the paddle out was tricky. A young Sicilian couple had been necking in their fur-lined parkas on one of the benches, too consumed with their passion to notice the danger she faced.

"Inconsistent, but there were some fun days," she finally said.

The quiet music Joe was playing sounded familiar somehow, but she couldn't place it. When she snuck a glance, his purposeful fingers told her that playing music was more than a pastime.

"What about you guys?" she asked, plucking a tiny shell from the sand.

"Santa Cruz," Marty said.

"Steamer Lane," she replied, imagining the pictures of the famous point break published regularly in surfing magazines. With the right conditions, waves at Steamer's peeled in long, clean lines, and unlike many spots, were sheltered from northwest winds.

"Ever surf it?" Marty asked.

Lorna shook her head. "Never been to California," she replied.

"What?" Joe stopped playing. "Every surfer needs to surf Steamer's."

"Is that so?" Lorna replied, raising an eyebrow. What did Steamer Lane—with its hundreds of overly possessive locals who beat up outsiders just for checking the waves from the cliff—have over her secret spots in the Northwest? Surely not resident whales and powdery sand touched by only one set of footprints.

"You coming to Bukuya tomorrow?" Joe said. "Could be epic."

Lorna took a deep breath. "I'm in," she said.

# THREE

Joe followed Marty up the dark jungle trail, trying not to trip. He was especially wary of the big spider webs he'd seen strung between branches.

"So what's her story?" Marty said, peering back at him.

Joe's stomach did a loop around his liver. He knew Marty was talking about Lorna. "She's lived in Sicily," was all he could think to say. Meanwhile the image of her silhouette—lean and curvy in all the right places—backlit by a teal-green wall of tropical water played in his mind. He'd also noticed her stormy eyes and the handful of faint freckles dotting her slightly rounded and very cute nose.

"I don't think she likes to talk about herself," he said. She had seemed slightly uneasy, as if nervous about something. It bothered him, especially after she'd blown everybody away in the water that afternoon. It seemed odd that someone so confident in the water could be uncomfortable on land.

Marty bumped into something and cursed. "She's smokin' hot," he said as he continued walking.

"Easy, killer," Joe said as his left toe jammed into a root. He grimaced. "Aren't you almost married?"

"Emphasis on the *almost*," Marty replied. "And you've got a little hottie waiting for you at home. So what? Why not have a little fun?"

In the dark, Joe scowled at Marty's back. Francine could wait as long as she wanted; he was done with her drama. When they'd met at the Salt Shaker, back when he was just the opening band, he'd fallen for her long, curly hair, hazel eyes, and tall, tanned legs she liked to show off with short skirts. Looking back, he guessed that dating someone in a band had gained her some sort of status among her friends. That was how she was. The idea of seeing her again made his head feel weird, light and heavy at the same time, like it was lopsided and needed to be shaken to get everything evened out.

"I'll bet she's a wildcat in the sack," Marty said as they neared the dorm's soft lights.

Joe gave Marty's back a shove. "Too bad you'll never know," he said.

# FOUR

Lorna woke early from a deep sleep, and went for a run along the beach. The air was clean and cool compared to the afternoon before. After changing, she grabbed some melon slices and a cup of murky Nescafe from the buffet in the main bure and packed a lunch from the spread laid out for guests going to Bukuya.

On her way out of the dining area, she noticed a tiny office tucked behind the bar, complete with a large computer and fax machine. A pale-faced man with thinning hair and bright, cornflower-blue eyes was speaking into a phone. The man turned and saw her. "I think she's right here," he said into the phone, then pressed the receiver into his chest. "Are you Doctor Lorna Jacobs?" he asked her.

Lorna nodded.

"It's for you," he said, extending the phone in her direction.

Lorna frowned. *What the hell?*

The man turned back to his computer. His nameplate in front of his keyboard said "Shaun Freeman, Manager."

Lorna put the phone to her ear. "This is Dr. Jacobs," she said.

"Lorna!" a familiar voice said. It sounded like Yoko, one of the residents in her program at the University of Washington Medical Center. Lorna could hear the sounds of the E.R. coming through the receiver: the shuffling of busy feet, computer keys tapping, the faint wail of a siren, the constant chatter.

"Yoko?" Why was Yoko calling? "What's wrong?"

"Your mom is here."

Lorna froze. An image of Alex sitting in the waiting room, scowling, flashed into her brain. Alex hated to wait. "Well, I'm in Fiji," she stammered and then remembered that everyone in the E.R. knew about her trip. Why was Alex in Seattle? She hadn't visited since Lorna's college graduation six years ago. And why was Alex in her E.R.?

"I told her that, but she won't listen."

"Wait, is she there just to see me, or is she a patient?"

"Both," Yoko said, sounding flustered. "I guess she came in saying that she was your patient and demanded to see you. They told her that you weren't here. Then she tells them that she's a relative, and she's only here for a day. I think they thought she was sort of crazy. They told her that this wasn't a place for family visits. Then, she sort of collapsed."

Lorna's pulse popped into her ears.

"I might be breaking privacy laws telling you this, but she did say I could call you."

Sharing patient information illegally was a sure way to end a career as a physician and could put you in jail. Lorna squirmed at the thought of putting Yoko in danger.

*Collapsed.* Alex was as tough as nails. Lorna began to get a bad feeling.

"She's got right upper quadrant pain. I'm waiting on blood and ultrasound results."

"Gall stones?"

"That's what I think."

Lorna knew it could also be appendicitis, cancer, or indigestion. "Does she want to talk to me?"

"I don't know. She's at ultrasound right now."

"Okay," Lorna said, hearing the sound of Veda's outboard motor enter the bay. *Epic Bukuya.* She tried to turn off her doctor brain, which was already running away with Alex's test results, chasing down a diagnosis, recommending treatment.

Should she skip the trip to the reef? Bukuya was an all-day event. By the time she got back, Alex might be discharged.

Or in surgery. Or admitted for a biopsy. Or . . .

Surfers from the main bure and from the path leading from the guys' dorm began to file down to the dock. An undeniable urge tugged at her heart. This might be her only chance. Bukuya was a fickle reef pass that sometimes didn't break for weeks or even months. She had only three more days to experience something that felt as vital to her as breathing. Alex, of all people, would understand. After all, her motto had always been: "When Neptune throws you perfect barrels, everything else can wait."

"I'm sort of heading out for the day," Lorna said, cringing at how awful it sounded.

"Oh, right. How's the surfing?"

"Pretty good." The surfers were filing down the dock.

"Okay, well, we'll take good care of her."

"Thanks," Lorna said. "I'll check in when I get back," she added before rushing out of the office to her bure.

Lorna stuffed her lunch, a hat, and a full water bottle into her knapsack, tucked her board under her arm and raced down to the dock.

The minute Veda pulled up, the group clambered on board, and the boat sped from shore, engine roaring. Lorna tried to piece through the conversation with Yoko, but it was such a jumbled mess her head started to pound. Alex had gallstones, and yes, it was painful, but it was an easy fix. Yoko would treat her, and then Alex would take off again. She had said she was "only here for a day." Typical Alex. In such a rush, unwilling to slow down. Even if Lorna left today, she would miss seeing her because Alex wouldn't wait. And why should she cut her trip short? Alex had never done that for her. Lorna watched the endless expanse of choppy seas, her butt bouncing against the hard seat.

After a long ride, the reef appeared on the horizon as a barely distinguishable mound of white fluff. The boat's engine masked any sound coming from the eruption of waves, making it impossible to evaluate the conditions. Veda simply pulled the boat to a stop in the deep channel, far from the impact zone. The boat became a flurry of bodies slathering sunscreen and donning rash guards and reef booties. Lorna was the first to jump off the boat, and set off with hard strokes.

A few surfers passed her, but Lorna didn't watch them. She knew that she needed to focus, get her head in the right place. The rumble from the waves intensified while a slight offshore wind whispered across her bare calves. She watched peaks rise up and break evenly, left to right like falling dominoes. Were the waves six feet high or ten? A twinge of anticipation fluttered through her insides. *Alex*, she thought, imagining her in ultrasound.

Alex had brought Lorna to her first big reef wave when she was ten years old. How scared Lorna had been. She remembered the speed—so much speed—like flying, with thunder at her heels. Playing with an energy force so pure and terrifying, yet beautiful, had given her a rush like nothing before. She had raced down the line and over the lip, flying high above the water for an instant before plunging down, feeling electrified. Something had changed that day. Surfing became her own thrill, not just something she did to get Alex to notice her.

Lorna reached the takeoff just as another surfer from their group dropped into a wave, his silhouette black against the pale blue wall. A tremor of fear and anticipation went through her. She caught a fleeting thought: *if only Alex were here.* But Lorna knew that wasn't possible. Alex would never come to a place so commercialized. Besides, after a childhood of chasing Alex from wave to wave, waiting for her to come home only to wake up in the morning to find her still gone, being dragged to surf spots that were remote, scary, and dangerous, Lorna had sworn she would never surf with her again, never wait for her again, never go looking for her again.

But Alex was at that very moment in her E.R., asking for her. *She needs me, really needs me. And not just to pay the energy bill on time or fix the leaky faucet.*

Lorna paddled the remaining distance to the lineup. The horizon was lined with dark ridges of approaching swell for as far as she could see. A light mist seemed to hang in the air from waves exploding to bits against the reef, and the bright sun turned each droplet into shiny prisms, the effect like being inside a fizzing rainbow. The fast current pushed her away from the lineup, and she had to paddle back into position almost constantly. There was no time for small talk or jokes, and no room for error.

When her turn for a wave came, she let another surfer take it. Another turn passed, but out of the corner of her eye Lorna watched the surfer drop into the sparkling sheet of pale-blue water. The wave exploded against the reef, its mist dusting her face and lips. Her heart wanted to be on that wave. Why was she letting someone else ride it? Here she was at a world-class reef on a perfect day. *When Neptune throws you perfect barrels, everything else can wait.*

Lorna made up her mind.

A peak steamed towards her. She spun for it, paddling deeper while making a slow turn toward the reef. In an instant the wave was looming, roaring like a jet engine. The offshore wind seemed to shear the top layer from the slope of heaving water, blinding her with ocean spray as she stroked into the drop. She punched to her feet and crouched low, blinking her eyes clear. The frosty blue lip reached forward, and she felt as much as heard it folding over her. The lip began to throw perfectly in her peripheral vision, and she tucked inside. Her breath echoed as the walls closed in on her; she watched the end of the tube, willing it to stay open. The room of glassy water shone pale green, yellow, turquoise, and her heart leapt with elation. Time seemed to slow down, yet the reef shimmering below the surface flew by so fast she knew that, if anything, time was speeding up.

Suddenly, she burst into sunlight. The channel still seemed far away, so she arced high for the lip then soared back down, as the thundering wave chased her heels. Sparks of joy erupted inside her chest, tingled over her skin. Again she turned, this time getting airborne off the crest. In the deep channel ahead, she spotted a surfer paddling back out, his head turned her way. The slope of her wave softened, and Lorna carved a long upward turn to exit, the collapsing lip booming shut behind her.

In the channel she found it was Joe who had watched her. "How'd you learn to surf like that?" he asked, his eyes wide with bewilderment.

Lorna relived the freedom and thrill still pulsing through her body before answering. For this moment, everything was right again. Her cheeks hurt from smiling. Her lungs were full of sweet air. Her scalp tingled with the delight of living in the moment, of being inside that beautiful wave. She didn't answer him right away, wanting to savor these gifts, a while longer. Because answering him meant letting in the heartbreak, the bitterness that accompanied it.

She stroked past him. "From my mom," she said, her throat tightening. She hurried back into the lineup.

Thoughts of Alex wouldn't leave her alone. Why after so many years had she shown up? Was it because she knew she was sick and needed Lorna to help her? Or was she just dropping in to visit, and something made her ill? Either way, it irked her. On today of all days, Alex pops out of the ether to ruin what was supposed to be her reward for working hard, pinching pennies, and waiting. *This is why I needed her out of my life*, Lorna thought. *Even from thousands of miles away she can still get to me*. Lorna poured her frustration into her surfing, pushing herself harder with each wave, taking off deeper, later, forgetting about the consequences.

But she should have known not to lose her focus at a place like Bukuya. Although it was almost lunchtime, she ignored her hunger. She was riding a wave far inside when her mistake became clear. She cruised over the lip, expecting a thrilling paddle to escape the next wave. Instead, a monster set was charging full-tilt for the reef. She cursed herself and dug hard strokes for the horizon, but the other surfers were already way ahead of her. Even with a perfect duck dive, she realized that her chances of escape were slim. Sprinting, her strokes hard and straight, she visualized punching through: the board sinking, her body submerging, the board's nose scooping beneath the churning tunnel of water while her body pressed against the deck. Then she would surface on the other side, unscathed.

She noticed a surfer in perfect position to catch the first set, the wall of which was a darker, thicker blue than anything she had seen that day. Ahead of her, the other surfers cleared the lip. She was alone. The surfer stroked into the wave, and at once she knew it was Garth. The indigo wall eclipsed the sun, and she felt as if it would swallow her. She sensed Garth flying down the line. Pushing the nose of her board under, she took a lasting breath.

But in a split second it all went wrong.

She was yanked up inside the wall of water. Then the powerful wave heaved her backwards over the falls and slammed her down. The rest of the wave poured down like a waterfall, pressing on her like a ton of bricks. Then she was yanked and bashed over the reef while stinging bubbles and coral ripped at her skin. She tried to be loose, to be calm even though she couldn't shake the image of the thick, dark wall, and the others behind it. Finally, the chaos of water eased, and she charged upwards through a thundercloud of water. Pulling with powerful, desperate strokes, she craved air with every fiber of her being. Surfacing with a gasp, she searched the foam for her board. But the board wasn't a board anymore—it had snapped, and only the tail section remained.

Panic erupted in her brain as her eyes took in the incoming wave, so massive it seemed to drain water right off the reef. There was nowhere to go, no place to hide. The frothy water hissed all around her as the horrible sucking roar of the wave intensified. She inhaled a lungful of air and dove.

The exploding wave blasted her like a freight train, forcing air from her lungs and ripping her upwards, churning her in a fizzing mass of cloudy water. *Keep your feet under you*, a voice inside her head reminded as foamy bubbles everywhere confused her up from down. Powerless, she waited for the wave's calm, but it didn't come. Her lungs begged for a breath. Over and over she tumbled. Feeling dizzy, she remembered Joe's warning: *Some guy died there last year. Hit his head on the reef.* She hoped to see light, but there was only froth. When the pressure eased, she swam in the direction she thought was up, desperate for air.

She broke through the surface with a gasp, but another wave was bearing down on her. With only a split second, she filled her lungs. It wasn't enough though, and when she dove, she had to force herself to stay down as the wave crashed over her, steamrolling her as before. At the surface again, she inhaled too soon and got a mixture of foam and air. The choking, irrepressible spasms brought a new kind of panic as the next pile of churning white water rushed at her like an avalanche. She was drowning.

# FIVE

"Something's wrong," Joe said to Marty while searching the channel for Lorna. The rogue waves had caught them all off guard except for Garth, who seemed to have been expecting them all day.

"Maybe she's back at the boat?" Marty said, his brow furrowed.

Joe had already assessed that Lorna wasn't there. In fact, there was no sign of anyone. Veda was likely taking his customary nap.

Joe began paddling for the channel, convinced of trouble. When he spotted the broken tip section of a surfboard deposited on dry reef far inside, he increased his pace. Then Lorna surfaced, the bottom third of her board trailing behind as she side-stroked towards the channel. The relief he felt in seeing her quickly faded. She was rasping out a shaky cough, and her shoulder was red with blood.

"Hey, you okay?" he called out, alarmed.

She looked his way, but her haunted eyes gazed straight through him.

He covered the last few strokes to her and scooped her across his board, intending to let her float for a minute, catch her breath, but she grabbed onto his neck. The additional weight pulled him from his board and they slid into the water. Treading water with his feet, he grabbed hold of his board and got her onto it. She was shivering and moaning something nonsensical, the pitch rising and falling with each breath.

He noticed that her leg was bleeding.

"We're going to get you to the boat, alright?" he said.

By then she had come around somewhat, although she was still coughing.

"Can you paddle?" he asked.

"Yes," she said, and repositioned herself on the board. She saw the blood from her leg then. "Oh, no," she said, her voice desperate.

He had gotten a good look at it already: a deep slice on her lower leg. It was probably from her fin; it was so easy to get tangled up in your own board, happened all the time.

"It doesn't even hurt, isn't that weird?" she laughed in a light, frilly sounding way.

"There's nothing we can do out here," he said, anxious to get her going.

At this she seemed to refocus.

"I'll swim," he said as an encouragement.

They made their way to the boat; Joe shouted for help as they neared.

When Veda saw the blood he blew the air horn—the emergency signal—and got on the radio. Lorna was helped from the water and laid on the floor.

Joe held a towel against her cut.

Lorna winced. "How bad is it?"

The blood was already soaking through the towel. "You'll be okay," he said.

"Bullshit," she said in a shaky voice.

The last of the surfers scrambled onboard and the boat pulled away from the reef.

"How deep is it?" she asked.

"Deep," he said, feeling flustered. His only first aid experience came from a weekend seminar he'd taken during college to meet outdoorsy chicks.

"Take this," she said, pulling a long-sleeved T-shirt out of her bag. She was propped up on her elbows, her face pinched. "Fold it lengthwise, flat. Wrap it around," she hissed, watching him do what she asked. "Tight."

"You sure?" Joe had to shout now because of the engine noise and wind. Her leash was still attached to her ankle, and the tail end of her board was nearby, snapped cleanly from the tip.

"Has it stopped?" Lorna asked after a moment.

Joe noticed the heel of her hand pressing on the inside of her thigh. "I think so," he replied even though he wasn't sure. She looked pale, and scared. Her long-sleeved rash guard was torn at the neck, her trunks pitted and frayed on one side.

"Don't let them take me to some clinic," she begged, her gaze boring into him.

Joe didn't know what she was asking.

"I know what those places are like, Joe," she said, her mouth quivering a little. "Promise me!"

"Okay," he said quickly but without knowing what he could do to prevent such a thing.

At this she seemed to relax a little.

"And bring this," she said, straining to pull a green nylon bag from a faded backpack. "My stuff's probably better than anything they've got."

Joe put the bag next to him and Lorna lay back. Covering the remaining distance to land seemed to take an eternity.

Joe and several surfers carried Lorna to Shaun's old jeep idling by the shore. Lorna felt surprisingly light in his arms, a realization that filled him with dread. He told himself not to be such an idiot; Lorna was going to be fine.

Shaun drove like a madman up the dirt track. Lorna lay curled up on the bench seat while Joe sat next to her against the window, feeling helpless.

His damp rash guard and trunks stuck to his skin. His eyelids itched as the salt dried on his face. He glanced at Lorna's bare shoulder peeking out of her torn rashie, noticing the rows of bright red scratches from the reef. Her knees and feet were similarly beat up. She was shivering.

"Are you cold?" he asked lamely, looking around for something, anything that could keep her warm. Except for the spare gas can and a sheathed machete rolling around in the back, the jeep was bare. He dug in her small green bag that he'd remembered to grab—looking for what, he didn't know—and was shocked to come across packages of needles, vials of drugs, a sturdy pair of scissors, and a brick of gauze pads. Lorna kept shivering. It was at least ninety degrees and the windows were wide open; he closed the ones he could reach.

"Is there a hospital in Suva?" Joe said to Shaun over the loud engine noise after they'd hit the main road. He didn't know if this was a strong enough suggestion to avoid the clinics Lorna feared.

"Yes," Shaun said, his mouth stiff. He glanced back. "How is she?"

Joe's stomach flipped over. "I don't know. She's cold."

Shaun ran a hand through his already rumpled hair. "Fuck," he muttered.

"Do you have any water?" Lorna said so softly Joe had to ask her to repeat it.

"Water," Lorna said again, her stormy blue eyes unreadable and her cheeks tight with pain.

Joe spotted a half-empty clear plastic water bottle on the front seat and grabbed it.

Lorna sat up a little and drank from it, her hands shaking. As soon as she returned the bottle, the jeep hit a pothole. The jostle nearly threw Lorna from the bench and she cried out.

"More?" Joe asked her, holding up the bottle.

Lorna's eyes clouded. "Oh no," she muttered, then leaned over the bench and retched up the water.

Her teeth chattered and she curled tighter into the seat.

Joe was overwhelmed with the need to do something. He pulled her closer and hugged her shaking body. "It's all right," he said, hoping some of his warmth was reaching her. He didn't know what else to do. Suva was still a ways off. "It's okay," he tried, but she felt distant to him, her body stiff and straining for something he couldn't give her.

Joe sat in the small waiting area, elbows on his knees, listening to the wall clock tick. After he and Shaun had carried Lorna into a room with four unoccupied beds partitioned by curtains, a team of men and women quickly swarmed in. Lorna's shredded rash guard was cut from her in two seconds, and a needle was poked into her arm.

After Joe ran the incident down for a woman he assumed was a nurse, she asked them to wait outside.

"Stay with me," Lorna had begged, her eyes desperate.

Joe was confused; the doctors were in charge now. What could he do but get in their way?

"No!" Lorna said as he let go of her hand and the doctor drew the curtain.

"Is she gonna be okay?" Joe called out as he was led to the waiting room.

"And who are you?" the nurse asked.

"I'm her friend," he said, realizing that he meant it.

"So what happened?" Shaun asked once Joe joined him in the waiting area.

Joe dropped his head and sighed. "A big set came in. Everyone made it over."

"Except for her?"

Joe nodded. "I'll bet she got held down." He shuddered, imagining it. "Her fin cut her leg."

Shaun sat back, crossed his arms. "Maybe it was too big for her. Maybe she shouldn't have gone out in the first place?"

"She handled herself fine," Joe grumbled. The image of her flying out of that green barrel into the sunshine would be with him for a long time. Shaun wasn't a surfer, so he didn't have a clue what he was talking about—Lorna knew what she was doing.

So why had she been caught inside?

# SIX

Lorna received a hero's welcome back at the hostel. Over a plate of reheated fish casserole, she tried to downplay the bags of IV fluid, the antibiotics, and the layers of stitches. She secretly enjoyed the attention, but the celebration of her bad positioning on that fatal wave made her feel coddled, patronized. She was terrified that they thought of her as the girl who couldn't hold her own. Was it just some cruel twist of fate that the biggest set of the day had come through when she was feeling reckless? It didn't matter; she was out of the game now.

Lorna realized with bitterness that she had to call the E.R. She swung over to the phone and Shaun helped her dial.

Yoko came to the phone after a short wait. "She left!"

"What?"

Yoko sounded out of breath. "I sent her to CT. She never came back."

Lorna lowered herself into a chair. The only reason Yoko would send Alex to CT was if the ultrasound showed something bad.

"What did the CT show?"

"I can't tell you." Lorna could practically hear the anguish in Yoko's voice. "Before, when I called you, she had asked me to. Now that she's gone, the HIPAA laws take over, and I can't share her results," she added.

"Cancer?" Lorna said.

The line buzzed with Yoko's silence.

Lorna grimaced. It had to be cancer. Yoko probably saw liver lesions, and the CT showed a mass on her pancreas. A trickle of sweat ran down Lorna's lower back. "Did she leave an address?"

"Nope."

"Anything?"

"Nothing."

"So, whatever is on that CT, she doesn't know about it."

"Right."

"Fuck." Lorna sighed. There had to be some way she could gain access to Alex's results. Maybe Yoko was just being overly cautious, or maybe because Alex claimed to be Lorna's patient she would be able to read the medical report that would be sent via email.

With frustration, Lorna put the issue aside. She would be home in three days and could sort everything out then. But then what? Lorna didn't know how to reach Alex. She hadn't exactly left a forwarding address.

Conflicted, her fury growing, Lorna hobbled to her bure and found Joe waiting on the steps. The awkwardness of her gait with the crutches made her feel flustered and graceless, on top of everything else she was feeling. It only worsened when he offered to help her.

"I can do it," she said, ignoring his hand.

"Okay," he replied, and let her shuffle up the steps.

She sat with him, trying to find a position that resembled comfort. She was hot, and her salt-crusted hair felt stiff. Her head itched. In fact, she felt itchy everywhere, and wondered if this was due to the Vicodin or the very long day.

They sat in silence, just breathing, and she wondered what he wanted. She didn't know how to act now, after everything. It embarrassed her that she had latched onto him so tightly during the ordeal, like a child. Would she have latched onto one of the other surfers, or was there something about Joe she trusted? She wished then that she'd accepted the additional narcotics from the hospital. It would make this horrible awkwardness go away.

"About today . . . " she began. "I'm not normally such a wuss." She sighed nervously. His compassion and attention had hit her brain like a drug. So why was she suddenly so scared of him?

"Wuss?" he replied. "I'm beginning to think you were raised by wolves."

Lorna pushed the heels of her hands against her eyes, trying to block out everything: her certainty of drowning at Bukuya, the fear of being abandoned at some backwoods clinic, and what she'd learned from Yoko.

*Alex has cancer,* she thought. *She's going to die.*

"Do you need anything?" Joe asked.

Lorna almost screamed in anguish. *Yes!* she wanted to say. *I need the world to stop spinning.* She realized that he was still there because he wanted to continue taking care of her. "No," she groaned.

Joe sighed and the silence stretched between them.

Lorna closed her eyes for a moment, pushing away the pain. "Thank you for your help today," she said evenly. "But I'm fine now," she added, scrambling to her feet to prove it.

"Are you?" he asked, his gaze soft, kind.

Lorna ignored a sudden yearning to bury herself in his arms. "Yes," she said and hobbled into her bure. She watched through the window as he walked away, his shoulders sagging.

Lorna swallowed a clump of Advil and wondered how she would pass her remaining days with a bum leg. Maybe she should call the airlines, go home early. Surfing with her stitches and soreness wouldn't be the same as before. She could go home, have a rest, find a way to read Alex's medical report, maybe try to contact her. Or maybe she should stay at Vunde Bay. She could pass the time doing normal things that people did while on vacation: read a book in a hammock, take out a kayak or an outrigger canoe. She had a sudden image of her younger self, riding in Alex's outrigger when the waves were flat. Her mom would stroke past wild patches of jungle alive with birds or over reefs teeming with fish while Lorna peered over the side. No matter how bored, or hungry, or restless she felt, Lorna never complained because she knew her mom would simply stop taking her along.

Her heart heavy, she got into the shower to wash away her humiliation, the dried blood, and the antiseptic smell of the clinic. The doctor had expressed his worry about her plan to surf again soon, but the cut had missed the tendon, so Lorna ignored his concerns.

Protecting wounds happened to be her specialty.

# SEVEN

The next morning, Joe found Lorna eating alone, a whole carafe of coffee and stack of toast dripping with butter in front of her.

"I see the cooks are spoiling you," he said, leaning against the edge of her booth. He was careful to avoid asking about her leg.

She seemed surprised to see him. "Didn't you go surfing?"

"I have other plans." He sipped his coffee.

"Let me guess. The Hostile Nautilus?"

Joe looked away. Why did she have to say that? "No."

Lorna looked chastened and was quiet for a moment. "It looks like it's getting windy," she said finally. The horizon had changed from the flat blue expanse to a dark, fuzzy line, and low clouds were gathering in the distant sky.

He paused to sip his coffee again. "I've hired a boat. Want to come with me?"

Lorna eyed him. "Where?"

"A village. It'll be cool. You'll see."

She seemed to think for a moment. "All right," she said.

Joe waited outside her bure while she gathered her things, and then they walked together down the dock to an idling boat. Lorna swung along swiftly on her crutches. He wanted to help, but remembered her reaction to his offer the day before, so kept quiet.

They cleared the shallows then sped into the open sea, aiming east and away from the surf breaks. A few minutes into their journey a cluster of tiny islands appeared in the distance. Lorna watched the horizon, her eyes squinting against the spray. Her skin had tanned, and the freckles across her nose seemed to have multiplied.

Suddenly, a school of flying fish leaped from the water, their translucent scales glowing like pearls against the darkening sea. They appeared to pause midair, hovering next to the boat for an instant before plunging back into the water. Joe looked to Lorna, hoping to share the moment, but she was watching the distant horizon.

The boat slowed as it approached a tiny beach located on the north side of the middle island. Through the trees Joe could see the outlines of tiny houses. He had agreed to come to Fiji for Marty, who wanted one last hurrah before getting married in June. They both loved to surf, and Fiji was the ultimate adventure. But Joe also wanted to experience life beyond the touristy front of the resort, and best of all, he wanted to hear the music he'd read so much about.

Joe hopped into the shallows and helped pull the boat onto the crushed shell beach. Lorna understandably stayed in the boat.

"Wait," their driver told them, holding up a palm. He disappeared up a faint dirt path into the trees.

"Wait for what?" Lorna asked, looking confused.

"He's probably getting permission," Joe replied with a shrug. He scooped up a few shell pieces and skipped one into the turquoise lagoon, but it caught the tip of a tiny wave stirred up from a gust of wind and disappeared.

"From who?"

"The chief," Joe replied. He waited for the wind to subside, then hucked another shell and counted four skips. "We can't just go barging onto their island." He skipped another shell. "They used to be cannibals, you know," he said to get her to smile. It worked. *That's better*, he thought.

Lorna leaned her crutches against the side of the boat and slid carefully out. Joe scooped some more shells. "So, that stuff you had me bring to the hospital," he said after choosing a large pink one. He glanced at Lorna. "Are you a nurse or something?"

"Nurse?" she replied, raising her eyebrows. "Why do you think that, because I'm a girl?"

"No," he replied quickly, cursing himself for such a stupid assumption. Of course, she could be a doctor or a medic. Why *had* he thought she was a nurse?

She grinned and Joe realized that she was teasing him.

"I'm a resident," she said, squinting into the jungle. "In the E.R."

Joe fingered a long curve of white shell in his palm. He realized why he hadn't guessed right: because doctors didn't have cute, freckled noses, weren't unbelievably foxy, and they didn't charge stand-up barrels. Doctors were nerdy, impatient, and at best, patronizing. Lorna was none of those things. He realized that he'd never met another woman like Lorna, let alone a doctor.

He realized why Lorna had begged him to avoid "some clinic." He thought about Lorna working in a fast-paced emergency room, cutting people open, digging for bullets, restarting people's hearts. "Isn't it scary?" he asked.

Lorna gave him a thoughtful glance. "Sometimes," she replied.

"Why'd you want to be a doctor?" he asked.

She glanced at the narrow opening in the jungle where the boatman had disappeared. "It's a long story," she said with a sigh.

A blast of wind skipped sand through the grass. "Looks like we've got time," he said.

Lorna looked uneasy but it passed. "I thought I was going to be a marine biologist. I was applying to schools and everything. But when I was seventeen I was in a car accident," she said. "It was when I lived in Sicily." She shrugged. "Driving there is not like driving anywhere else. They're so reckless, impatient. And they drive these tiny little cars, without seatbelts. The roads are narrow and windy. When accidents happen there, people die." She seemed to be studying the seam of her shorts. "I was a passenger. A car was passing a truck on a blind curve, it came right at us. It had just rained . . . "

Joe felt the shells he was holding cut into his palm.

"I didn't really know the guy driving. I was just hitching a ride home from swim practice." She looked up at him. "His name was Jeremy."

"Oh," Joe said and then regretted how lame it sounded. "I'm sorry, Lorna," he added.

She looked past him, at the ocean. "I didn't know how to help him. There was blood everywhere, and he . . . " She stopped, and a look darkened her face. "Everyone told me that he would have died anyways. He had too many injuries," she said finally. "But I never forgot that feeling of helplessness." She looked at him. "The doctors who took care of me in the E.R. were so calm and in control. They had all the answers. They knew what to do. I decided I had to be one of them someday."

The boatman returned and led them onto a worn dirt trail. Joe followed Lorna who swung along, breathing hard. They passed a few tin-roofed shacks built on low stilts. Nearby, slatted wooden racks held ropy lumps of yellow-tan kava root, curing in the heat.

"Bula!" a woman sang from her porch. Several shy children peered from behind her long skirt. Lorna and Joe returned the greeting and continued through the village, scattering chickens at every turn, and followed by a growing number of barefoot children in faded, loose clothing. Their dirty brown faces glowed with mischief as they giggled and hid behind the lines of laundry drying in the wind.

"This is probably a lot like Hawaii," Joe said to Lorna. He was still thinking about her story. What would it be like to watch someone die? He shuddered.

Lorna swung along a few paces. "Maybe in the past, but not anymore."

"How long did you live there?"

"We—I—moved when I was eight."

"You been back?"

"A few times." She didn't elaborate.

"You ever surf Pipe?"

Her reply was a nervous laugh and he worried that he'd said something wrong.

They descended a windy path through a section of jungle, the leaves stirring in the wind. Now and then he snuck glances at Lorna to make sure she was getting along okay. The path opened up to a large grassy clearing, with a school at one end near a length of beach. The village's main bure, a long, large, single-story building, stood at the other end.

They crossed the clearing on a dirt path compressed by generations of use. When they came to the building, Joe could see the beginnings of a kava ceremony underway. His heart beat faster, and he sprang up the steps behind Veda. But Lorna hung back, her high cheeks rosy from her awkward, swinging gait.

"Come," the man replied, beckoning to her with both hands. "Now we drink kava."

"What's kava?" she asked.

"It's part of a ceremony," Joe said, interrupting. "They make it for us."

Lorna's eyes were pained. "A ceremony? Yikes. Can I pass?"

Joe paused, uneasy. Turning down kava was an insult. How could she not know that?

But the boatman's deep, dark eyes sparkled, and he smiled. "Come," he said.

Lorna looked like she was going to say something, but didn't. She tried to move up the steps on her crutches, but it was painful to watch.

"Upsy-daisy," he said, and scooped her up. Her look of alarm somehow only lifted his spirits higher.

Inside, they were seated in front of a large man Joe assumed was the chief, circled by villagers. An elder kneaded the ropy kava root repeatedly in a huge bowl of water, which turned a thick and dirty-looking brown. When the brew was ready, a woman offered Joe the first cup, which he reached for with both hands.

"Bula," the woman said warmly. "We welcome you."

Joe replied "Bula," to the villagers and tipped the bowl back, opening his throat to the tangy, thick drink. He returned the cup and clapped the customary three times. The woman returned with a bowl for Lorna.

She took it, her gaze darting around the room. "Bula," she replied seriously. Her face grimaced with distaste as she swallowed.

The woman repeated the offering for the others. Grinning, Joe turned to Lorna and was startled by her stiff jaw and distant eyes.

After the ceremony, the villagers assembled against the far wall for what Joe had so hoped to enjoy: their music. Joe couldn't help grinning like an idiot as a buzz of anticipation ran through him. Two men held guitars. A group of children joined in, lining up in front of the adults. The choir opened with a hymn so pure and sweet, it gave him goose bumps. Joe focused on the children's voices and their smiles. He watched the women sway, their long dresses shifting side to side, and he chuckled almost at the tingling sensations of joy lighting through him. Just as he thought the song was ending, the tempo changed and the children began clapping, stamping their feet to the new beat, their voices ringing higher, stronger, the walls seeming to pulse. The men's deep melody filled the space, their ebony-black eyes sparkling.

Stamping feet shook the floor. Still the harmony sweetened, the women's voices striking a perfect melody with the rich, deep notes from the men, the guitars adding a kind of backbone to it all. The music suddenly stopped, and a kind of yelping, yipping cheer erupted from the choir—an almost unnerving, war-like cry and he felt like joining in, opening his mouth and filling the air with whatever thundered out. The villagers' faces glowed with welcome and joy in the stillness, but they were quick to begin again, the next song faster, and that highlighted the women's high, clear notes.

With his mom being a music teacher, he'd grown up hearing all kinds of music, but listening to it in this way, with the wind and the waves and the wood rattling beneath his feet, vibrating his heart, was something different altogether. It was beautiful, a gift. He turned to Lorna, expecting to see her smiling, but tears were streaming down her face and her eyes were lost. Alarmed, he reached for her hand, but she scrambled to her feet and hobbled out of the building.

Joe couldn't bear the thought of going after her—not only would leaving be an insult, he couldn't possibly abandon the concert.

He refocused on the music but the mood was spoiled. By the time he found Lorna at the edge of the beach, his temper was red-hot.

"What the hell?" he asked, dropping her crutches in the sand. Maybe it was no big deal to her: the music, the hospitality, experiencing the culture, actually being a part of it, something so rare in this world. "These people have put their whole day on hold for us. And this is how you show your thanks?"

The wind ruffled her curls and he noticed her red eyes. "My mom is dying," she said.

Joe's anger melted away. "What are you talking about?" he finally asked, the wind stealing his words.

Lorna watched the ocean for a long moment. "And she's disappeared."

# EIGHT

Lorna felt heavy and tired, as if from some epic shift in the Pit. During her first year of residenwcy, she sometimes fell asleep at the bus stop. A noise would wake her to a kinked neck and a moment of panic—what had she missed? She felt like curling up on the crushed shells and having a long nap.

"How do you know she's . . . ?" Joe asked, looking uneasy.

Lorna told him about Yoko treating Alex.

"But that doesn't mean that she's dying. What if it is gallstones? Or something else?"

"Then why did she need a CT? It's something bad, Joe." Lorna knew from experience just how bad.

Joe seemed to think about this. "Why did she leave the E.R.?"

Lorna sighed. What was Alex's true purpose for being in Seattle? "She got her pain meds. Why stick around?"

"That seems weird."

"That's Alex."

Joe seemed to watch her for a long time. "You're sure she's not still in Seattle?"

Lorna shrugged. Truthfully, she wasn't sure of anything. But if even if Alex was on her deathbed, staying in Seattle was unlikely. "She's not a city person."

Joe's brow wrinkled in confusion.

"The last time I saw her was at my college graduation. She wanted me to come see her newest discovery. Some big wave spot she'd found, I bet."

"Do you know where it is?"

Lorna shook her head. "At one point she said something about south swells. I'm pretty sure it's Mexico. But she wouldn't come out and tell me." Lorna grabbed a fistful of shells and threw them. "She's been searching for waves her whole life. She could be anywhere, Joe."

"So what are you going to do?"

"I don't know."

"Lorna," Joe said, touching her arm. "She needs you."

*She needs you.* Lorna remembered chewing on that idea at Bukuya. But it couldn't be true. That same image of Alex filled her mind, the one of her emerging from the surf. She would be smiling her wicked half smile, her long straight hair draped like yellow silk down her back, and her electric blue eyes laughing.

Lorna thought of all the times she had needed Alex. "I don't think so," she said.

"C'mon," Joe scoffed.

Lorna hugged her knees close. "I'm pretty sure she wasn't in Seattle to see me. She was there for some other purpose, and I was an afterthought."

"It couldn't be a coincidence that she went to your hospital."

That was the strange part. "She must have looked me up somehow."

"See? She's reaching out."

"No!" Lorna shouted, more forcefully than she intended. "You don't know what she's like."

"She's still your mom," he said, his jaw clenched. "And she might be sick. Who's going to take care of her?"

A village member gathered them for a tour of the island. After hearing a farewell song on the beach, Joe delivered his parting gifts of guitar strings and boxes of crayons. Then the boatman returned them to Vunde Bay, before speeding off into the breaking storm.

Lorna swung alongside Joe who had been quiet since they left the island. "The ceremony and everything was . . . special," she said, feeling like her words were coming from far away. Did he understand? She hadn't meant to be rude or burden him with her problems. Or selfish—why hadn't she brought gifts for their hosts?

"Thanks for coming," Joe sighed, barely meeting her eye. He walked away from her, his head down and shoulders slumped, as if defeated.

Lorna brushed back new tears. She'd always been able to take care of herself. What was happening to her?

Sometime in the night, Lorna woke to the sound of palm fronds clattering and rain pelting the roof like gravel. She lay awake listening to the storm, imagining miles upon miles of frothy blue ocean and wind-waves crashing over reefs and shorelines. In Hawaii, when she was eight, they'd evacuated because of a hurricane. The wind had forced the palms sideways, while incredible amounts of water crashed onto the beaches and flooded the roads. The storm surge had destroyed their house—the bottom floor filled with sand and bits of everything imaginable: broken chunks of plywood, a shredded tarp, automobile parts, glass bottles, a brand-new tennis racquet. Soon after, the navy moved them to Bremerton, and nothing was ever the same.

Lorna closed her eyes and saw her mom walking up the sand after a session, hair slicked back and that cocky expression in her eyes. She'd be telling Lorna about the waves, her board tucked under her arm, her hip cocked and tanned skin sparkling with silver beads of ocean water. Meanwhile Lorna would be hopping up and down, impatient. "Take me," she'd say. "Please?"

Lorna hated the saltwater stinging her eyes but found that she got used to it. She would stay out for as long as Alex's patience lasted, obsessing over every detail, wanting desperately to be good enough. A few days before her eighth birthday, Alex towed her outside the breakers, and Lorna caught her first real wave. She expected the experience to bond them and that her mom would take her along when she went away. But she didn't, and it hurt even more because Lorna knew what she was missing. Meanwhile she would go to school and her dad would go to work on the base, each of them pretending that Alex was working extra shifts, or housesitting, or had just lost track of time.

What Lorna had never been able to figure out was how easily she took her mom back when she did come home. As if she'd suddenly woke up from a coma. Lorna would sit and listen to her stories, all the while her stomach churning with anxiety and self-doubt, her brain sizzling with the need to yell and cry and demand answers she knew would never come. But then they'd go surfing, and everything would be right again. For a while.

Lorna swung her legs off the bed, ignoring the pain, and grabbed her crutches. After slipping on a pair of shorts, she went to the door. Outside, the blackness enveloped her and rain blew into her face, wetting her lips and soaking her camisole, streaking down her legs. She swung up to the main bure and collapsed into a chair, breathing hard. A dim light shone from a bare bulb above her but the building was empty. Was everyone asleep? She imagined Joe in the guy's dorm, curled up beneath his mosquito net. Or was he awake, thinking of her? *Forget it*, Lorna thought. She groaned, restless, stirred up by something she couldn't identify.

Outside, the air hung thick and misty, and a fresh wind cooled her shoulders. The black night enveloped a churning ocean, the palms raging in the wind, the fat raindrops pounding the jungle, the roof, the white-sand shallows.

The ashtray on the window ledge held a few roaches from hand-rolled smokes. After rooting around for a light, she lit the first blunt, but it tasted of straight tobacco. Coughing, she stubbed it out. The second was potent, and she sat back, sucking on the dregs until nearly burning her lips.

Lorna sat for a long time, unable to clear the spinning thoughts from her head.

Finally, the rain pelting the roof lessened to a gentle tapping, and she ambled down the stairs with her crutches to return to her bure.

Lorna had sworn to stay away from Alex, and yet the shocked look on Joe's face had unnerved her. But Joe didn't understand what she'd been through, and how hard she'd worked to exist outside of Alex's shadow. She had been better off since she had said goodbye to Alex.

Maybe she needed to say goodbye to Joe, too.

# NINE

"I'm getting gangrene," Marty groaned from his bunk.

Joe lay in a hammock in the gentle morning heat, his fingers finding familiar chords. Inside the dorm, surf trunks of all colors hung from bed frames, towels lay on the floor in lumps, duffels in various states of emptiness were strewn in the middle of the room, on unoccupied beds, atop empty board bags, or half-zipped beneath beds. Surfboards lined the far wall like a picket fence, black leashes sat coiled or in tangled bunches on the floor, empty beer bottles littered every surface. The room smelled of coconut surf wax, sweaty T-shirts, and faintly of pot.

"You shoulda put lime on it like I told you to, pussy," Joe replied. The reef cuts had begun to ooze, and Marty's foot was squishy and bloated.

"Why won't you go ask her!" Marty cried. "She's a doctor!"

"You go ask her," Joe said. How could she turn her back on her mom like that? Had he been completely wrong about her?

"I can't walk!"

"Shoulda thought about that before your trek to the Nautilus." He peered at his friend. "Was it even worth it?"

Marty didn't meet his eyes. "Man, you are so cold," he replied, shaking his head. "*So* cold." He hobbled out of the dorm. "At least I'm making an effort and not moping around here all frickin day."

Lorna unscrewed the fins from her spare board and slipped them inside the pocket of the board bag. She swallowed her last sip of Nescafé and then wrapped the board's rails in foam piping. She remembered Joe's expression on the beach the day before. He would never understand what it was like. Alex was gone, surfing away her last days, alone. There was nothing left to do, but go home and try to forget she'd come.

She wondered if she would be able to forget about Joe.

A knock at her door made her jump. Lorna found Marty on her porch, the mischief she normally saw in his eyes replaced with a serious stoicism that got her attention immediately. She was about to ask if something was wrong with Joe when he blurted, "Could you have a look at this?" his gaze falling to his barely weighted foot. The reef cuts she'd seen before were red and swollen, and yellow pus was caked around several of them.

She invited him in, her body responding to the purpose: her spine straightened and her mind quickly organized a plan. She felt in control, ready.

He followed her lead and hobbled to her small kitchen, where she helped him onto her counter near the sink. "I think there's something's growing in there," Marty said.

"Doubtful," she replied, pulling on a set of Nitrile gloves from her kit. Marty grimaced as she examined his cuts, poking and prodding. Lorna filled her sink with hot water.

"Ow," he cried as she eased his foot in. "That's hot!"

"Good," Lorna replied, giving him a look. She pulled out a bottle of Keflex from her kit and shook one pill into his palm. Marty swallowed it dry. She handed him the bottle. "Twice a day till they're gone. Even if it starts to feel better. Okay?"

He nodded. "Thanks," he said.

"Don't thank me yet," she said, unwrapping a preloaded iodine sponge.

Marty's body stiffened as she began to scrub. He clenched his eyes shut.

She thought of the pack of U.S. Navy hospital corpsmen who befriended her after the accident. She had become a volunteer in the emergency room where they pulled duty, and at first their shared love of surfing brought them together. Because she was lonely in Sicily, she endured their racist jokes, bad manners, and constant need to one-up each other by doing stupid things that almost always ended with severe pain. Besides, the accident had changed her. Miles was the first one to understand this, and their friendship bloomed. The corpsmen became her everything: they taught her how to stitch up reef cuts and relocate shoulders, how to roll a spliff, how to blend in, and from a few, how to get laid. They never pried into her past, and she never asked about their battlefield nightmares. She would never forget how much they had helped her.

"You have fun at the island yesterday?" Marty asked after she'd rinsed his wounds. His forehead shone with sweat.

Lorna's brain shifted gears sluggishly. She wondered what Joe had told Marty. "The people were kind," she said finally, remembering the island's peaceful feel. "I can see why some people think it's paradise." She pushed thoughts of Alex out of her brain.

"Joe wants to record their music."

Lorna raised her eyebrows. Slowly, it all fell into place. Of course, Joe was a musician. That's why he had been so upset at her behavior. The singing had been beautiful, of course, but it must have been something almost otherworldly to Joe. It made her feel even worse about how she'd behaved. Joe had been right to confront her. As usual, she had misunderstood everything.

"You ever seen Six Foot Savior play?" Marty asked, as if he'd been able to see her thoughts.

Lorna applied a poultice made with sugar and water and began dressing the wounds. She had never heard of a band called *Six Foot Savior*, but that didn't mean much. She'd had no time for nocturnal adventures. The last live show she had attended was years ago at the Crocodile Café on a hot summer night. She pictured Joe on a stage, belting out songs and jamming on his guitar while a crowd cheered. "No," she replied, frowning. *Six Foot Savior?* It sounded strange. But then Joe as a rock star sounded even stranger.

"Well, you should." Marty's voice faded. "Before Joe gives it up."

"Why would he give it up?" Lorna replied, peeling off her iodine-stained gloves. She realized that she was ready to reclaim her position in the E.R. Practicing medicine felt good, safe.

"He says he's over it. That it just doesn't fit him anymore."

Lorna considered this. She knew that feeling—of wanting to change. But to be brave enough to make it happen was something much more difficult.

"I know," Marty said, shaking his head. "Cat's got a screw loose, if you ask me."

Lorna's heart fluttered. "Maybe not," she said to herself. *More like someone worth holding onto.*

After Marty left, Lorna finished packing and swung on her crutches to the main bure hoping she could still scrounge some breakfast. The grass sparkled with drops of rain from the night before. The winds had softened but the sea looked confused and dark. Without waves, Lorna wondered what everyone would do all day.

Garth grinned at her as she hobbled up the porch steps. "You know, doc, I've got this horrible rash on me arse," he said. Laughter erupted from the other surfers playing cards with him. "Maybe you'd have a look?" Garth added.

Lorna noticed the empty beer bottles and roaches in the ashtrays and had the answer to her question: they were halfway blitzed and it wasn't even ten o'clock in the morning. Annoyed, Lorna went to the buffet inside and, while balancing on her good leg, stabbed a golden pancake onto a plate and spread peanut butter on it, then a swirl of syrup. Lorna was tired of Garth's game, whatever it was. After breakfast she wanted to transfer to a nice hotel near the airport where she could get drunk by the pool and forget all the stupid mistakes she'd made at Vunde Bay. She grabbed a fork and then realized she couldn't carry it and the plate *and* swing on her crutches at the same time.

Garth came up next to her. "I figured out who you are," he said, startling her. "You look like her, you know. Especially when your hair is wet."

She studied his sly grin. "What are you talking about?"

"Alex is your mum, isn't she?"

Lorna's mouth dropped open but no words came out.

"She's got a sweet setup down there." His eyes sparkled. "I'm thinking of heading back this summer. I have a few weeks off from the tour."

Ice crystals formed in her bloodstream. "I . . . " The words in her head piled up on each other, she couldn't make her mouth work.

"You should join me." A tense look passed over Garth's face. She almost missed it; she was so used to his arrogant smirk.

The ice crystals tumbled through her insides, tickling the back of her lungs, burning down her spine. She tried to imagine traveling with Garth. To see Alex after six years. Alex who might be sick.

One of Garth's eyebrow arched. "You two can get caught up, and she could show us her secret spots."

Behind them, the patio screen door slid open. "You gettin' those beers or what?" called a voice.

Garth jerked his head in the direction of the porch. "Keep yer panties on," he called out. The screen door slammed, accompanied by a muttered curse.

Lorna tried to move closer. "I . . . haven't seen her in . . . a while," she stuttered. "Where did you say she is?" Her stitches throbbed but it felt distant to the blood pulsing in her ears. Somewhere inside her brain, alarm bells were blaring.

Garth's grin widened. "It's this tiny town. Rio something. I was with some team riders. Our coach set everything up. South swells will be peaking any time now."

*You look like her.* She hadn't heard that for a long time. "Huh," she mumbled.

Garth grinned, his old brazen self returning. "Think it over," he said, handing her a scrap of paper with an email address scribbled on it, before striding off towards the bar.

# TEN

## The Nautilus

The Aussie girl in the red bikini looked at Joe with awe.

"He's starting his Australian tour in a few weeks. You should come to a show," said Marty, grinning at Joe. "We'll get you backstage."

Joe's face felt hot. He had only intended to keep Marty company and probably carry him home, too, with that foot of his. But this was too much.

"Wow, yeah," the girl said, wide-eyed. She had a sharp nose and straight, dark hair, and her Aussie accent-melody made *I've* sound like *Oive*. Words were different, too, like *pissed* meant *drunk*, not angry. Marty's bird had already coiled her hand around his arm. She was curvy and blonde, a skimpy sundress covering her white bikini.

"He'll probably play something for you if you ask nice," Marty said, winking at Joe as he was led away by the blonde girl. Shelby? Sharla? Joe hadn't been paying enough attention.

"I'm Genevieve," the girl in the red bikini said once they were alone. "But everyone calls me Viv," she added, giving him a playful smile. "Wanna go for a swim?"

At the water's edge, Joe stripped off his T-shirt and flip flops and waded a few feet, then dove after the girl. In contrast to the cool breeze, the water was blissfully warm. Joe swam beneath the sea and kicked along the sandy bottom, past Genevieve's blaring red toenails planted in the sand. He thought about Lorna's hurry to leave the village after the ceremony, and surfaced feeling frustrated. She was so willing to help Marty—practically a stranger—but give up on her own mother? A mother who might be dying. Why would Lorna think her mother didn't need her?

"You're a surfer, yeah?" Viv said, standing in waist-deep water, her wet hair slicked back, her tan skin beaded with water.

He made a water spout with his fists. "You surf?" he asked. A sudden breeze gave him goose bumps.

"Yeah, right," she said, rolling her eyes.

Joe gave her a look. "Why not?"

"I dunno, there's heaps of sharks, right? And it looks so . . . " Her pretty face twisted into a frown. "Hard."

Joe dove again. *This is going to be a long day*, he thought. He burst through the surface and spotted Viv swimming toward a floating dock.

"Come on," she said, her pink lips curled into a sly smile. Joe treaded water for a moment and glanced to shore where Marty and Shelby/Sharla sat on a large flower-print towel, the girl rubbing sunscreen on his back. Marty's eyes were closed and he swayed with her touch. Joe sighed and swam towards the dock.

Viv climbed the ladder, swinging her hips.

"So have you been getting any?" she asked, cocking her head. His eyes were drawn to her nipples making perfect buttons in the center of her top.

"Um." He shook his head. "Sorry?"

"Waves. Have you been getting any good waves?"

"Oh." He stepped onto the dock. "Yeah."

She lay down. He noticed how her hipbones lifted the fabric of her bikini bottom from her slender abdomen. Sitting with his back to her, he looked out at the choppy horizon and wondered what

Lorna was doing. Why couldn't he figure her out? He remembered that first day when he apologized for dropping in on her. How had she answered? *Just make sure it doesn't happen again.* He grinned, realizing that she had been messing with him. But then she'd begged him to stay with her in that clinic. How could someone so confident be so scared? And if being alone scared her, why did she seem to prefer it? Then she had confided in him about Alex. That had to mean something.

"Sing to me." He felt a hand brushing his back.

Joe closed his eyes. He had to get out of here. "Um, I gotta go." He stood to dive.

"Oh," she said, looking hurt.

Joe dove in and swam for shore. Viv came up next to him, looking fretful. "There's a guitar in the commons," she said once they were wading through the shallows. "I'd really love to hear you play."

He looked at Marty lying belly-down beside Shelby/Sharla, their bodies touching, laughter rising over the sand. Marty glanced his way, raising an eyebrow while Viv waited by his side.

Joe sighed. "Can we go for a walk instead?"

Viv seemed to grow an inch. "Okay!"

He picked up his flip flops, and Viv pulled on a wrap skirt, tying the knot carefully over her hip.

They rounded a point of land, and Joe noticed a thin ribbon of white offshore that marked the outer reef. The pale aqua water inside the sheltered lagoon shimmered over dark rocks and broken bits of coral, creating a calico patchwork of blues and blacks. Occasionally, a gust of wind scuffed the surface and fluttered the leaves of the palms.

"So, what do you do back in Oz?" Joe asked.

"I'm an actress."

"Really?" Joe said, blinking at her.

"Well, I want to be," Viv replied quickly. "I've been in a few ads, and when I get back I'm going to read for a really good part. It's a miniseries." They walked in silence for a moment before she added: "You think it's stupid."

"No, no," Joe said. "I mean, you gotta follow your thing, you know?"

"Yeah," she said.

The sandy crush of their footsteps blended with the sound of tiny waves caressing the shore. Joe picked up a piece of shell and skipped it into the lagoon. If Alex was dying, why wouldn't she need Lorna? Joe remembered the hurt in Lorna's eyes, as if rejected.

"So do you write your own songs?" Viv asked.

He shrugged. "I do covers, too." She wasn't going to try to get him to play again, was she?

"I had to sing for an audition once. It was terrible."

"I'm sure it wasn't that bad."

"Oh, it was awful. Even my parents said so."

Joe wondered if Marty was still on the beach with Shelby/Sharla, or if they had gone somewhere else. He didn't think he could hang out much longer. He was getting a picture of Lorna and her dilemma, and it pained him. *She can't give up,* he thought.

"You've got a girlfriend."

Joe looked at Viv. "What makes you say that?"

"I can tell."

He remembered the way Lorna's features calmed in the waves, as if surfing those giants cost her no effort at all. He wondered what it would be like to hold her, kiss her.

"I've got something that might help you take your mind off her." Viv wound her hands around his waist and pressed up against him. The feel of her body sent a warm flush across his skin. Viv's serene eyes gazed at him, and he lowered his head to kiss her. She opened her mouth to him, and he rubbed her slender shoulders, her back. The tie of her bikini was in his hands; he loosened it. Her breath quickened in his mouth. She pressed against him, her hands stroking his lower back. The string came undone, and he felt around to her perfect breasts, the nipples hard against his palms. She gasped into his mouth, her fingers working at the string of his board shorts.

He pulled away suddenly. *What am I doing?*

Quickly, she retied the strings of her top. Her eyes didn't meet his but he could see the shock on her face. He turned away and didn't look back.

"Well, if you change your mind," she called out behind him.

Joe shook his head and kept walking.

When he returned to the beach, Marty and Shelby/Sharla lay close together, talking, Marty rubbing her arm. His expression changed from leisure to alarm as Joe walked past them.

"What's up?" Marty said after he caught up.

"I can't do it, man," Joe said, shuffling into his flip flops.

"What? That little hottie not good enough for you?"

Joe kept walking.

"What happened?"

"Nothing."

"Whaddya mean? Looked like she was all over you."

Joe made a face. "I guess."

Marty stopped, his eyes open wide. "Did you . . . already?"

"No!" Joe faced him. "I left."

"*What?*" Marty grabbed handfuls of his thick blonde hair. "Dude! *What* is the matter with you?"

"I'm so not into this."

Marty sighed. "It's Lorna, isn't it?"

Joe kicked a pebble.

"Shit," Marty said.

"Yep."

"Well . . . " Marty glanced back to the beach. "Godspeed, man." Joe hit fists with his friend before turning to go.

The sun beat down on Joe's shoulders as he walked. He replayed the time he and Lorna had spent together and knew he'd misinterpreted everything. She was confident in the waves, but shy, awkward even, when it came to talking about her feelings. She wanted to help Alex but was afraid of getting hurt. Joe needed to see her. Something *had* passed between them during that trip to the hospital. She'd pushed him away after that, and now he knew why. She was scared.

The road smelled of rotting guavas and cow shit. He passed a Fijian man, walking with an ox and a little kid. They wore dirty clothes, and the kid's upper lip was glossy with yellow snot. The old man greeted him with, "Bula!" and a smile missing several teeth. The kid just stared. "Bula," he answered, moving on with quick strides.

Finally, the turnoff with Vunde Bay's faded sign came into view, the crushed shell drive weaving into the shaded jungle. He quickened his pace, feeling hot and sticky from the hike. Birds hooted and cawed from hidden perches, sounding an alarm at his intrusion. The road snaked down alongside a trickling creek, and its musical sound made him acutely aware of his thirst. Finally the frothy turquoise ocean came into view, and with it the familiar faint, steady growl of the waves.

# ELEVEN

Panicked, Joe pounded on Lorna's door again. Why had he been such a dick yesterday? What if she had left? "Lorna!" he called out, not caring if anyone heard.

The door opened partway, revealing Lorna dressed in a blue tank top and shorts. God, she was beautiful.

"Oh," he said, feeling limp with relief. He realized he had rehearsed nothing of what he wanted to say. "I'm so glad you're here." He reached out and stroked her forehead, his fingers trembling.

Her tense features relaxed and her stormy eyes closed. He wrapped his arms around her and held her. After a long moment, she looked up at him. He kissed her, a light, soft kiss that awakened a feeling of lightness inside his chest. She kissed him back, and the feeling expanded, zipping into his toes, his shoulders. She pulled him inside.

They kissed their way towards the bed. He told himself to slow down but it was no use—he had already pulled off both of their shirts. The feel of her soft breasts against his chest was no help. He wanted her. He was sweaty and hot after the long hike, while she was cool and smooth and smelled fresh, like the skin of an apple. His fingers couldn't figure out the buttons on her shorts, so she had to help, which made her laugh between his kisses.

He caressed the soft scoop of her low back and lower, beneath the edge of her panties. He sat her on the bed and kissed her neck, behind her earlobe; his hands fell in love with her breasts. She made soft noises into his ear and arched against him. He had a sudden fear that he would ejaculate at that very moment. *Stop!* He told himself to calm down, to think of something else. *What's the matter with me?* But he didn't want to think of anything else, he wanted to savor every inch of her. He could taste the sun on her skin and smell the vanilla scent of her hair. He wanted to hear what other sounds she might make. Her fingers undid the knot in his trunks, and he kicked them off. Her touch feathered over his hips and pulled him close. He groaned.

The responsible part of his brain sounded the alarm. "Do you have . . . ?" he mumbled.

As if she could read his mind, she reached over the bed to her duffel and pulled out a silver package. He kissed along her collarbone to her nipples. She gasped, her fingers curling through his hair. He was fully erect against her inner thigh that was smooth and warm; he could feel the damp fabric of her panties as her hips nested against his. She took him in her hand and the shock of her touch was almost painful. He slid her panties down and tasted her there. She gasped and gave in to his caresses, moving with him, weaving her fingers through his hair. "Please," she whispered, pulling him up. She slid the condom on, and he thrust inside.

She breathed a joyful little sigh and her eyes closed. Their bodies seemed to know the rhythm so he let go, enjoying the freedom and the thrill bubbling up inside him. He suckled her nipples, and her breaths made sweet little gasps of surprise. His yearning skyrocketed and he kissed her mouth, tasting the waves and the sun and the mist. Her lips opened in pleasure, and he watched in fascination and delight, feeling her climax begin. She gripped his backside, urging him until she cried out, her hips tense against his. When it ended, she laughed, a sweet, wonderful laugh that filled him with happiness.

After a moment of rest, he grinned. "Let's do that again," he said.

"Yeah?" she said, her eyes like sparks in the dim room.

On top, she rocked slowly against him. The sensation of watching her in control sent a new pulse of desire racing through him. "You feel so good," he said, his hands caressing her hips, her smooth belly.

He rose to kiss a nipple, his mouth taking in her softness, his teeth teasing. Lorna's head fell back and she closed her eyes. Joe stroked her, kissed her, his breaths fast and sharp. They moved slowly, passionately. She came again, sighing softly this time, the waves of pleasure shuddering through her. He felt his own climax rising and grasped her hips. Her shoulders relaxed, and her chest arched, moist in the humid room. Wave upon wave of ecstasy flooded through him. Their bodies slowed, and he reached up to kiss her, his fingers tangling in her wild curls. Lorna fell softly against him, breathing hard.

Lorna blinked her eyes open. She rolled to her side and stared at him, seeming to take him in for a long moment.

Joe grinned at her. "Hi," he said.

"Hi," she said, grinning back. "How long did I sleep?"

"About an hour," he replied.

"And you just lay there, watching?" she asked, giving him a look.

"I went through your pockets," he teased, stroking her shoulder.

"What?"

Joe kissed her, his body still buzzing from what they'd done. He already wanted to do it again, and felt himself harden.

"Mmm," she said. "Maybe a shower, first?"

This time he explored every inch of her, and when at last they collapsed, spent and satisfied, dusk had fallen.

"Food," Lorna groaned.

They dressed silently, and Joe could feel the shift in her mood. He was thrilled at how they'd spent the rest of the day, but had it brought him closer to who she really was?

She went for the crutches as they left the bure, but he convinced her to ride piggyback instead. She laughed, and though he pretended to huff and puff, he was glad to have her arms around his neck, her breath on his cheek.

They arrived at the empty kitchen and Joe lowered her to the shiny floor. "Hello?" Joe called into the dim space.

"Did they get a night off, or something?" she asked.

"Maybe, but where's everyone else?"

"They've gone to town," a voice said from the back door. Shaun shuffled into the room, his red face crinkled with concern. "You didn't hear?" he asked, unloading a large box. "I guess someone's had a baby," he added, waving a hand at the empty kitchen.

Joe looked at him, trying to figure out which one of the surfers was having a baby.

"In the village," Shaun said distractedly. "They might not be back for a day or so."

"Who?" Lorna asked. "The surfers?"

"No, the cooks," Shaun replied.

Joe looked at Lorna, who shrugged.

"You can rummage in the fridge," Shaun said. "You might find some cold cuts, there's bread on the counter." He pointed at the far corner where Joe saw a plastic tray containing humped rows of sandwich bread. "I can open the bar but then I'm off," Shaun added, wiping his brow, his wrist smudged with black grease.

They ate their mystery meat and limp iceberg lettuce sandwiches on the end of the dock as the last colors faded from the sky. A tiny wave washed over the reef outside the bay, hissing gently before fading back to silence.

Joe sighed. "I could live here," he said, washing down a bite with a sip of beer.

"Here?" Lorna replied.

Joe took a quick survey of the endless water and the creaky dock. "Okay, we might need a bed," he replied.

"Just a bed?" Lorna joked, raising her eyebrows. "Not a roof? Walls?"

"Okay, a roof might be nice."

"Don't forget a fridge."

"Who needs a fridge? You'd have fresh fish every day, and there's cassava root and mango growing everywhere."

Lorna wrinkled her nose. "I don't like cassava."

"Okay, you can have a fridge then."

"And a bed," she reminded.

Joe traced her delicate kneecap with his finger. "Of course," he said, and kissed her.

They sipped their beers in silence as the waves cascaded over the distant reef. A breeze cooled his skin. He wondered if Lorna had thought any more about Alex, but he wanted to hold on to the sweetness of the moment, the romance and the warmth of her, content, it seemed, by his side.

"So, are you giving up music?" she asked.

Joe squinted at her, surprised. "Marty tell you that?" He shrugged as he considered his answer. "I'll never give up music. I just might not play in a band." He leaned back.

"Why?"

"I don't know. It's a weird life." The sun had melted into the horizon and the sky's pink hue burned slowly to crimson. He could feel her studying him. He tipped his beer back for the last sip.

"You get laid a lot, don't you?"

Joe sputtered, choked. "What?"

"C'mon, tell me!" she howled, her eyes dancing playfully. "It's not like I'll be upset."

Joe looked away. Was he blushing? He sighed, deciding to go down this road with her. "At first I thought, hey, I must be somethin'," he admitted. He shrugged, adding, "I had some fun." Then he looked at her and the memories of his recklessness, his carelessness faded. "But it got old. I mean, these girls, they just want to party." He shook his head. "They don't care about anything, not even themselves." He turned to her. "People should be good to each other."

Lorna's smile faded and she looked away.

He watched the first of the stars twinkle out of the dusk. "Besides, the money's no good," he added, half-jokingly.

"So?" she replied as another wave spilled over the reef. "What do you need a lot of money for?"

He exhaled heavily. In truth, if the band kept increasing its popularity, he could make good money. But it felt dirty somehow, tainted. "I don't need a lot, but it sure would be nice to have something saved up. I want to build a house someday. I want a family." He looked at her, feeling nervous. He hadn't shared this with anyone, and knew it sounded corny, hokey.

Lorna frowned, looking serious.

"Life's short," he said, refusing to defend himself. She would either get it or not. "If you don't plan for what you want, for what really matters, it won't happen."

Lorna's stormy eyes connected with his, and her face was serious, as if he had said something profound. A breeze skimmed the surface of the ocean and washed over them before ruffling the palm leaves lining the shore.

"So that's what you want? To punch a clock so you can go home to your housewife and your two-and-a-half kids?" Lorna said.

Joe shook his head. "No. That's not it at all." He sighed. "When I was six my parents took me and my sisters out of school and drove to Central America. We spent a year traveling, surfing, sailing. My parents helped the locals create a sanctuary for endangered birds. When I was twelve we spent a summer in the Alaskan bush, building a school." He glanced at her. "I want to do things like that."

"A regular Swiss Family Robinson, huh?" she asked.

He shook his head again. "Wouldn't it be cool to sail around the world?"

Lorna shrugged. "Sure."

"Buy a piece of land in Peru, right in front of a killer break?"

"It's cold in Peru!" she joked.

He sighed. Life was what you made of it, not what people told you to make of it, or expected you to make of it. Joe believed that you could have it all if you worked hard and had the patience and determination to see it through. But he didn't want to do it alone.

"So you're quitting the band?"

He twirled his empty beer bottle in his lap. "I started the band because I love making music." He remembered the way they had agonized over song lyrics in the beginning and how the melodies had been the result of hard work and a lot of soul. "It's not about that now. Playing gigs at these crappy little clubs, with cigarette smoke in my eyes, people getting into fights, and girls doing coke in the bathroom. I'm just over it." He placed the empty bottle aside and looked up at the explosion of stars now burning brightly above them. "I want to start thinking about the future."

The sound of car wheels on gravel up at the main bure broke the moment, and Joe heard the surfers flood onto the grounds with their loud banter, laughter, and slamming car doors.

Soon the surfers were shuttling several cases of beer and a large bottle of liquor down to the beach.

"Oi!" Garth howled. "Are we interrupting?"

A party was soon underway, and Joe felt they had no choice but to join in. He carried their empties, and Lorna hobbled behind him to the shore. Soon, a pipe made its rounds and the boisterous group, with Garth as the ringleader, carried on.

Then Marty stood at their side, wearing his Cheshire-cat grin. "Have a good day, Lorna?" he asked, passing her the pipe.

She paused but her bright eyes betrayed her. "Yeah," she said, glancing at Joe. "I did." She inhaled from the pipe before passing it to Joe.

Joe lit the bowl and inhaled, thinking of how little he'd learned about Lorna. But maybe it was a start.

# TWELVE

Lorna left the party and hobbled to the main bure for a pit stop and to refill her water bottle. All the extra-curricular activities from the day had caught up to her. She was sweating and grimacing now with each step. *But it sure was fun*, she thought, marveling at how much had changed in the past few hours. When Joe had shown up at her doorstep, the look on his face had knocked her flat. She realized how much she had hoped—somewhere deep inside her—that he would come. A rush of heat flooded her skin when she remembered how he made her feel. *Like he knew exactly how to touch me, kiss me.*

She was on her way back to the party when the green glow of the office computer caught her attention. The door was unlocked; she looked both ways before entering the tiny room. What Garth had said earlier was spinning in the back of her mind. Where had he and Alex crossed paths? Maybe she could use the computer to find out. "Rio something," she said aloud. She poked a key and the computer slowly whirred to life.

Lorna lowered carefully into the hard plastic chair. She started at Garth's website and got distracted by his bio. He was sponsored by Billabong, and from what Lorna could tell he seemed to be struggling. He hadn't made a quarterfinal in over a year and hadn't won anything since his rookie season. His opening page showed him riding a massive wave. It seemed strange that he could ride such a giant but not win a contest. Maybe that's why he had come with a photographer and had hogged all the big sets: to prove something.

Lorna tried an Internet search with Alex's name and the word *Rio*. Nothing. She tried *Alex Morneau* and *surfing* and listened to the computer whir. Rio something had to be in Mexico, or Central America maybe.

The search results loaded. Nothing.

She tried one more: Surfing, Mexico, Billabong.

Bingo.

A link to a blog on Billabong's website described a surf camp along the Michoacán coast, located in a tiny town called Río Limón. *She's got a sweet setup down there,* Garth had said. Alex was running a surf camp? It seemed so unlike her, yet that had to be it. Lorna clicked a link to a map and when it loaded, it showed a road-less, blank area on a bump of coastline.

When Lorna returned to the crowd, Joe was playing his guitar. She slipped into a hammock. To her surprise, some of the surfers knew the words to the songs. Lorna felt disoriented. Was Joe famous? She felt stupid for not asking more about his music and wondered if she'd heard his songs on the radio.

The guitar melodies and his rich voice melded with the sound of the night wind and the tiny waves tapping the shore. She couldn't always make out the meaning, but she sensed sadness and hints of bitterness; humor, too, and joy, as she could tell by a certain softening in his voice or crispness at the edges of the words. The music put her at ease, making her feel dreamy. She thought back to Joe's goals: marriage and kids and adventure all tied together with a big, shiny bow. He was a dreamer, for sure. But she admired him for pursuing a dream that defied convention—quitting an easy party life for diapers and maps of National Parks. She imagined Joe driving some station wagon, playing punch bug and I-Spy with a gaggle of kids and his adoring wife, a natural wonder herself, smiling at him as she led a round of "Rain drops on roses and whiskers on kittens . . . " Lorna looked up at the stars, wondering how many road trips Alex had taken without her. Was it just too much trouble, or did freedom trump responsibility?

As Joe played, she could see it change him—in the sureness of his hands working the strings, in the way his body seemed more alive, as if channeled by something. He didn't seem shy or deferential or even quiet; he was taller, more powerful, a force almost. Every now and then his electric eyes sought hers, and she knew that he was thinking about her, about what they had done. It almost frightened her the way she wanted it too, and how she knew it couldn't possibly last.

Joe took a break and more beer bottles hissed open; conversations splintered, but the mood stayed charged.

"Well, girls," Garth suddenly pronounced. "The tour calls, so tonight's me last night," he added, raising his beer.

Cries of surprise and dismay filled the darkness. His eyes swept past hers. "Next time I see you arseholes, it will be from the podium!" he shouted.

With this the group rose up in a kind of riot, lifting him up and rushing towards the water. Shocked, Lorna watched the mass of bodies plunge into the dark abyss, chests and arms and legs smacking the water as they thrashed, shouting, their words echoing to the horizon, filling the night.

"No swim for you, huh?" Joe asked from the shadows.

Lorna released a long breath, putting Alex and Río Limón out of her mind. In two days she would be home and could sort everything out. Until then, there was Joe, warm and real and waiting for her. "Nah," she said easily, swinging carefully out of the hammock to grab Joe's hand. "I'm wet enough as it is," she replied, enjoying the shock in Joe's eyes.

Joe lifted her over his shoulder and made a break for her bure. She beat at his back in mock protest, laughing. As he charged up her steps, she caught sight of Garth wading from the water, his gaze steely, his lips set in a hard line.

"Why do you call her *Alex*?" Joe asked after.

Lorna rolled to her side. "When I was a kid, I had to go find her. She'd be off surfing somewhere, and so I'd go looking. 'Have you seen my mom?' I'd ask. 'Who's your mom?' they'd say." Lorna smoothed the sheets. "'Alex,' I'd say. At some point it became easier to ask, 'have you seen Alex?'" But Lorna knew it was also easier to be left behind by a person named Alex.

"What are you going to do?"

Lorna could feel her shoulders tense. "I know where she is now. Garth told me."

Joe looked at her, surprised. "Garth?"

"He's surfed with her in Mexico, part of some team trip he did last year. I did some research. It's in Michoacán, in this tiny town called Río Limón."

"Wait, how did Garth connect you to your mom?"

Lorna imagined Alex pulling a picture of her out of her wallet to show Garth, but pushed the idea away. Alex would never do such a thing. "I sort of look like her."

Joe looked pensive for a moment. "So, if the results at the hospital show something . . . bad . . . at least now you can go tell her."

"I'm not going there, Joe."

"Why?"

"Because I can't! I'm broke, and I've used up every last hour of vacation time for the next year." Alex had chosen to run away from her problems, just like she always had. Lorna needed to move on with her life.

"I'm through chasing her down." She had made up her mind. "If she's sick, she should have stayed in Seattle. It's too late now," Lorna said with bitterness.

"What about it being too late for you?" Joe said, stroking her hair.

Lorna wished they could go back to talking about cassava and surfing in Peru. "It's already too late," she said, her jaw tense.

"Look, whatever happened between you two . . . " He grimaced, like he was holding back. "This could be your chance to make it right."

"Nothing can ever make it right!" she said. "You don't know what it was like, Joe!"

"Then tell me," he said. "Let me help."

"I don't want your help," she said, swiping back angry tears. "I have to do this my way."

Joe's eyes were dark when he looked away. "Then what are we doing here?" he said. "I thought . . . "

"You thought what?" Lorna asked.

"Forget it," Joe said, getting out of bed. He yanked on his shorts and grabbed his T-shirt. "When you're through playing games, you let me know," he said.

"I'm not playing games!" Lorna said, her fury rising.

"Then let me in," Joe said from the door.

Lorna paused, wanting to scream, to cry. *I can't*, she thought as she watched him walk out the door.

# THIRTEEN

Joe served himself and Marty coffee from the buffet then shuffled towards an empty booth far from the kitchen. A handful of other surfers were bent over their bowls of cereal or wedges of melon, their hair scruffy, their T-shirts already limp in the early heat. Joe recognized one of them as Garth's photographer. Piles of luggage and surfboards were stacked by the door.

"Get any sleep last night?" Marty teased in a low voice after they were seated.

Joe gave his friend a warning look. He was not ready to talk about Lorna.

Marty chatted on about the open-air bar near the harbor, where they had watched MTV and hit on girls the night before. Joe remembered Lorna's soft skin against his.

" . . . she ends up smacking him right across the face," Marty said in a low voice. "Too many martinis."

"You guys were drinking martinis?" Joe asked, realizing that Garth wasn't in the room with the others. It still seemed crazy that he knew Alex.

Marty looked at him blandly. "Garth was buying."

"How's your foot?" Joe asked, leaning out to get a look.

Marty shrugged. "Looks like good surf today." He squinted at Joe. "We should go."

Joe had seen the latest swell report—a new groundswell was arriving, and from the looks of the luggage pile, they were about to be blessed with a nearly empty lineup.

"Hell, yeah," Joe replied eagerly, draining his coffee. A morning session with Marty was just what he needed, even though there was a little voice in the back of Joe's mind telling him to stick around, maybe find a way to talk to Lorna. *Later*, he thought. *After I figure out what to say.*

"Then let's hit the Nautilus after. Charlotte promised me a massage." Joe studied the bottom of his stained cup.

"You got some play already, so don't get all high and mighty," Marty said, wagging his finger.

A sudden rush of heat filled Joe's his cheeks. Not because Marty was right—being with Lorna would never in a million years be qualified as "getting some play." He wanted to be done with that kind of experience altogether, and hadn't being with Lorna felt like more than that? Even though things got heated, it only made him want her more. She was fighting against something inside; he could help her. He toyed with the idea of offering to go to Mexico with her. *Don't be stupid*, he thought. *What is wrong with me?*

He felt like he was in that moment just before dropping in late on a wave. He might make the drop and score the ride of his life, or go over the falls and get crushed. He was there, deciding: go for it or pull back. Then he realized that the decision had already been made. *I'm going over the falls*, he thought.

"Let's go," Joe said, inhaling a shaky breath. Marty gave him a shrewd look, then stood and followed him out the door.

# FOURTEEN

## Wailoaloa Beach Hotel, Nadi

Lorna ordered another drink and tried to get into her book. She took a dip in the pool. She completed an entire collection of Sudoku puzzles. After four cocktails, she fell asleep in her lounge chair and woke shivering. The sun had lowered below the hills and the pool was deserted. She gathered her things and limped to her room where she took a long shower. Feeling ravenous, she raided her mini fridge for junk food she ate on her bed while watching reruns of *ER*— shouting at the television when the actors made mistakes that real doctors wouldn't. As always, it amused her to catch all their flaws, but it both made her miss her job and dread her return.

It was better that she left this way. Joe wouldn't have to go through an awkward goodbye, and he wouldn't have to see her cry.

# FIFTEEN

May 25th, 2004

University of Washington Medical Center, Seattle

During Lorna's first shift back in the E.R., she discovered with anguish that she had indeed been cc'd on Alex's medical report. However, it was easy to avoid it. Her leg was throbbing and her body felt wrung out. The jetlag made her brain feel sluggish, and at three a.m. she collapsed on the lounge couch. When a nurse woke her with "G.S.W., four minutes," she bolted upright, guzzling a half-liter of water as she hurried toward the ambulance bay.

In the end, it took her almost a week to get to the report. The shifts were jam-packed with interesting patients to treat, the jetlag messed with her sleep, and her sore leg meant she couldn't go running to release the tension. Deep down she knew she was avoiding the report, and then one morning she ran into Yoko in the locker room at shift change.

Lorna's eyelids felt like they were made of sandpaper. Her stomach was churning from too much coffee and the stale almonds she had found in her backpack.

Yoko was in a rush and only gave her a passing, "Hey," while tying up her long, black hair and hurrying out.

Alex's medical report had been riding around in her backpack, unread, for days. On the bus home that evening, she took several deep breaths and smoothed the creases from it. Then, she began to

read, first slowly, then a second time, flipping to the critical find-
ings, trying to see it differently and with alternative outcomes. Then
she slumped against the cold window, and cried.

*Primary adenocarcinoma.* Pancreatic cancer.

Vunde Bay had sent her an email with a link to their photos
page. Unable to sleep after her first night shift, she had opened the
link and scanned the pictures. Her gut lurched when her eyes passed
images of Joe. She clicked on one of herself making a cutback high
on the face of a turquoise-blue wall, her features so grave she barely
recognized herself. That's when she realized how easily Garth had
made the connection. In that picture, with her wet hair slicked back
and her face that way, she looked like Alex.

Alex, who was somewhere in Mexico, sick and not knowing
why. With no one to take care of her when things got bad. And they
would. Even without a biopsy, there was no doubt in Lorna's mind:
Alex's cancer was real, and without treatment, she would be dead in
six months, maybe sooner.

What should she do? She couldn't ask for leave so soon after her
trip to Fiji. Plus, she couldn't just abandon her residency whenever
she felt like it. And there was the problem of being broke. With a
grunt, Lorna remembered Garth's bizarre invitation. It still bugged
her, though she couldn't say why.

Memories of Joe wouldn't leave her alone. The feel of his strong
body holding her, of the easy way they had laughed and talked, and
the tenderness he had shown her were still imprinted in her memories. If only *he* had offered to go with her to Mexico.

If only he had been real.

Would this keep happening to her? Meeting someone like Joe
only to lose him? She remembered how she'd fallen for Miles, who

was kind and made her laugh. Over time, their friendship developed deep roots, but the pain of his rejection still haunted her.

She remembered the way Joe had looked at her when he left. Like she had hurt *him*, when it was the other way around.

Lorna tried the phone number listed for Alex's surf tour business, but it only rang and rang. She found an email address, but her awkward message, "Hey, it's Lorna. I hear you were in my E.R. Can you call me?" bounced back with *mail undeliverable*. After two weeks of failed attempts, of worrying, thinking, wondering, Lorna started having trouble sleeping. Each day, she felt more and more like a zombie. Her judgment felt cloudy, her reactions sluggish. Worried she might make a mistake that could hurt someone, she upped her caffeine intake and began babbling her thinking process out loud to her fellow residents and any other physicians who happened to be nearby. She began to get strange looks; some avoided her. When she tried to sleep at night, she saw Alex bent over in pain, or stuck in some jungle clinic with doctors who wanted to dig out her appendix or give her Pepto-Bismol.

She went to her chief.

"Are you willing to risk your career for this?" he asked.

Lorna was sweating in the air-cooled room. *No*, she wanted to say. "Yes," she whispered, her jaw sore from clenching it.

The chief sighed. "I'll give you a week."

Lorna held back a sob. "Thank you," she replied.

After getting high in her tiny apartment that overlooked a sunless alley where a neighbor was attempting to grow tomatoes, Lorna sold her truck to a man whose wife was so pregnant her husband had to drag her into it backwards using her armpits. They had just moved from somewhere. Lorna wished them good luck and did not watch them go.

The next day, Lorna bought her ticket for Morelia, Mexico. Although she was packing a carefully assembled medical kit for Alex, with special medications like Ambien, Percocet, and Midazolam, plus some general must-have drugs like Keflex and Phenergan, she felt completely unprepared for the journey that lay ahead. It felt like a trap.

*And I'm willingly walking right into it.*

# PART II

# SIXTEEN

June 12th, 2004

Seascape Golf Club, Santa Cruz, California


Joe slipped the flask from the breast pocket of his tux. "Here," he said to Marty, whose white face and frightened eyes needed fixing fast.

Marty tipped back the flask then grimaced with a tight sigh, then sipped again. On the manicured greens beyond the banquet room, a group of old men finished their round of golf. "What if I'm making a mistake?" Marty asked, looking Joe square in the eyes.

Joe's insides did a somersault. "You're not," he said, picturing Jen getting ready in a spare room similar to theirs. Like Joe's sister Annabelle, would Jen be freaking out, too? Crying because the napkins were ochre instead of French cream? Anxious about the invisible tan lines on her shoulders? "Jen's the best thing that will ever happen to you," he added, eyeing him shrewdly.

Marty took a deep breath. "I know," he replied. He returned the flask, and Joe took a quick sip before returning it to his pocket.

"But this is it," Marty said, the whiteness in his cheeks gone but his eyes dull, resigned.

Joe sighed. Yes, this was it for Marty, but only because he'd wanted it this way. Jen would make a good wife for him—besides being pretty and smart, she would keep him honest, and maybe that's what Marty, at his core, knew that he truly needed. And because Marty wanted it, Joe wanted it, too. "That's the best part, man," Joe said. "This *is* it, the happy ending, where you ride off into the sunset with the girl," he said, smiling.

Marty smiled, too. "Yeah," he replied, straightening. "Let's do this," he said.

After his speech, Joe slid the mic back into the stand and returned to the table, where the plates had been cleared. Jen covered his hand and gave it a squeeze, her bright blue eyes sparkling. Joe swallowed the guilt of knowing things she did not and would never know, and gave her a quick smile in return.

After dessert, the tables disappeared from the dance floor and the band—nobody he recognized, thank God—warmed up. Marty took his bride's hand and led her to the floor for the first dance, Jen's small body floating, her cheeks shiny from her huge smile. He knew she'd probably dreamed of this day since she was ten years old. He wanted this to be her happy ending, too.

He headed towards the bar for something stronger than beer, greeting friends, shooting the shit with a few guys he hadn't seen since high school. Marty joined him some time later, his tie loosened a notch, his cheeks flushed. "We've got one last picture," he gushed, grabbing Joe's arm. "Jesus, you'd think we were documenting the first lunar landing or something."

Marty handed him a cigar. "We gotta smoke these and look like assholes."

They walked down a carpeted hallway and through glass doors to a small balcony, where the photographer stood poised with a large camera. She lined them up against the railing, fussed with their boutonnieres and ties, lit the cigars, and fired through a series of shots, then left in a rush.

Joe leaned over the railing. "These aren't so bad, you know," he said, puffing on his cigar.

"But they're not that good, either," Marty said, exhaling smoke upwards.

The setting sun had turned the edges of the golf course's manicured lawns and sculptured trees to a soft and uniform gray-green, the sky a faint but sickly orange.

Marty produced a tiny pipe from his inside pocket.

"You'd better put that away before someone sees you," Joe said, looking around.

Marty made a face. "What are they gonna do? You know how much this shindig is costing?" He stubbed out the cigar and tossed it over the railing. Joe lost sight of it halfway to the pavement below.

"Costing you? Or Jen's daddy?" Joe teased.

Marty lit the bowl, illuminating his scowl.

They shared the pipe, then Joe leaned back, watching the sky as the faint pinpricks of starlight emerged from the dusk. The night enveloped them, smelling cool and dewy, and faintly sweet from the honeysuckle coiling up the side of the building.

Marty sighed and gave Joe a long and serious look. "You still thinking about Lorna?"

Joe's heart hiccupped and he was suddenly warm despite the cool sea breeze. "I just wish. . . " He closed his eyes, and Lorna was there, her sweet laugh, her heavy heart.

"I feel like it's my fault. You went surfing with me that day instead of . . . "

"Naw, I needed to clear my head." *But I never meant for it to be goodbye.* And he'd been dazzling her with his maturity, his sincerity, and spiel about "being good to each other." What a load of crap! God, how could he have blown it so badly? He'd judged her from his high and mighty position of chief dickhead. "She was right to go," Joe replied.

Marty pushed back from the railing. "You could still find her . . . "

Joe had already dismissed this idea. What would he say? *Hi, remember me, the asshole who walked out on you in Fiji?*

"Well, I've got a party to crash," Marty said. They bumped fists, and Marty slipped back inside.

Joe rested his forearms on the railing and remembered what Marty had said after Lorna left: *Dude, you only knew her for like, a few days? It wouldn't have worked out, anyways, she lives in Seattle. She's a doctor. You're playing gigs or swinging a hammer. Let it go, there are other mermaids in the sea.* Marty was only telling him to go after Lorna now because he knew Joe wouldn't. Joe shook his head. In his way, Marty meant well. He was trying to help him get over Lorna. But Joe had a frightening feeling that he never would.

"Hey stranger," a soft voice said from behind him.

Joe turned to see Francine, smiling shyly. She'd put up her hair, and her sparkling green dress exactly matched the color of her eyes. "Hey," he managed, swallowing the dry lump in his throat.

"Marty said I could come, but I wasn't sure I should," she said, stepping closer.

Joe noticed that her shoulders were already tan but looked frail somehow. *Probably because I'm comparing them to Lorna's,* Joe thought. He forced a smile. His feet ached from the tight shoes he had been wearing since early afternoon, and the mixture of wine, beer, and Jack-and-Cokes were beginning to make his head throb. He either needed to keep drinking or pound a gallon of water. Upon seeing Francine, he decided to keep drinking. "Of course you should come, we said we'd be friends, right?"

He resisted the urge to rub his temples. "You missed most of the party, though," he said, his voice sounding hollow, shaky.

She joined him at the railing. "You look nice," she said.

Joe suppressed the inexplicable urge to laugh. "Thanks," he said, which with his held-back laughter sounded like a cough. "So do you," he added, not looking at her.

She didn't reply.

"No date, huh?" he asked.

"Nope, just me." Her smile wavered.

Joe nodded, more to himself than to Francine. He couldn't get Lorna out of his mind. So many things he hadn't gotten the chance to say to her, so many things he had wanted to ask her. "Fuck," he moaned.

"Huh?" Francine said.

"Sorry," Joe said, pushing off the railing. "I'll see ya," he mumbled, already halfway to the door.

Joe gripped Marty in a bear hug. "Congratulations, man," he said, releasing him to Jen, who slipped her delicate hand in his. "Take it easy on him tonight, alright?" he teased her. She laughed. "No way," she replied over her shoulder. They rushed through a tunnel created by guests crowding into the lobby for their departure, their cheers roaring as tossed confetti fell like snow.

Joe watched the limo drive away. The milling crowd dispersed. Some guests were moving back to the dance floor; some were making their own exits. Across the room he spotted Francine, her eyes sweeping the room until finding his.

Joe cursed under his breath.

"Can I help with anything?" she asked after approaching. The question surprised him.

"Um," he replied, clenching his sweaty palms. "I'm supposed to put all the gifts in Jen's mom's car . . . "

"Okay," she said.

They accomplished the task quickly and with few words. The chilly night air gave Francine's slender neck goose bumps. She seemed to blush when she caught him looking.

"Drink?" he asked as they finished their last load.

"Maybe we could just talk?" she replied, hugging herself.

In the pit of his stomach, Joe knew her coming here, acting this way, looking the way she did meant only one thing. But there was nothing she could say that would convince him to try something he had lost faith in.

# SEVENTEEN

Morelia, Mexico

Lorna left the stuffy airport to steamy mist and darkness, still unsure about the bus station's whereabouts. Had the man at the desk said yes, it was possible to walk, or yes, she should take a bus to get there? Her years of Latin and combat Italian were little help when it came to deciphering Spanish. Warm rain tickled her face and she wiped her eyes with her palm.

A short man with a mustache stepped from the shadows. "Taxi? I take you good hotel," he said, thrusting a worn brochure into her hands.

Lorna recoiled, letting the brochure fall to the wet pavement.

The man scrambled to pick it up. She watched him make a quick assessment of her meager belongings: a grimy backpack and small black duffel. "You come for *mariposa*? I take," he said, unfazed.

"No," Lorna barked, setting off into the night. On the plane, she'd flipped through an article about the butterfly sanctuary south of Morelia, so she knew what *mariposa* meant.

The man was right on her heels. "No safe you go," he said, his tone different now, urgent.

Lorna stopped.

The man's worried eyes pleaded with her. "Where you go? Bus? Hotel? Please. I take." He glanced into the darkness then back at her.

Lorna was exhausted. "Bus station?"

The man nodded eagerly. "Sí, Señora," he said, reaching for her duffel. "I take."

Lorna pulled it close. "I got it," she said. The man led her across the street to a small tan car.

A flicker of anxiety tickled her gut as he opened the door for her. The moments leading up to the car accident in Sicily flashed through her mind. It had been raining so there were new potholes. After a curve in the road an approaching truck suddenly appeared in her lane.

"How far is it?" she gasped, pushing the image away. She resisted the urge to ask him about his driving record—something she had once done to a med school colleague. He had taken it the wrong way, and a rumor bloomed that she was a snob.

The taxi man's eager eyes pleaded with her; he didn't understand.

"*Kilometres,*" she tried. "*Quanto?*" That didn't sound right, was it Italian?

The man pursed his lips a moment. "Oh, si, *kilómetros. Tres . . . quatro,*" he said, waving his hand in the direction leading away from the airport. Lorna grimaced. The stitches had been removed four days ago, but her leg was still sore. Walking four kilometers would cost her.

She slowly lowered into the cab. Her T-shirt and jeans, both drenched from the rain or humidity or both, stuck to her skin, and she had difficulty bending her knees. The worn, lumpy seats sagged beneath her and the cab smelled of greasy food and stale cigarette smoke. Lorna sat rigid, afraid to touch anything. Her lungs felt like they might drown.

The man checked his side mirrors and pulled away from the curb.

She smoothed back her wet curls and wiped her forehead with the back of her wrist. The streets were dark. Lorna noticed the absence of any taxi-like equipment in the car. No license laminated on the dash, no radio, no meter, just a colorful Jesus talisman, surrounded in yellow fringe, hanging from the rearview mirror.

Lorna hugged her backpack and kept one hand looped through the handles of her duffel. "I only have five dollars," she said, which was a lie; she'd stashed the cash from the sale of her truck inside the hidden pocket of her backpack. Not the safest place, but the wad was too big for her shoe.

"*No hay problema,*" the man said. They stopped at a red light. Mariachi music blared from the open door of a bar across the street. The taxi's wipers scudded across the windshield.

While the man drove, taking a series of turns, she discreetly attempted to pull out a five-dollar bill. Wasn't this taking a long time for something "no far"? She realized she was clenching her jaw again. "Has it been raining a lot?"

The man took a quick left turn without signaling, which threw her back against the seat.

Lorna yelped; her hands reached out for the door handle.

"Sí," the man said, apparently not noticing her reaction. "It is rain season now, Señora." He gestured to the sky.

Lorna opened the window several inches and breathed the moist, jasmine-scented air. Of course, it was the rainy season, the same weather that would bring the big summer south swells. She was sure that was the draw of Mexico for Alex—big waves, empty coastline. She could almost feel Alex's anticipation, could picture her studying swell predictions, hoping, calculating. Lorna knew the ritual because she did the same with her own favorite breaks. Lorna's stomach did a nauseating flip when she realized that this season would likely be Alex's last.

The taxi stopped at a curb, and the man's big brown eyes watched her curiously from the rearview mirror. He pointed to a dark and empty ticket window; behind it, light spilled out from a tall, open building.

Lorna extended the bill over the back of the seat, but he didn't take it.

Lorna shook the bill at him, her anxiety mounting. She wanted to get out of the cab. "It's all I have," she said, cursing herself for fumbling around in her pack earlier. Did he suspect she had more?

But the man shook his head, his lips tight. He pulled his wallet from his back pocket and removed a picture of a teenage girl with long brown hair and a shy smile. "No safe," he said, glancing out at the night. "*No ande sola.*" He shook his finger at her. "Okay?"

Lorna glanced at the dark streets and released a long breath. "Okay," she replied, stepping out of the taxi. "Gracias," she added, but he had already pulled away from the curb.

She boarded the bus just before midnight after waiting in agony for almost an hour. Restless and jittery; she'd spent most of her idle time pacing inside the small pool of light granted by the overhead bulbs in the bus bay.

As Lorna queued up to climb the steps, she was surprised to see a small, uniformed woman handing out sack lunches to the passengers. She was further surprised by the bus's clean and new interior. Shuffling down the aisle, she took in the other passengers: a handful of tired-looking older men and a few couples, one with a baby sleeping in a sling. The bus driver secured the luggage bins outside and then dropped heavily into his seat.

She was putting her life into this stranger's hands. Foolishly, she had read about the many speeding, reckless trucks that prowled these Mexican highways at night. How would the driver stay awake? At exactly midnight, they rolled out of the station and down dark and empty streets. The bus's interior lights were turned off, and soon the bus merged onto a highway. The driver lowered a screen shading the passengers from oncoming headlights. With no way of knowing why the bus swerved and accelerated, Lorna began to sweat.

Using her duffel as a pillow against the window, Lorna tried to get comfortable. The hum of the bus engine and occasional splashing of its tires through water flowing over the road soothed her, but she was wide awake.

Her mind returned to Fiji and her rides at Bukuya, the water so crystalline blue. She remembered Joe watching her, and her chest tightened. *When you're through playing games, you let me know*, he'd said. An ache spread to her shoulders, tightened her chest. She pulled her duffel tighter as the space behind her heart cramped, like a hot pebble lodged somewhere deep, unreachable.

She unzipped her duffel and wriggled her hand inside the Ziploc bag containing the drug kit she'd assembled for Alex, looking for Advil to combat her growing headache. In the pitch darkness she hesitated. What if she grabbed the midazolam instead? Or the precious Dilaudid she couldn't afford to waste?

*This is a fool's errand, and I'm the fool*, she thought. Alex could refuse the drugs or the plan to move to a hospital. Or what if Lorna couldn't find Río Limón? Even if she did find it, Alex might no longer be there. She imagined a phone ringing in an abandoned office space.

Lorna used the blue light of her watch to check the vial in her hands. Valium. *Why not?* After swallowing the tiny pill with a few sips of lukewarm Coke, she sat back and watched the rain slash against the windows, shivering as the silent air conditioner gave her goose bumps.

Sometime later, as the road traced hairpin turns up the side of a mountain, Lorna regretted eating the squishy sandwich, scented with Miracle Whip, the thin piece of meat and slice of tomato so entombed in the bread they were impossible to separate. She managed to hold on until a rest stop where she threw it up in a clump of shrubs, the mountain air cool against her hot cheeks.

At dawn she changed busses in a small town that, compared to Morelia, seemed to be part of a different world: banana trees extending for miles, hummocky, rolling hills, ancient cobblestone streets and a central square lined with benches in front of a grand but faded church. While strolling the streets in search of coffee and something to eat, she enjoyed the fresh breeze mixing with the aroma of roasting corn and the astringent odor of mop water drying on the sun-starched cobbles. Skinny stray dogs lifted their heads from the dirty gutters as she passed, their ears twitching from mites. Rounding a corner, Lorna watched a woman in a house dress smoke a cigarette from her balcony, mop in hand and a TV blaring from inside. At the mini-mart two men in polyester pants, Western shirts, and spurs sauntered onto the street, their sweat-stained cowboy hats pulled low.

After a quick egg-and-burrito breakfast and a tepid cup of Nescafé that she mixed herself in the tiny eatery that seemed to double as the family's living room, she hiked back to the station. She boarded her bus, which was crowded with brown faces and two middle-aged white women who ignored her when she passed. After choosing a seat near the back, she swallowed an Ambien and fell asleep soon after the wheels began rolling.

# EIGHTEEN

"Río Limón?" she asked the driver of the tiny, beat-up truck.

During one of her stopovers when Lorna had gone to exchange money, she had missed her southbound bus, the only one until the following day. Lorna had been walking for an hour and her leg was on fire.

The driver discussed something in rapid Spanish with his wife before the man's curious eyes met hers. "Si, Señora," he said, nodding to the back of the rusty pickup idling at her feet.

Lorna took a deep breath. The words of the Morelia taxi driver rang in her ears. What if she was kidnapped? Or raped?

She climbed in the open bed and got as close as she could to the back window. The truck merged onto the road, and the relief to be seated flooded her legs and feet, making her feel lightheaded. When a cloud of dust engulfed her, she clamped her eyes and mouth shut, ducking her face into her T-shirt. The first pothole sent her flying into the stack of wire cages strapped down with a section of rope; she tried to calm her rapid heartbeat by thinking of the sea. *The warm, blue sea.* She held onto the edges of the wire cage with one hand and tried to grip one of the truck bed's ridges with the other. She conjured the sound of waves combing a quiet beach while her butt rammed the truck bed with each successive pothole. It took every shred of self-control not to jump out of the truck. But she had chosen her driver well: the man didn't swerve, or overtake other vehicles. If she didn't die of dust inhalation or a shattered pelvis, she might be in Río Limón by nightfall.

Was she ready?

Lorna gave the couple a hundred pesos and quickly moved away from the roadside and its dust, faded soda cans, and speeding semis. The ocean had been peeking at her through the thick trees during the journey, but how many miles down this road would she limp to reach it? And if Río meant river, where was it? The Lonely Planet guide she'd brought offered only little assurance:

This sleepy beach village used to have a mellow vibe, but recent reports show that it's become quite dangerous, sup-posedly due to drug-related activity. There are no ATMs or hotels, so plan accordingly. If you should find yourself stranded, friendly Eduardo at the north end of the beach rents *palapas*.

The gravel crunched beneath her feet as she climbed a slight rise that seemed to extend into the horizon. Finally, at the top, a large, fenced field, with a brown-and-white horse and its colt graz-ing nearby, gave her an excuse to rest. They raised their heads but did not approach. The air hummed with insects, and the breezes stirring the trees smelled of alfalfa and uncollected garbage stewing in the sun. Then, through the thick green trees ahead, Lorna finally saw the ocean's blue sheen. The low sun told her only a few hours of daylight remained, yet her feet refused to move. What would she find at the end of this road?

She watched the mother and colt nibble the field and shift their feet. She could hear their powerful teeth ripping the grass from the earth. The colt nuzzled the underside of the mother, but she nudged him away, her tail swatting forcefully at the flies.

Lorna readjusted her pack straps and let her heavy feet propel her toward whatever waited.

The gravel transitioned to honey-colored sand as the road leveled. Long, wispy shadows from palm trees danced over her. Wildflowers grew in clusters of bright purples and reds along the chain-link fences. Her hands gripped her pack straps so tightly they cramped; her T-shirt clung to her like a second skin. Would Alex see her first? Call out to her in the street? Lorna avoided looking in the windows of the buildings she passed and mumbled a meek *hola* to an old woman sitting on her shaded porch. Would Alex be watching TV in one of these sitting rooms, her door left open as a form of air conditioning, her blonde hair flipped over the back of a faded orange couch? Or would she be surfing the beach break with the local boys, berating them in playful Spanish, disarming them with her wicked grin before dropping in on a wave? Or would she be coming out of the grocery store, clutching a sack of groceries and looking frail?

Lorna passed a few small, cement-block buildings, one with a wire fence guarding several copper-colored chickens pecking at kernels embedded in the gray dirt. The sidewalks were empty; the few stores she passed—a paint store, a tiny market ironically named "Mini Super," and what looked like some kind of machine shop taking up an entire block—were all closed. The street that had delivered her from the highway ended here, at a T intersection. Across from her was a row of whitewashed buildings, separated in the middle by a breezeway that led to the beach, and what looked like an open-air restaurant. Lorna crossed the street, her leg throbbing, and wondered if Alex was watching her. She stepped beneath a large, thatched-style roof, the sand gritty beneath her running shoes, her heart thumping. She walked to the end of the breezeway and inspected the empty tables and vacant chairs. Was the restaurant closed for siesta or for the season?

The beach dropped off gently to the turquoise shimmer of the sea, the golden sand punctuated by palm trees. Her eyes adjusted to the shade beneath the thatched roof as she stepped past a large open sink, cutting board, and a set of half doors she assumed were restrooms.

The sun's glare heated her face as she walked from the damp coolness of the restaurant to the sand, kicking off her shoes as she continued on, unable to resist the pull of the ocean. She disregarded the possibility of finding Alex in the water—the ocean was as flat as a lake. In fact, the beach's only visitors were several large birds disemboweling a fish carcass near the shore. Palm leaves shimmered in the breeze above her as she transitioned to the hot sand. She dropped her pack and duffel in a patch of shade and rushed into the clear blue water. Tiny ripples lapped the beach, leaving lacy edges of foam. She waded up to her shins, hitching her jeans against a surge that lapped the shore behind her. Lorna closed her eyes and savored the salty scent, listened to the hush-crush of the waves meeting the beach then sliding back into the sea. She took another step forward, her toes curling into the coarse sand, and inhaled again. Soon she was kicking away from shore, diving under the little swells, bursting up to the surface. She glanced back at the little village, her skin slippery with salt and road grit, and noticed the purple-black clouds billowing behind the mountains.

Flanked on both ends by high points of land covered in vibrant greenery, the tranquil sea swayed beneath her. If this was indeed Alex's paradise, where were the waves? And where was Alex?

∿∿∿

Lorna sipped the last of her beer and paid the boy. She consulted her Lonely Planet guidebook's dictionary again before asking him, "*Estoy buscando . . .* "—she hadn't found the word for woman— "*una donna?*" She unconsciously slipped into Italian.

The boy pointed at the women's restroom.

Lorna shook her head and tried again. "Estoy buscando Alex?" She hoped that meant *do you know Alex?*

The boy blushed, shook his head.

Lorna flipped through the pages of her book, looking for other words that might work.

"Hotel?" the boy asked, his eyes hopeful.

"No," Lorna replied. "Una gringo . . . " She closed the book. "*Mi madre.*" Lorna grabbed a lock of her own hair. "*Bianca.*" She pantomimed long hair, feeling like an idiot. She could see an older man peeking out at her from behind the kitchen. Didn't anybody here speak English?

Still the boy shook his head.

"*Estoy buscando mi madre bianca.*" Lorna groaned in frustration. "Oh!" she cried. Of course, the boy would surely know the white woman who surfed. "*Olas?*" Wasn't that the word for waves? "Estoy buscando mi madre bianca qui amore olas!"

The boy backed away, looking spooked.

Lorna pinched the bridge of her nose with her fingertips. *Am I in the wrong town?*

The rain began just after she left the open-air restaurant in search of Eduardo and his palapas. Lorna knocked on the door of the trailer. The salt that had dried on her face from her swim was now stinging her eyes and crumbling from her temples; her calves were splattered in kicked-up sand that itched. A loud creaking precluded the door being thrown open, revealing a thin man with hollow eyes and thick stubble. Blue light and rapid Spanish from a television filled the dingy space beyond.

"Eduardo?" she asked.

"Sí," he grunted, looking her up and down.

"Er, palapa?"

The man shooed her with his arms and slammed the door shut.

Stunned, Lorna looked around at the night, listening to the rain patter on the metal roof of the trailer and *pat-pat-slap* on the palm fronds overhead. She was so tired her bones hurt.

*There is no ATM or hotel, so plan accordingly.* Lorna gritted her teeth. She pounded on the door again, ignoring a mild sense of panic.

Eduardo opened it, glaring.

Lorna thrust her Lonely Planet at him. "I have nowhere else to go, okay?" she said, her voice hard. She felt like chucking the book at him for good measure.

Eduardo glanced longingly at his television then grabbed a set of keys from a hook next to the door and rushed past her. "Vamos," he hissed.

Lorna scurried after him to a whitewashed building with three doors. He stabbed his key into the middle door and pushed it open, stepping over a concrete threshold and flicking a light switch. A single bulb glowed dimly to life from the center of the ceiling, revealing a bed and a sink. The bed was a concrete platform topped with a thin, plastic-sheathed mattress, and the tiny sink's dripping faucet had made a rust streak that looked a hundred years old.

Eduardo turned to her with his hand out. "Quinientos pesos."

Lorna blinked.

The man sighed heavily then held up five fingers followed by making two hollow fists. Five hundred pesos, or about thirty dollars. Thirty dollars? Wasn't Mexico supposed to be cheap? Her meal had cost eight dollars, the beers being the most expensive part.

Lorna shivered despite the stuffy warmth of the room and the thick humidity. "Are there sheets? A blanket?"

The man's eyes didn't flinch.

Lorna looked outside at the pouring rain before digging the correct bill from her pocket.

The man snatched the money and quickly departed, not bothering to close the door.

Hours later, Lorna woke to the sensation of someone touching her and screamed, swinging at her intruder. But after touching nothing, hearing nothing, she slid out of bed and switched on the light. The room was empty, but a cluster of tiny black turds near the sink didn't make her feel any better. She turned off the light and smoothed down her extra clothes doubling as a cover sheet and tried to relax back into sleep.

But sometime later, yells outside her door and the *thud, thud, thud* of someone's fist against wood woke her again.

Lorna sat upright, her heart pounding.

There was a sound like a gunshot, then an engine revved and sped away. A door slammed and footsteps slapped past her room on the wet walkway.

Lorna considered crouching on the far side of the bed but remembered the mouse turds and whatever else might be down there. Paralyzed, she waited for her door to burst open, but after a long moment, there was nothing more.

After a while, Lorna curled up again, slipping on her sweatshirt and covering her legs with a towel as she began to shiver. *Some paradise*, she thought. With no waves and no Alex, come sunrise she'd be on the first bus out of this nightmare.

# NINETEEN

## Río Limón, Mexico

Lorna woke well into the morning, her cheek wet from the puddle of drool she'd left on the mattress's plastic sheath. Disgusted, she sat up to wipe her face with her sleeve then peeled off her sweatshirt; the room was stifling. Ignoring the irksome kink in her spine, she slipped into her flip flops and shoved the rest of her things into her pack. After running her fingers through her matted curls, she approached the door and listened. Hearing no sounds, she opened the door an inch and peered both ways.

The wet pavement shone brightly beneath a pale blue sky dotted with puffy white clouds. Boats idled at the edge of the bay, and the air was so still she could hear the fishermen's voices carry across the calm water. With no sign of the previous night's activity, Lorna closed the door softly behind her and hurried down the walkway.

On her way back to the main part of town, the slight offshore breeze brought the smell of frying meat and wet grass. She left the beach—walking in the sand made her leg ache—and made her way to the potholed road that paralleled it. A long, crumbling building with bars on the tiny windows bordered the road. To her left, towards the mountains, was a length of scraggly jungle. She kept on until she intersected with the road she had walked down from the highway. After her terrifying night, she was ready to leave on the first bus, but her empty stomach had other ideas, and her head screamed for coffee. One block away was the beachside restaurant—and someone there was singing.

The man who had peeked out at her from the kitchen the previous night greeted her without surprise, wearing a faded blue T-shirt and a white apron wrapped around his wide middle. His thick black mustache twitched with his *buenos días*. He nodded toward a table at the edge of the beach.

"*Huevos?*" she asked.

The man nodded curtly. "Café?"

Lorna gratefully agreed, and the man hurried away.

After Lorna finished off the platter of scrambled eggs, mixed with tomatoes and peppers and bacon, plus the entire stack of fresh tortillas, the man reappeared from the kitchen. He removed her plate but stood at her side, seeming to pause. "*Estás buscando las olas?*" he finally said, his shiny dark eyes sharp, inquisitive.

The question disarmed Lorna. She'd been preparing to ask about the bus station, or the possibly of another Río Limón located somewhere along the coast.

"Sí," she replied slowly.

The man tipped his head sideways, towards the ocean. "*Vienen.*"

Lorna squinted at him, not understanding.

"*Con la lluvia.*" He squinted at the sky. "Lluvia," he said again, pantomiming falling rain with his free hand. "*Siempre vienen.*"

Lorna blinked but the man offered nothing more. She watched him retreat to the kitchen, where she could hear chopping and the lilting melody of his song.

Lorna washed up in the tiny sink and wandered back to the town's main intersection in search of a bus station. The collection of cement-block homes with bare dirt yards, some with chickens, one with a goat tied to the low branch of a gigantic tree extended in a straight line up the long hill toward the highway. She entered the Mini Super and asked the clerk, a plump woman with brown hair slicked back into a tight bun, about a bus. The woman pointed in the direction of the highway. Lorna sighed. But when did the bus come? The woman shook her finger sideways at Lorna as if to scold her. "El Domingo," she said.

Lorna didn't understand. "Donde Río Limón?" she asked. Was there another town with the same name?

The woman's brow wrinkled. Finally she pointed to the south.

Lorna's heart skipped a beat. "How far?" she asked. Could she get there by bus?

The woman blinked.

"*Con autobus?*" Lorna asked, pointing to the road.

The woman stepped through the open doorway. Lorna followed. The woman pointed to the jungle south of town.

"*Cinco minutos*," the woman said before returning inside to assist a trio of preteen girls buying bubble gum.

Lorna hurried south, passing the restaurant and the length of an apartment building to a huge slash pile of dead palm fronds, mixed with trash and pieces of rebar, scraps of wood, an empty paint bucket, soggy mounds of toilet paper, and the thin white sleeve of a condom. Inching carefully between the pile and the end of the building toward the beach, Lorna took a few steps in the direction of the water. She walked further. Was there more of a town beyond?

Still confused, Lorna continued until the dune descended to a shallow valley. Hidden by the curve in the beach and the height of the dunes, a trickling creek flowed into the ocean, making an opaque, turquoise blur where the waters mixed. Beyond, the bay curved to a rocky point. Lorna blinked at the stream. She squinted at the horizon and at the point for signs of habitation.

Slowly, Lorna realized where the clerk had sent her, and laughed out loud. The river. The woman had sent her to El Río Limón.

Lorna was not sure how long she sat at the edge of the creek, plunking pebbles into the current. The sand at her side was hot to the touch; she closed her eyes from the sun, diffuse through a thickening band of haze but still searing, and swatted at the tiny insects biting her ankles. *Domingo.* Sunday. There were no busses on Sunday. After a while, a new sound penetrated her jumbled thoughts, and she turned her head toward the ocean.

Waves.

She sat up and squinted at the sea, but the shore lay hidden from her position. Rising up, she watched a ripple speed toward the beach. She watched in disbelief while the ripple peaked and crumbled, the tumbling lip folding on itself, curling, crashing into a mash of whitewater. The slush pile of foam washed up on the beach and melted into the sand. Another wave peaked and folded. Lorna scrutinized its size: thigh high maybe? Breaking over the sand bars from the river, most likely. A rumbling thunderclap stole her attention; she glanced at the clouds hovering like a black curtain over the mountains. Rain. She thought back to the mustached man at the restaurant. *Lluvia* meant rain!

Lorna grinned as another set, this one bigger than the last, rose up and crumbled perfectly along the beach.

*Las Olas vienen con la lluvia.* The waves come with the rain.

She had found the waves of Río Limón. Lorna felt a rush of emotion. Alex was here; she had to be.

Lorna gathered her things and stepped quickly over the soft sand toward the town, but before she reached the closest building, the darkened skies erupted, pelting her with hard raindrops. She raced to the cover of a palm tree as the sand around her turned from yellow to tan-brown. The drumming of the drops on the palm fronds sounded like marbles hitting a metal roof; the rain came so fast that a sheen of water spread over the sand, and her circle of protection quickly shrunk. Raindrops bounced up from the ground and dripped from above. Under attack, she sprinted for the building she'd strolled along after breakfast as silver spikes of rain stung her skin. After ducking under the building's tiny awning, with the duffel slung over her shoulder and gummy sand crowding into her flip flops, she stood against the wall and caught her breath. Lightning split the sky followed by a crack of thunder, making her jump.

Through the dense haze of rain, Lorna saw a slender figure running into a building on the other side of the restaurant. Lorna inched along the wall, squinting down the beach. The woman was Caucasian. Lorna's heart skipped a beat. The woman raced toward some kind of entrance Lorna hadn't noticed before, her arms laden with boxes. When the woman slipped inside her mysterious doorway, Lorna noticed her blonde hair tied up in twin buns and her face, which was too young to be Alex's. But surely she spoke English and would know if Alex was near.

A flash of lightning brightened the darkness before a deafening boom exploded almost simultaneously. Lorna flattened herself against the wall, which must have been a door because she suddenly found herself inside a room. A Hispanic man sat behind a desk, facing partly away from her. A phone was pinched between his ear and shoulder while his fingers typed furiously at a keyboard. Besides the computer and phone, the desk held only a small stack of papers and a plastic fuchsia-colored cup holding two writing utensils. The rest of the room contained a wastebasket in the corner overflowing with crumpled paper and soda cans, a narrow couch, and a stand-up fan in the corner that stood motionless, its metal cover furry with gray lint.

"Yeah," the man repeated several times in lightly accented English. "Just get here," he said. "Gonna be epic, man," he added then hung up.

Lorna stood dripping wet in the doorway, an apology on her lips.

The man frowned at a fax machine near the computer that was squeaking out a shiny length of paper.

Swell report? Weather? *The waves come with the rain.* Lorna's brain felt jammed—there was something going on here, something familiar.

"Er, I," she stuttered. What to ask first? Was there another place to stay besides "friendly" Eduardo's? Was this really Río Limón? Who was the woman with the boxes? "Is Alex here?" she finally blurted.

The man examined her briefly before calling out, "Alejandra!" to the door behind him.

A tanned face with blue eyes stepped into the room, bantering something in Spanish to the man. Her blonde hair was cut short and gray at the temples. Her bare arms were lithe and strong, and she had replaced her usual board shorts for Wranglers and a buck knife clipped to one hip that was cocked just enough to be coy. But the shock in her electric blue eyes when she saw Lorna was genuine.

"Mom," Lorna whispered.

# TWENTY

"Oh!" Alex said, blinking. "You're here."

Lorna's nose stung as the tears swelled behind her eyes. Her thoughts mashed together like a ten-car pileup, making her head throb. She balled her fists, thinking, *That's it? After all this time? Oh you're here?*

Alex's gaze shifted to behind Lorna. "Are you alone?"

Lorna realized that the moment for her mother to come to her, to embrace her, had passed. The deep breath she needed caught in her throat. "Yes," she finally answered.

"Good," Alex said, then glanced at the Hispanic man who had been watching her shrewdly.

"This is Lorna," Alex said to him and then added, "Lorna, Carlos."

Lorna felt sick. Not, "This is Lorna, my daughter," just, "This is Lorna."

"Are you okay?" Alex added.

"Me?" Lorna said, a little too forcefully. "I'm fine." Her fists were wet with rain and sweat. "How are you?"

Alex shrugged her lips. "All good."

"Good," Lorna said flatly. Her heart was beating so loudly her ears hurt.

Thunder rumbled in the distance and rain splattered against the walkway, thrummed against the sand, the palm fronds, cascaded off the overhang like a waterfall. A breath of humid wind puffed into the room, carrying the sound of waves pounding the beach.

"Well, just so happens I was headed out," Alex said. Her eyebrows arched. "You need a board?"

Lorna's fingers tingled as she released her fists. *When Neptune throws you perfect barrels . . .* "Uh, sure," she replied, which got her a scowl from Carlos and a trademark wicked grin from her mother.

"Let's go," Alex said.

Twenty minutes later, Lorna was gripping the bow of Alex's small boat, squinting into the warm rain, with two shortboards spooning in the bottom of the boat.

"That's Monkey Point," Alex shouted over the engine's whine, pointing to the rock outcropping just north of the tiny harbor.

Lorna nodded even though she couldn't detect anything monkey-like about the craggy brown jumble. They curved to the south, the boat cutting through water alive with skipping, bouncing raindrops. On any other day, a boat trip to new territory with smooth swells approaching, and her mind would be buzzing with excitement. Today it was screaming to go back, sit down, talk, make a plan. How easily Alex had dominated in that sweltering office. They should be packing up for Acapulco or Guadalajara, not going surfing.

"Where are we going?" Lorna shouted.

"Buzzard's. Around the point," Alex replied, looking ahead to the bluff guarding the southern edge of the bay, the one Lorna had squinted at from the banks of El Río Limón, hoping for signs of habitation, of Alex.

They passed outside of the river's mouth where Lorna had skipped rocks just hours ago, a thought her brain couldn't grasp.

"That's El Boca," Alex shouted, pointing as a green bump of swell rose up and exploded in a messy pile, its thick lip curling and tumbling forward in an opaque mash of green-white water. To Lorna's surprise, two surfers bobbed in the lineup.

"Where'd they come from?" Lorna said, amazed. Río Limón had seemed like a dead-end, disconnected from the world.

"It's probably Oscar and Pico," she said, watching the two figures. "Our two locals." One surfer gave them a nod, his sideways grin a white beacon against the stormy green-blue of his surroundings. "Surfing is still kind of an unknown thing here," Alex said, as if reading her thoughts.

They soon rounded the steep, crumbling cliff, the boat passing through confused currents and conflicting waves that spat ocean spray into her face. Lorna wiped her eyes and blinked back the warm salt, her fingers gripping the gunnels. Alex slowed the boat as they neared a jumble of rocks on the other side of the point. Brown cliffs rose up from the dark cobbled shore, with a layer of faded vegetation edging the top. Along the empty coastline to the south, palm trees hung limp over cocoa-brown sands.

A wide lump of swell appeared outside, rising slowly, the choppy surface smoothing as it stretched into a clean, slate-blue slope. The lip curled outward as its belly tucked beneath it, engulfing the rocks before it began to break, collapsing inch by inch to rejoin the ocean.

Alex grinned at Lorna. "Good, huh?" she said.

Lorna didn't have a chance to answer because Alex quickly steered the boat to deeper water and set the anchor. She exited the boat in a flash, paddling hard for the takeoff. Left with the crush of waves and the gasoline/seawater mix sloshing around in the bottom of the boat, Lorna picked up her loaner board and jumped over the side.

"Don't blow your takeoff—there's urchins," Alex called out to Lorna from nearby the rocks where she sat upright, her hands circling in the water, as if trying to maximize contact with the medium she loved so much. Her words were barely audible over the growing rumble of the waves and the choppy water slapping against the underside of her board.

Lorna couldn't stand it any longer. "Alex!" she shouted, her dry throat squeezing tight around the rest of what she wanted to say.

But Alex spun, paddled a few strokes, and was gone from sight.

Lorna reached the takeoff and sat up, rotating her feet against the current and watching for Alex to reappear from behind her wave. Lorna caught her breath, wondering how Alex could have so much energy.

Alex hadn't reappeared. Could she be in trouble? A peak came her way, and Lorna paddled for it, a gust of offshore wind misting her face as she leapt to her feet. But the foam ball was right on her heels, so she crouched and aimed for the cleaner section ahead, remembering Alex's warning about the urchins. The wall opened up, and she carved a smooth turn, racing into the bowl; then she pivoted, smacking the water with her palm as she made for the lip. Still no sign of Alex; was she already outside?

Breathless after several more turns, she kicked out before the wave collapsed, and paddled back out. Alex was already paddling into a new wave; Lorna watched her late drop and quick recovery, her seamless connection of turns, her total focus and spontaneity, and the smile on her face. Lorna's heart filled with despair. *How can I do this?* she thought with horror as she duck-dove a cresting wave. *How can I take this away from her?*

A sudden rush of anger heated her neck as she broke through the surface. *Hasn't she had it her way for long enough?* Lorna was overwhelmed with an urge to punish Alex, to take glory from the

news she was about to share. The heat rose to the back of her skull
and began to throb. She imagined the look of despair on Alex's face.
Would she cry? Beg? Seek comfort in Lorna's arms?

Lorna raced back outside only to find Alex dropping in on another wave. Groaning, Lorna sighted the next wave and rushed to
drop into it, racing forward, staying high, gripping her outside rail,
watching for Alex to appear in front of her. Alex's rooster tail of
spray fanned out over the back of her wave, as if meaning to taunt
her. Lorna arced high and sent spray of her own. A slow burn began
in her wounded leg. Again she dipped low to high, grunting with
the effort, biting her lip and engaging her core muscles, feeling aggressive, reckless. To her dismay, she sighted Alex paddling over the
far end of her wave for the outside, her eyes on the horizon. So
Lorna tried harder on the next wave and the next, until she could
feel her quad muscles and obliques crying for mercy. Her leg felt like
it was on fire. Each time Alex seemed to be outdoing her, surfing the
wave farther inside or taking off later, pulling tricks like floaters and
airs. It was maddening. Hadn't she stopped competing with Alex
long ago?

"Man, Carlos is going to be so bummed he missed this," Alex
sighed. She and Lorna had finally met up in the lineup after a mara-
thon of waves, each of them breathing hard. "He likes El Boca better
though. No urchins there." She smiled.

Lorna looked away. She didn't want to hear about Carlos.

"He's a beautiful body boarder, just wait till you see him surf,"
Alex continued.

Lorna swallowed. They'd be gone before she'd have the chance
to see such a thing.

"You've got quite an aggressive cutback, by the way. Don't think I haven't noticed."

Lorna hated herself just then for how her mother's praise could still make her feel good. She knew her twelve-year-old self would have done a million cutbacks to hear such a compliment again and struggled to ignore the urge to do so now.

"I hope you've been working on your lefts. This one's the only right-hander we've got."

Lorna thought of the waves along her beloved Washington coast, point breaks, bays, river mouths, all of them left-breaking. On her most recent trip to Fiji she'd surfed Bukuya and Vunde's— both lefts. Lorna realized she was gripping the rails of the board and tried to relax.

"We just got back from a scouting trip in Oaxaca. Funny that you came today," she said. Lorna could feel Alex's gaze on her. "Perfect timing actually, with this swell coming and all."

Lorna picked at a blob of old wax on her board's deck. Alex made it sound like Lorna had dropped out of the sky, instead of doing all of the soul-searching about whether or not to come, traveling for days, and sleeping on buses or the previous night's cement-block palapa. The mattress must have had fleas because she'd been scratching her legs and forearms all day. She knew that Alex would never think to ask about such things.

"I got clients coming in tomorrow, though. But you can tag along," Alex said.

"Tomorrow?" Lorna asked, looking up. *Tag along?* Lorna remembered the seasonal surf tour business that Alex was supposedly running.

"Ten guys." Alex spun for an incoming set.

Lorna had had enough. "Alex!" Lorna interrupted.

But Alex continued. "Starting a surf business wasn't exactly my first choice, you know, but it made sense." She tossed Lorna one of her sideways grins, her cheeks beaded with mist. "I keep the numbers small. But the word is out and I can't keep them away!"

"We need to talk about—" Lorna shouted over the rumble of the wave now rising outside of the rocks, but Alex was paddling for it and Lorna needed to sprint outside to clear it. She launched over the lip and caught a glimpse of Alex dropping in, her inside hand skimming the wave's face while her eyes focused down the line. Lorna paddled for the takeoff and spun just in time to catch the second wave of the set.

After kicking out, Lorna saw Alex waiting for waves just inside of the rock jumble. Lorna sighed and stroked towards her.

"Some kids from Quicksilver came last year. You should have seen them! The talent they have, it's amazing!" Alex said as she drew near.

Lorna watched her spin for another wave, and hung her head in defeat. How much longer did Alex want to stay out here?

Outside, another large set wave began to break. She scrambled towards it then duck-dove beneath the feathering lip. Surfacing, she scouted the rain-stippled surface for Alex and spotted her standing, far inside with tight lips and scared eyes. Lorna knew that look: Alex was in pain.

Lorna sprinted towards her, pulling deep strokes through the water. But Alex had recovered and was stroking hard for the outside. Lorna turned sharply around to follow. "Are you tired?" she said, fast on her heels. "Is it your stomach? Are you okay?" she asked. When Alex finally stopped far outside, Lorna's lungs ached from the exertion.

Alex had slid off her board. She propped up the sole of her foot for inspection. "Damn urchins," she uttered.

Lorna could see the tiny black specks embedded in Alex's skin.

A roll of unbroken swell passed beneath them. Moments later, Lorna heard it feather and break inside the impact zone.

"In the E.R., you had some tests," Lorna began, her heart pounding.

Alex slid back onto her board. "Don't," Alex said, looking into Lorna's eyes for the first time since leaving the office. Lorna saw then the dark patches beneath her lids and the sallowness of her cheeks.

"I didn't come all this way to catch waves," Lorna said, swallowing hard.

"I know," Alex said, her eyes solemn. "I knew the minute you showed up." She inhaled a slow, shaky breath. "But I just wanted to hold on to everything a little longer. I just wanted to come out here with you, just once, before . . . "

Another wave rolled beneath them then thundered as it broke along the empty shore. Lorna watched her feet dangle beneath her, the lack of sunlight turning everything below into a black mystery. Lorna's insides twisted into a slow and agonizing knot. *This is what it's like to see someone's spirit break*, she thought, feeling wretched.

"I always hoped you'd come, Lorna Kai," Alex said, her eyes fixed somewhere beyond the boat bobbing end to end in the rolling swells. "I know things were never . . . " She hunched her shoulders and sighed, and the gesture looked more like a shrug than the explanation Lorna had learned to stop expecting. "But I have a business to run, so if you're here to hover over me with doom and gloom, forget it," Alex said, paddling toward the boat.

Something gave way inside Lorna. Tears sprang from her eyes, but she swatted them away. *This could be your chance to make things right*, Joe had said. Well, he was wrong. But she'd known that already. Why hadn't she listened to her own advice?

Lorna began picking at the wax again. Hard shavings of it crowded beneath her nails, and the pain of it felt good, reassuring somehow. Ocean swells pushed and rolled beneath her. She let the tears fall but it didn't help. *This is what it's like to see someone's spirit break.*

Alex drove the boat to the tiny marina in silence, the rain lightening to a clinging mist by the time Lorna stepped onto the dock. Without looking back, she continued towards the town.

The crunch of gravel beneath the Ranger's tires did not slow her pace.

"Get in," Alex said through the side window.

"No," Lorna said, keeping her eyes ahead.

Alex sighed. "You know, that's always been your problem. You take everything so personally."

Lorna spun. "Yeah," she managed through lips quivering with emotion. "That's my problem."

Alex didn't flinch. "Would you just get in the truck? There's something I gotta tell you."

Lorna put her hands on her hips. "What?" she said. *To hell with this,* she thought. She would sleep in a bus station if she had to. Get to an airport. Never look back. Alex would die here, alone. Her choice.

Alex's eyes flicked away nervously. "You didn't leave anything in the truck, did you?"

Lorna felt the heat drain from her face, pulling her insides with it, down to the ground. She closed her eyes for an instant, remembering the black duffel and backpack tucked under the bench seat containing everything: her cash, the meds, her passport. Everything. She opened her eyes to Alex's bland look, noticing the cab's back window missing its sliding pane. She flung the passenger door open and reached beneath the bench, her fingers passing over spare tools and gummy bits of trash, not the lumpy shape of her duffel, the stiff nylon of her pack. She squinted into the space, hoping her possessions were just pushed back out of reach.

The space was empty.

Lorna covered her face with her hands.

"Welcome to Mexico," Alex said dryly.

Gone? Just like that? *Gone*? Lorna felt dizzy. Her tongue felt too big for her dry mouth. "Oh my God oh my GOD," she whispered.

"Lorna, get in," Alex finally said.

# TWENTY-ONE

Lorna waited through the long clicks, followed by the strange ringing tone. Gina answered on the fourth ring.

"Lorna!" she replied, sounding breathless. "Sweetie, how are you?"

"Um, good," Lorna replied. She waited as her dad's second wife scolded one of their children, followed by a small voice of protest and more muffled discipline from Gina.

"Sorry about that," Gina said quickly. "Piper's on treat restriction, and Jordan thinks he can build forts in the living room," she added.

Lorna toyed with the stiff plastic phone card Alex had given her, digging its rounded corner into the dust-caked metal shelf below the phone. She tried to picture the ever-changing faces of her half-siblings, but they were a blur.

"Is my dad there?" she asked, unsure how long her phone card would last.

"He left last week, hon. On the *Truman*."

Lorna's spirits sunk. "For how long?" Lorna wondered if the *Truman* was headed to the Middle East again, but let it go. She had stopped trying to understand the U.S. Navy a long time ago.

"Three months at least," Gina said with a sigh. Lorna could hear water running and Gina's muffled voice again—something about staying at the table. "You okay?" Gina said to Lorna. "Need me to get him a message?"

Lorna considered asking Gina to wire-transfer five hundred dollars to a Mexican Western Union but quickly dismissed the idea. Gina's life was complicated enough; Lorna was afraid she'd wire the money to Manzanita instead of Manzanillo. Besides, Lorna didn't want to explain where she was. Gina didn't have that kind of time. "No," Lorna replied, wondering how the hell she was going to get out of Río Limón with no money and no passport.

"How's Seattle?" Gina asked.

Lorna consciously relaxed her jaw. "Great," she replied.

"Good," Gina crooned. "I'll tell your dad you called, okay?"

When Lorna finally tracked down her ex-boyfriend and fellow resident, Keith, he was at home and sounded groggy, like he'd been woken from a deep sleep.

"Sorry," Lorna said sheepishly. He must be on nights.

"How's Mexico?" he said, his voice thick with sleep.

"Um," Lorna stalled. "I'm in a bit of a jam," she said.

"Too many margaritas will do that," he grumbled.

Lorna didn't want to use up her few minutes left on the phone card arguing. "Can you loan me some cash?" she asked.

Keith laughed bitterly. "You know who got stuck with your shift when you took off?" He paused. "Me. Now buzz off."

"But I'm—" Lorna tried.

"The answer is no," Keith said. "Goodbye," he sang and hung up.

Lorna knew that her navy corpsmen friends would help if they could, but Miles was probably just getting back from his honeymoon, and the others from their group were out of reach. Jess was in nursing school, Trent was a medic in Philadelphia, and Stig was probably on a desert tarmac somewhere, orchestrating an evac. She had no contact info for any of them, nor did she have the courage to track them down for a loan.

Lorna spent the night on Alex's office couch, swatting at bugs, itching from the fabric and the flea bites from Eduardo's and wondering if Alex was sleeping or tossing restlessly in the apartment above her.

Carlos shook her awake. "I got five guys coming in and my driver's AWOL. Can you go to the airport and get them?" he asked, grabbing a set of keys from the desk.

Lorna scrambled to a sitting position. "What about Alex?" she asked.

"She is . . . unavailable."

Unavailable. Was she sick? "Does she need—"

"Can you do it or not?" Carlos put his hands on his hips.

Lorna saw herself gripping the steering wheel, honked at for driving slowly or pulling off the road to catch a breath. She remembered the bus ride from Morelia and the driver's aggressive tactics. Busses like that would be everywhere. What would she do? Then she saw the dorky sign she'd be holding at the airport, waiting for a group of bad-mouthing surfers to come tumbling, drunk and horny out of an airplane. They'd ask her to stop for beer then pester her for information about the waves while she white-knuckled the steering wheel and tried not to act like a paranoid freak. The humiliation of it made her jaw ache already. She remembered Alex's: "If you're here to hover over me with doom and gloom, forget it, Lorna Kai."

"Sure," Lorna sighed.

The van's jerky brakes and loose steering added to her anxiety; the rearview mirror dangling sideways from a half-broken plastic clasp didn't help, either. Plus, the vehicle had no map, a fact she found maddening, irresponsible. At a confusing intersection, she didn't realize she had chosen the wrong spur until almost half an hour later and had to backtrack. There had to be a shortcut, but without a map she needed to follow the hand-scrawled directions Carlos had given her, with the flight number and the guests' last names.

Emergency *mordida* money, as Carlos called it, was tucked into her shorts pocket. He had said, "If the *federales* pull you over, just act dumb. Ask to pay the fine there instead of going to the station. They'll go for it."

*And if they don't?* Lorna thought, her eyes glued to the road, her back rigid in the squishy seat. She could see herself in handcuffs being led into a Mexican prison, the other inmates banging their metal cups against the bars as she passed.

Lorna quickly grew panicky. The tight corners, jarring speed bumps through the endless string of tiny villages, the semi trucks crowding her rearview as she descended winding, narrow roads—their massive metal grills looking ready to swallow her whole—the cattle crossings, and the van's ineffective air conditioner all made her feel small and out of control. The city of Manzanillo confused her even further. She followed signs for the airport but seemed to drive forever, leaving the city behind. She passed a massive supermarket called Mega and almost rear-ended a car that swerved suddenly to enter the turn lane. She slammed on the brakes just in time while boxes of something from the back toppled over, and her head snapped forward. Cursing the tight brakes, she rubbed her neck.

She never needed the sign she'd imagined holding—the surfers easily stood out in their flip flops, faded T-shirts, and trucker-style caps. Behind them waited an impressive pile of surfboards tucked into tattered silver or once-white travel bags. Lorna instructed them to load up while she raced to the restroom inside. She ran to a stall and puked in a toilet that smelled of piss and doused cigarettes.

If any of the surfers were curious about her or the waves, they didn't let on. And during the drive, they either slept or listened to their headphones. Lorna's knuckles ached from gripping the wheel, and her mind felt woozy and unsteady from focusing so diligently on the road: looking for cops, for speeding busses, for the plentiful potholes or sudden road diversions. Just as she crested a long curve, she almost plowed into a stalled truck parked halfway in the road. She swerved hard, praying for no oncoming traffic. Once safely back in her lane she glanced back at her cargo, but all seemed unconcerned. She exhaled but her nerves were fried.

By the time she turned down the sandy road to Río Limón, the setting sun had left a purplish bruise on the horizon. The van's cooling fan kicked on as she stepped onto the curb, her legs shaky and her back wet with sweat. She walked to the office, but the windows were dark, and the door was locked. Frustrated, she stepped back and peered up at the apartment. No sign of activity. At the street, the surfers were spilling out of the van, gathering their gear. Lorna registered their low voices, a loud yawn, and someone's sudden laugh. Anxiety crept into her consciousness as she wondered where she would take them. For the first time she wondered where on earth they would stay. Lorna raced up the stairs, but the apartment too was locked. She yanked on the doorknob. "Alex!" she called out, thumping on the door. Where were she and Carlos? Lorna cursed. She laid her head against the door and closed her eyes. What now?

She returned downstairs and surveyed the surfers, who were quickly rallying after the long drive. Accustomed to late nights spent partying, she wondered how they would survive in Río Limón. And what would she do with them until Alex or Carlos appeared?

"You guys hungry?" she asked as her empty stomach churned.

They walked to the open-air restaurant, and the plump man in the apron brought a bucket of beers on ice, a stack of fresh tortillas, and a small collection of salsas. Lorna was too tired to be surprised by such swift service. A few of the surfers seemed to speak some Spanish—more than she could manage—and the plump man left with their order. In the background, Lorna heard a wave crumble outside of El Boca and had a sinking thought: Could Alex be surfing?

"I'll be back in a bit," Lorna said stiffly to the surfers. "Don't leave your stuff unattended, okay?"

Lorna walked the street toward the harbor. If Alex's boat was missing, Lorna would be the first thing her mother would see upon returning. "Goddamn it, Alex," Lorna muttered as she broke into a run.

Through the dim lights of the harbor, Lorna could just make out Alex's boat. So she was on shore somewhere. Lorna hadn't noticed Alex's dusty Ford Ranger parked on the roads. Was she with Carlos? Lorna had no idea how to find him, either. She thought of asking around for Carlos—*you know, the one with the dark hair and stocky build?*—and cursed. There had to be at least ten guys named Carlos even in this small town, and they were all stocky with dark hair. She kicked a rock and turned back towards the town, her mind spinning.

Returning along the beach this time, Lorna considered her options. The group could stay in Alex's apartment if she could jimmy the lock. She guessed there had to be a bed, some floor space, bedding. Did Alex have blankets? Or should she keep them at the restaurant until Alex showed up? Could a few of them sleep in the van? Lorna couldn't send them to Eduardo's. What if something happened? Even more terrifying was the problem of what she would do with them in the morning. Lorna had never operated a boat; she barely felt familiar enough with Buzzards to take them there. Would they be satisfied with paddling out at El Boca? Surely not. These surfers were hungry for serious waves, not some scruffy little beach break. Lorna realized that if Alex didn't show by tomorrow morning, she would have to tell the surfers to go home.

Or maybe she should just tell them now. Wouldn't that be better? Surely they could be somewhere else, with someone who knew what they were doing.

Nearing the restaurant, Lorna slowed to a walk, noticing a small entrance lit by a bright bulb. Squinting, Lorna read the indistinct sign above the door: Hotel Las Olas. Her heartbeat quickened. Why hadn't she noticed this entrance before?

Instantly she remembered the woman in the skirt heading into a building the moment before she found Alex. Lorna peered again at the doorway and then down the length of the building, past the restaurant to where a dim overhead light illuminated the surf tours office door. The woman in the skirt had to be connected to this hotel. *Las Olas veinen con la lluvia.* Hotal Las Olas. Hotel of the Waves.

Drawn in, Lorna passed through an arched hallway to a small side room containing a wooden desk with a collection of miniature, brightly painted wooden animals, a phone, fax, and what looked like a pile of mail or some kind of documents. Behind it sat an empty wicker chair. Large watercolor paintings of waves and beach scenes hung from the walls. The space had a feeling of calm and warmth. Where were the owners? If it was a hotel, where were the guests?

"Hello?" Lorna called out, continuing down the hall to a tiny courtyard, open to the sky, with a pebble floor and lush plants clustered in the corners and dangling from hanging baskets. She knew the showerhead and floor drain in the courtyard's far corner catered to surfers; they could rinse away the sand and salt. Above, she could make out a row of rooms on the second floor. Suddenly a pair of feet descended a circular metal staircase located to her right. A man with shoulder-length white-blonde hair and a goatee nearly collided with her as he came around the last of the steps.

Lorna blinked at him.

"Hola," he said, though Lorna was pretty sure he was 100 percent Southern California White. Despite the leather sandals instead of flip flops and a collared shirt in place of the usual faded tee, she had him pegged as a surfer. She could see it in his broad shoulders and the crow's feet creasing the edges of his eyes, too deep for someone so young.

"Are they here?" SoCal asked, looking past her as another set of feet clanged down the staircase.

"Who?" Lorna asked, puzzled, following his gaze.

"The Billabong kids?" SoCal said slowly, his eyes squinting in confusion at her.

Billabong *kids*? Wasn't this guy a kid, too? Lorna's brain geared down as it snagged on a detail. She realized that Garth must have traveled here in similar fashion, with his team.

Just then a slender, tall woman in flip flops and a loose tank dress stepped from the staircase. Lorna realized it was the same woman she'd seen ducking into the doorway in the rainstorm. "Hola," she said to Lorna, embracing her in a soft hug. Lorna felt herself stiffen at the sudden gesture. "You must be Lorna," the woman added as she stepped back. "It's so great you're here to help," she said. Her straight blonde hair hung to below her shoulders, and when she smiled at Lorna, her light brown eyes twinkled. "I'm Becca," she said. "And this is Seth."

"So, is Alex here?" Lorna asked. *Los Olas vienen con la lluvia.*

"Up here," a voice said from above. The metal stairs clattered as Alex rushed down. "Did you bring them?" she said, sounding breathless.

Lorna fought her mounting humiliation. "I didn't even know this place was here," she said.

"So where are they?" she said, her voice urgent.

A look of panic passed between Seth and Becca when Lorna told them about the restaurant. Alex pushed past Lorna, cursing. Seth and Becca followed.

"I'm sorry!" Lorna called out when she caught up. "I couldn't just leave them in the van!"

"Ricardo will probably charge us five bucks a beer *and* give them hepatitis. I need them healthy," Alex replied, giving her a scathing look. "Next time ask me about shit like this, okay?"

"There was nobody here to ask," Lorna said, hating her pathetic, pleading tone. "And there's not gonna be a next time, okay? Do you know how dangerous those roads are? And the drivers aren't any better! You knew I would hate it, but you got me to do it anyways." Lorna waited for an apology, but Alex only grunted. "You're welcome," Lorna grumbled to the empty beach.

Alex rushed to greet the surfers, her tone cheerful, low-key. Lorna hung back in the shadows, her breaths unsteady and her nerves fried, hearing the surfers laugh at Alex's opening joke: something about how hard it was to find good help these days.

# TWENTY-TWO

Lorna sat on the beach, listening to the crashing waves. Had driving the shuttle been some kind of test? If so, had she failed? It didn't matter; she was leaving.

The quickest way to get a passport was through the U.S. Consulate in Guadalajara, more than 500 kilometers away. She should have tried to visit there as part of the trip to Manzanillo earlier, but there had been no time to prepare; she needed money, passport photos, and documents. And according to Carlos, she needed to be there before dawn to get in line. She would have to take an overnight bus to arrive early enough. Or she could go through the smaller consulate office in Acapulco, only 300 km away, but the process could take weeks.

"Hey," said a soft voice behind her.

Lorna turned. Becca held two beers, and offered one to her.

Lorna took the beer and Becca joined her on the sand. There was a quiet, lithe way that Becca moved, almost as if she floated rather than walked. The way she folded up her long legs lotus-style made Lorna wonder if she was some sort of yogini or ballerina, maybe.

"I heard about your stuff getting stolen," Becca said.

Lorna sighed, lamenting the loss of the meds she'd brought for Alex. She imagined the crackheads having a heyday, or had they just thrown the vials out? Or sold them. "Yeah," she replied.

"I might be able to get some of it back for you," Becca said.

"How?" Lorna asked.

Becca shrugged. "It's a small town. Sometimes people tell me things."

Lorna dug her toes into the cool sand. She glanced at the hotel door behind her. "I've walked past this part of the beach before. Why didn't I see your place?" she asked.

Becca grinned. "Because we just arrived yesterday and only put the sign out this afternoon. When you showed up tonight, we were still getting ready."

"You're only here in the rainy season," Lorna said, feeling slow. "Because of the waves." *Hotel Las Olas.*

"For the last three years." She beamed. "We have to shutter things up tight in the off- season. Safer that way," she said casually, as if it was no big deal.

Lorna remembered the sense of calm inside the hotel, and the warmth, like another world compared to Eduardo's and the ramshackle town. The surfers would be happy there. "It's nice."

"Thanks." Becca sighed. "I'm really glad you're here . . . " She glanced in the direction of the restaurant. "Is Alex okay?"

Lorna's heart thump-thumped.

Becca gave her a serious look. "She's gotten really thin. She seems, I don't know, down, I guess." An invisible wave rumbled in the distance. "She hardly surfs unless she's guiding."

Lorna realized that Alex had coerced Becca and Seth into uprooting their lives in order to serve her goal. And now she was sick and hadn't bothered to think about how it would affect anyone else. It was the same old selfishness that Lorna had run from.

"And lately . . . " Becca stopped, her face drawn with worry. "She's been holding her stomach like it hurts."

Lorna hugged herself on the sand. "She came to see me," Lorna said and explained Alex's visit to the E.R. "But I was in"—Lorna stopped as a sudden image of Joe popped into her mind—"I wasn't there. I thought maybe she needed medical care and wanted me." Alex's medical report flashed through her brain. "But now I don't know. Maybe she stopped in to invite me here, or maybe she needed help with the business?" Lorna shook her head. "But then she ended up getting admitted."

Becca cringed. "Maybe she's been working too hard. She goes like a hundred miles an hour."

Lorna figured that everything Alex ate bothered her, that stress made it worse, that surfing for four hours with her estranged daughter probably made it worse. How was she going to convince Alex that she needed help? That she couldn't drag these nice people down with her?

"You can stay in our cubby room," Becca said, peering at Lorna. "It's not as nice as the other ones, but it's better than Alex's office couch."

"Thanks," Lorna mumbled, wondering if her offer was tied to making Alex better, something Lorna would be unable to do.

"Alex is tough," Becca said as she rose to her feet. "With you here to help, maybe she can rest. She'll get better."

Lorna swallowed a hard lump in her throat.

Becca floated away, leaving Lorna alone with the waves.

Lorna tapped Alex on the shoulder, ignoring the surfers, whose volume level had increased several notches since their arrival. Alex regarded her impatiently.

"Can I talk to you a minute?" Lorna whispered.

"Seems my driver wants to get paid," Alex boomed to the surfers, who chuckled. Lorna noticed that Alex wasn't drinking.

They walked into the shadows a few feet away. Lorna could hear Seth's voice and wondered if he'd come to collect the group.

"I can't pay you yet," Alex said, crossing her arms. "I gotta process their payments first."

Lorna screwed up her courage. Becca had said Alex was glad Lorna had come. "How did you get Becca and Seth to follow you here?" she asked. "What did you promise them? Money? Fantastic waves? Fame?"

Alex blinked. "I didn't promise them anything. They came to me."

Lorna didn't believe it. "If you really care about them, you need to hear what I have to say. You need to have a plan."

"You think I need you to make a plan?" Alex replied with sarcasm.

"Tell me about your stomach pain," Lorna said. "Have you been vomiting?"

Alex's eyes narrowed. "Who told you?" she replied, her gaze gone flat. "Becca," she said and then sighed. "Look, it's nothing. My system's just getting fussy in my old age, okay?"

Food intolerances were an early sign. Vomiting came later. What would Alex's CT scan look like now? "You're not old, Alex. Don't drag these people down with you."

"Enough!" Alex hissed. "We settled this already. Last I heard you were late for a bus," she said, striding past her.

Lorna lay on the narrow bed in her room beneath the stairs, a room she suspected had once begun its life as a closet with its slanted ceiling and only one tiny window. The humidity had made the cramped space unbearable, so she had propped the door open. Becca's fan was helping, so she decided to trade privacy for comfort. The exterior door to the hotel—made of metal bars—was secured, so she was safe. The muffled movements and banter of the surfers quieted inside the courtyard walls, but Lorna could not sleep. One of the guests was playing the guitar; it sounded familiar, somehow. Finally she realized it reminded her of Joe. Angry, she slammed the door.

Lorna rolled into the wall, pressing her sweaty skin against the cold concrete. Becca's cry for help stirred her thoughts. Lorna didn't know how to tell her that Alex wouldn't get better. At best, Lorna hoped to extend her time. Lorna squeezed her eyes shut. How had it come to this? Lorna had not considered that Alex would refuse to listen, refuse help. What would happen to Becca and Seth when Alex couldn't finish the season? Lorna decided that if Alex wouldn't listen to her, she needed to inform Becca. At least she and Seth could save themselves.

She wondered about Carlos and Alex's relationship. Business or pleasure? Lorna remembered the way Alex talked about him while they'd surfed Buzzard's yesterday. When Alex became too weak, Carlos would have to take over leading the tours. She realized that she would have to inform Carlos, too.

Lorna sighed. Maybe that was her way in—through Carlos. Maybe he would he listen to her, but would he help?

Lorna woke late after tossing in the hot room for most of the night. She got up to search for a cup of coffee and discovered from

Seth that the surfers and Alex had left at 5:00 a.m. and wouldn't return until late afternoon.

Lorna looked for Carlos in Alex's office first, but the door was locked, the window dark. She retreated to the street and wondered what kind of car Carlos drove. She spotted the plump man from the restaurant—Ricardo, Alex had called him—singing in an operatic voice while chopping in the open kitchen. When he saw her watching, he winked.

She sighed and approached the entrance. He wiped his hands on his white half-apron and met her halfway.

"*Donde Carlos?*" she asked, pointing to the office beyond the tables.

The man shrugged. "*Mercado?* Surf? *Durmiente?*" at the last suggestion he chuckled.

"*Vive qui?*" she tried.

The man jerked his head up while rattling off something in fast Spanish.

Dejected, Lorna returned to her room, where she found a stack of clothing on her tightly made bed and a small basket of warm muffins. Lorna's heart went out to Becca as she munched one of the muffins. Lorna couldn't let Becca get pulled into Alex's demise. She fingered a soft, yellow T-shirt resting on top of the stack. Underneath was a pair of faded board shorts, a few tank tops, a bikini, and even a loose linen tunic with a pair of lightweight, cropped pants. Lorna sighed. Becca had known she would need these. She changed into the bikini top and board shorts and the yellow T-shirt then padded into the inner courtyard looking for Becca. Not finding her at the desk, Lorna wandered up the circular stairs, past the rooms and then up a half-stairway to the open roof, where several rows of laundry hung stiffly from lines.

"Becca?" she called out.

A cool breeze brushed her cheek and stirred the laundry. She gazed to the east, where dark, billowy clouds seemed to grow by the minute. Looking down to the street, she took in the clerk outside the Mini Super, smoking a cigarette in her faded apron and scuffed leather shoes, the skinny dogs sleeping in the dirt, the few people on their way somewhere. Her eyes swept back to the ocean where shimmering rolls of swell steamed into the bay. The ridge of land separating the town from the tiny harbor rose up like the back of a serpent, hiding the boats.

Rumbling thunder brought her back to the roof. She began collecting the sheets and pulling down towels and clothing and tossing them into a laundry basket. She felt the first raindrops as she scurried down the staircase. Becca met her halfway with a honey-haired toddler on her hip. The splattering drops of rain were marking the pale walkway with fat, mismatched polka dots.

"Oh!" Becca said, out of breath from her dash up the stairs. A flash of lightning brightened the darkening sky, followed by a boom of thunder. The tanned child on her hip, wearing only a diaper and a faded purple tank top, hid her eyes in Becca's neck. "Thank you so much!" Becca said as they ran back to the first floor to cower in the office space. Raindrops splattered the inner courtyard, peppered the stairway, zinged against the metal drainpipe.

Lorna handed her the basket, eying the child curiously. "Thanks for these," she said, pinching a bit of her T-shirt.

Becca smiled and lowered the child to the floor, who raced to the doorway to watch the rain. "Glad they fit," she said with an appraising nod.

"Will the group come in?" Lorna asked, thinking of the surfers. "Because of this?" She eyed the dark sky.

"Not unless one of them gets struck by lightning," Becca joked. She said something to the child in Spanish, who returned to Becca's side.

"How old is she?" Lorna asked, her curiosity getting the better of her.

Becca seemed surprised. "Goodness! I completely forgot you two hadn't met." She gave the child's forehead a soft caress. "Fie, this is Lorna." The child peered at her shyly.

Lorna smiled at the child, whom she guessed to be about two. When Lorna had entered medical school, she had wanted to specialize in pediatrics, and she loved everything about it except when she began dealing with parents. They talked too much, were paranoid or careless, lied, were lazy, or even abused their children—something that wrecked Lorna emotionally every time, so much that she started having anxiety attacks and sleep problems. She'd had to switch.

The child buried her head against Becca's leg. "Da-da?" she asked Becca.

"He's in the kitchen. Would you like a snack now?"

The child rushed off into the rain. Lorna was secretly amazed that Becca and Seth, who seemed so young, had a child—here, in Mexico, while trying to start a business. It made her think of Joe and his Swiss Family Robinson plan. Her chest tightened. She pushed the image away.

"Um, do you know where Carlos lives?" Lorna asked Becca.

Becca squinted into the rainy courtyard. "Above the office," she replied.

Lorna gave her a sideways glance. *With Alex*, she thought, trying to hide her surprise.

She said goodbye to Becca and sprinted through the rain and up the stairs to the apartment. After catching her breath, she knocked on the door but there was no answer. Tentatively, she tried the doorknob, and the door swung open.

"Hello?" she called out. The place was still and quiet.

She stepped inside. The studio-style apartment's furnishings reminded Lorna of those seen on the curb affixed with a FREE sign: a double-sized bed, with a faded, thin coverlet, separated from the rest of the room by a flimsy wooden divider, a worn easy chair, ripped at one edge, a pea-green velvet couch, a dusty floor lamp, and a hammock in the near corner, suspended above a mound of surfing magazines.

The surprisingly spacious kitchen with a breakfast bar and stools, a full-sized refrigerator and cabinets offered only a hotplate for cooking. *How appropriate*, Lorna thought. Alex had never baked: not cookies, not birthday cakes, not even a casserole. If not for Lorna and *The Joy of Cooking*, they all would have starved.

Lorna found herself humming the catchy tune that the surfers upstairs had been playing the night before while she moved through the apartment. She stepped closer to an object hanging from the gray walls that looked out of place next to the surf posters: a large corkboard crowded with photos, postcards, and memorabilia such as beer-stained coasters, a wrapper from some kind of candy, a small earthenware pig on a cheap key chain, a twenty-pesos bill. *Great waves, good times, thanks again!* wrote someone named Zane in tight, angular letters. The mediocre photos, taken most likely with disposable waterproof cameras or cheap hand-helds, showed mug shots of guys on Alex's boat giving the "hang loose" sign or in groups inside some bar, grinning like idiots. Alex appeared in only one photo, cradling a sleeping baby. Lorna leaned closer, realizing it must be Sophie. The look of content in Alex's eyes made Lorna feel strange, like she was intruding.

An invitation made of thick, folded paper and with a gold-braided tassel dangling from the center crease made her blink in disbelief. *University of Washington*, it read in raised purple and gold print. It was from Lorna's college graduation, the last time she'd seen Alex.

Lorna's heart pounded as she saw herself that day, fidgeting in the hot black gown sticking to her skin due to the unseasonable June heat and the lack of shade. Her heels had already blistered from the new leather sandals Gina had insisted she wear. Alex had appeared out of the throng of people mingling outside after the ceremony, as if they hadn't been apart for years. Her father and Gina stood in silence while Lorna hugged Alex, out of surprise rather than a natural instinct. The stiffness in Alex's body made Lorna release her quickly.

"So what's next?" Alex had asked with her one-sided smile, shifting her feet on the hot pavement.

Lorna's hands trembled. "I start Medical school in the fall."

"Medical school? Wow." The surprise was clear on her face. Lorna could feel what was coming, knew the words forming before she heard them. "You got time for a little surf trip, right?"

Lorna's insides twisted, ached. Every fiber of her being wanted to believe that there would be more to the trip than just surfing, but she had told herself years ago that such a wish would never come true. "I don't think so," she'd said with difficulty. *I have a life now*, she wanted to say. *And it can't include you.*

Alex's eyes flashed with confusion, but the spark that always accompanied her descriptions of waves quickly replaced it. "I have a new spot." Her tone lowered. "Empty waves," she added, her eyes wide. "Good ones, too. The south swells have already kicked on. It's a perfect time to come down, Lorna Kai," she said, using her full name, something she only did to persuade. "Not much in terms of accommodations, but that's nothing new." She gave a little laugh.

Then her face calmed, and she looked at Lorna with a serious, grave face. "And I found something special. Something I've always hoped to find . . . it barrels perfectly, like Pipe, only bigger." She paused, as if replaying some epic session in her mind. "And it's off the map. No one knows it's there but me."

"Sounds great," Lorna said quietly. The mention of Pipe had filled her with anger and hurt. Alex had taken her there once on a big day. Alex had surfed with her buddies, ignoring Lorna who, in trying to keep up, mistimed her first takeoff, hit the reef, and almost drowned. Alex hadn't even come in, hadn't even noticed. Lorna had stuffed the remaining half of her broken board into the trashcan and hitched a ride home.

"But I've got to work," Lorna offered feebly, thinking of her boring ambulance job and the even more boring banquet-serving job. "And study."

"Study? You just graduated!"

Lorna blushed and looked at the ground. "Medical school is very competitive," she mumbled.

Alex gave her one of her "oh, please" kind of looks.

"If I take the summer off, I'll be behind," Lorna replied, trying hard to keep her cool. Alex hated it when she got emotional.

There was a long, awkward pause, and Alex's expression hardened. "Well then, good luck to you."

"Thanks," Lorna replied.

Lorna realized Garth's picture could be among the many notes and photos from past guests, but she saw nothing signed by him and no photos. She couldn't shake his presence, as if she could see his fingerprints on the things she'd already touched. Had he been here, in this apartment?

One particular photo of a steely blue wave curling over a tiny surfer caught Lorna's eye. Could it be Buzzard's, taken from the cliff? No, she decided. She saw no sign of land, and wondered if it was an outside reef, maybe. Lorna squinted. There was something sinister, even threatening about the wave. It was in the thickness of the lip and the shape of the barrel: wider, as if a slab of water had been sheared from the top of the ocean and yanked forward. The frothy lip looked hungry, and Lorna shuddered at the thought of getting in its way. Who was riding such a menacing wave, anyways? But Lorna knew before she registered the shiny blonde hair and the certain way the rider's arms were poised, the shoulders lining up just so: Alex.

Lorna stared.

Alex's perfect wave.

The one she'd found after a life of searching.

The one she'd begged Lorna to share that day outside the Pavilion, the one she proposed Lorna abandon her summer plans for. *It barrels like Pipe only bigger. And it's off the map.* The ideal recipe for Alex's perfect wave.

Had the graduation program and that particular photo been placed side by side for a reason? Lorna wanted to believe that they represented Alex's two true loves—her daughter and the wave of her dreams. But Lorna knew better.

Lorna wondered if the invitation to share that wave six years ago was the only way Alex knew how to connect. Not the way Lorna had always yearned for, but a connection all the same. Surfing might be the closest bond they would ever share. The thought filled her with anguish—because it might be true and because she'd so easily turned it down.

She stepped back, feeling drained and spooked, as if she'd seen something she shouldn't have. She moved on, searching the cupboards, under the sink, for what, she didn't know. So Alex liked coco puffs and hard boiled eggs, and her coffee maker's filter was furry with mold, so what? Lorna peered into the bathroom and scanned the pedestal sink, square- mirrored cabinet, and the shower the size of a telephone booth for signs of sickness. Blobs of toothpaste stuck to the sink in hard lumps, and the mirror was filmy, but the toilet was clean. She was about to leave when something colorful in the wastebasket caught her attention. Lorna grimaced, looked closer. *I shouldn't be doing this.* Grimacing, she removed a small strip of thick paper with specialized ends from the wastebasket. She recognized it immediately. It was a test strip for blood monitoring, the kind used by diabetics. Only, Alex wasn't diabetic.

Her hands shaking, Lorna replaced the test strip in the trash and let herself out of the apartment. Alex's condition was worse than she'd thought.

# TWENTY-THREE

From the stairs, Lorna heard the van door sliding open, followed by the sounds of the boisterous surfers heading for the hotel. She raced to the street, hoping to catch Carlos.

"I don't get it. He hasn't won a contest since his rookie year. How's he land a deal like that?" a blonde surfer was saying to a skinny, dark-haired surfer as she brushed by them.

"I don't know man, but that shit's fucked up," the dark haired surfer replied.

"He rode that big wave in Fiji," the blonde one said. "He told me he's gonna surf a fifty- footer."

"Fifty?" the second voice scoffed. "No way."

The hair on the back of Lorna's neck prickled at the mention of Fiji. Then she forgot all about it when Carlos started the van's engine.

She ran to the passenger door and hopped into the seat. "Can I ride with you?" she asked.

He studied her then put the van in gear. "I am driving to town," he said.

"Where's Alex?" she asked, buckling her seat belt. Vans were big, and safe, her rational brain told her.

"At the boat."

"Everything okay?" Lorna asked. The van smelled of surf wax and unwashed bodies. She rolled her squeaky window all the way down.

"Peachy," Carlos replied, keeping his eyes on the road.

Lorna raised her eyebrows. *Peachy?* "So, are you guys, like, together?" she blurted, unable to stop herself.

A look of annoyance passed over Carlos's face. "We're business partners, but we are also friends."

*Clear as mud*, Lorna thought.

Carlos accelerated onto the highway and immediately overtook a pickup truck with several stocky, brown-faced men standing upright in the bed. The sudden movement made Lorna nervous, and she gripped the door handle. The men in the pickup bed stared blithely forward as the van passed.

"So do you run the tours too, or do you just tag along?" Lorna asked, wondering if Carlos always drove this fast.

Carlos gave her a sideways glance. "Alejandra is the *heffe*, but I help, sometimes. I was fishing guide." They approached a small city that Lorna remembered from her drive to the airport. Carlos pulled the van into a service station and got out to fill the tank. Lorna relaxed her grip on the door handle.

"So could you run the tours yourself, then?" Lorna asked when he climbed back inside.

Carlos glared at her, clearly losing his patience. "It is Alejandra's passion to run the tours. Why would I take that from her?" He put the van in gear and exited the station.

Lorna shifted in her seat, eyes glued to the road. "In case she needs a break, or something."

Carlos sighed. "Why are you asking these questions? You should be worried about yourself."

"Myself?" Lorna replied, flinching as the car in front of them slammed on the brakes. *I'm not the one dying*, she thought. "I'm not the one in debt, taking everyone else down with me," she replied instead, thinking of Becca, Seth, and little Fie.

"Just because she does not give you money means that she is in debt?" he replied in a stern voice. "Ask yourself, why are you here?" he looked at her with narrow eyes. "Running here and running there with your frown and your questions, looking down on everything. You make things worse." He sighed. "Alejandra has been worse since you came."

Lorna's boiling temper made her sputter: "Do you have any idea what I went through to get here?" she said, her teeth grinding on her words. She remembered her journey—the bus ride, the night in Eduardo's, the theft of her possessions, and Joe's words about making things right—words that hurt so deep she felt shaky. "I'm here to help her!" she cried.

"Then start by being here, *Pajarito*," he said gently. "You will get nothing from her if you keep taking away."

"Take away?" Lorna said feebly, feeling drained. She looked out the window, her head throbbing. *What am I taking away?*

They passed through several stoplights then he coasted into a lot beneath a neon sign that read: *Farmacia Guadalajara*. Lorna watched Carlos enter the glass-sided building and join the queue of people waiting inside.

"What's that?" Lorna asked when he returned with a small plastic bag.

Carlos showed her a small box with green print, written in Spanish. "For the *erizo*," Carlos answered. "In her feet."

Lorna shook her head in confusion. *Erizo?*

"The little spines," Carlos said as he checked both ways and entered the highway again, in the direction of Río Limón. "Her foot is swollen, she hurts when she walks."

"Alex?" Lorna replied, her pulse accelerating. She remembered the soles of Alex's feet after they'd surfed Buzzard's. Urchin spines, broken off beneath her skin, were buried there, full of bacteria. *Erizo.* Urchins. Lorna felt a tingling panic, a thrumming buzz like electricity running through her belly. Later-stage patients often died of simple infections: pneumonia, bronchitis, staph.

"Some of the guests, too," Carlos said. "From today."

Lorna's pulse bounded, she felt suddenly out of breath. "Does she have a fever?" she began, discarding the surfers whose young, healthy bodies would heal without her help. "Has the swelling radiated? Have you noticed any redness extending from the wounds?" Lorna imagined the faint reddish line signifying sepsis.

Carlos shook his head but Lorna wasn't convinced he'd even looked for these things. "No, it is just the hurting."

"What's in the box, then?" she asked.

"*Ungüento,*" he said.

"Which is . . . ?"

"Like . . . " Carlos rubbed his skin as if to apply something.

"Lotion?" Lorna asked, incredulous.

"It is soothing," he replied, looking surprised.

"Go back," Lorna said quickly. "Go back and get her some Keflex, or Amoxicillin, some kind of antibiotic."

"But—"

Lorna lunged for the wheel. "She could have a staph infection!" she cried. Every cell in her body was alive with this purpose. They swerved to the left before Carlos regained control, sputtering in Spanish.

"Go back! Why aren't you going back?" Lorna cried, managing to get both hands on the wheel this time. They fought for control of the van while Carlos's curses shot at her like spears.

"Stop this!" he cried, his eyes blazing. "We are going to crash!"

Lorna released the wheel, stunned at her actions.

Carlos stopped the van at the side of the road, breathing hard. "And you wonder why she left you!" he fumed.

Lorna curled into the far corner, trembling. "I just want to help her," she whispered, stung. "I'm a doctor," she added, remembering the pride she used to feel in that word. Now it was merely a tool, one that seemed to become more and more obsolete every day.

Carlos smoothed back his dark hair and exhaled heavily. Passing cars hissed past his open window. He seemed to study his hands for a long time. "Alex has never needed antibiotics for this," he said, his dark eyes finally connecting with hers. "Either you are crazy," he said. "Or something is very wrong."

Lorna inhaled a deep breath, which did not calm her frantic heart. "There's a tumor on her pancreas," she said, unable to look at him. "It's cancer, and there's nothing we can do."

Carlos looked out the window for a long time. Lorna had seen his type before, the ones with brave faces who cried in private.

"She has been sick," Carlos said finally. "But I never thought . . . ." He inhaled a long breath, his face a tight mask. "You are here to tell her," he said, his eyes squinty and dark, as if they'd shrunk.

"She doesn't want to hear it," Lorna said. "I've tried."

"Tomorrow morning," he said, his lips tight. "She will be leaving early with the group. You will be on the boat waiting."

"Okay," Lorna said, wondering if she now had an ally.

Carlos drove back to the *farmacia* only to find it had closed for the day. He promised to return as soon as he could. Then he turned the van back onto the highway.

"I will say nothing," Carlos said as they turned down the road toward Río Limón.

"Thanks." The van's engine hummed in her bones, and suddenly Lorna knew why Alex hadn't been willing to drive to the airport. It must hurt. She wanted to see Alex and check for signs of infection but knew there was nothing she could do about it tonight.

"I need you to try something," she said, remembering a trick from her past. "It's not exactly soothing, but it will get the spines out," she added.

Carlos hesitated, his dark eyes hollow. But he pulled to the side of the road in front of the Mini Super like she asked.

"Can I have a few pesos?" she said, reaching for the door.

Carlos slipped a bill from his leather wallet and handed it to her. She left the van and after rummaging through the plastic tubs of vegetables outside the Mini Super, she settled on a few firm, medium-sized onions. After paying, she returned to the van. "Boil the onions till they're soft and falling apart, in a big pot."

Carlos frowned.

"Let it cool, but not too much, you want it as hot as she can stand." Lorna checked to make sure he understood. "Then soak her feet. The spines should slip right out, or disintegrate, whichever comes first." Carlos peered at her. "It should work," she said encouragingly. Truthfully, she wasn't sure. She'd been in Greece the last time she'd used it. Were the onions more potent there? In any case, as her corpsmen friends used to say, "Can't hurt, might help." It might be the only way she could get through to Alex, the only way she could communicate that she was not here to "take away," as Carlos had accused.

"Does she have a fever?" Lorna asked, wiping her moist palms on her thighs.

Carlos's eyes clouded. "I don't know," he said.

The thought of Alex's body working double time to fight an infection that could be licked in twenty-four hours within the walls of a hospital made Lorna feel useless, like everything she'd sacrificed amounted to nothing. She felt like hitting something, anything—a palm trunk, a mattress, the dashboard of the van—until it was reduced to a compliant, desiccated lump. "Well, don't let it get over a hundred and two. Or I guess that's about"—she worked the conversion in her head—"thirty-nine degrees in Celsius," she said finally. *If only I still had the Keflex,* she thought, grimacing.

Carlos agreed, looking grave, and put the van in gear.

# TWENTY-FOUR

Santa Cruz, California

"You sure you didn't tell anybody?" Joe asked Marty. The bartender put their beers down but waved off Joe's ten-dollar bill.

"Okay, I told a few people," Marty replied, grabbing his beer and slipping into the crowd.

Joe cursed under his breath and followed him into the next room, where the opening band had finished setting up. "It's not supposed to be a big deal," Joe said to Marty as they reached the stage.

"Don't you want to go out with a bang?" Marty said, facing him. Joe sighed. "Not really."

Marty shook his head. "You'll thank me someday."

Joe took a long sip of his beer as Marty hopped up to the stage to talk to Jake, the sound guy.

Already the bar was packed, and several people had given him the double-take look that he'd grown to hate. A group of girls he'd once partied with in a hotel hot tub spotted him. One of them gave him a babyish little wave and a wink. He pulled his trucker hat lower on his forehead and ducked out the back. This was turning into the kind of gig he had wanted to avoid. He stormed back to his Subaru, cursing Marty.

Doherty and Marshall showed up just as he was unloading his gear and quickly joined him in setting up behind the stage. Hefting his endless drum cases, cigarette dangling from his thin lips, Marshall gave him a grin as he ducked inside.

Doherty returned to the dark alley. "Looks like a good crowd already."

Joe slammed the trunk of his car. "Thanks to Marty."

Doherty pulled a joint from his breast pocket and raised his eyebrow.

Joe shook his head.

Doherty sighed and lit up, leaned against the brick wall. "I'm gonna miss this," he said.

Joe crossed his arms and looked up at the clear sky. He still remembered the epic day of surfing a perfect six-foot swell together that had given rise to their band's name and idea. At first, people thought they were a Christian band, which Joe found hilarious. But their first album's cover art of a six-foot barrel helped dispel the label. Their next album featured a cartooned-out massive Robin Hood, with Joe, Marshall, and Doherty as the arrows in his quiver. "You'll find another band."

"Not like this one," Doherty said, his eyes burning into Joe.

Joe hung his head. Hadn't they been through this?

"We're finally making money, man. People are calling *us* for gigs. I've gotten more ass in the last year than I probably ever will."

"Life's not about getting laid, man," Joe said, his voice rising.

"Maybe not, but it should at least be about having fun," Doherty said.

"What's that supposed to mean?" Joe asked.

"Did Fiji fuck with your head or something? Cuz ever since you've been back you've been acting weird." Doherty took a puff.

Joe remembered the morning light on Lorna's skin, and her laugh.

"First you start up with that drama queen Francine again. Then you say Six Foot Savior is done." Doherty shook his head. "I once knew this girl who trekked all over India and came back having seizures and shit. They found out she had a parasite in her frickin brain, dude. I shit you not. From drinking the water."

Joe reached for the joint, inhaled. "I don't have a parasite," he said after exhaling.

"You sure?" Doh said, taking another drag. He pointed to Joe's head. "What's the issue, then?"

Joe took the joint again. "The issue," he said, pushing thoughts of Lorna away. "Is regret."

"Well let me know when you get over it," Doherty mumbled before heading inside.

Joe remained in the alley smoking the last of Doh's joint. Quitting the band was the right move; he knew it the minute he'd returned from Fiji. His heart wasn't in it anymore. Joe killed the roach and flicked it into the street, looked up again at the city sky, too bright from its own lights to reveal the stars. He dreaded this night, couldn't wait for it to end. Tomorrow he was taking Francine camping. He wanted to get away from the noise and the people in the bar recognizing him, yelling out his lyrics, getting drunk and reckless and stupid. He'd play a good show, though. He owed at least that to Doh and Marsh. Plus, he wanted to play the song he wrote after Fiji. He needed to say goodbye.

Joe could barely see beyond the stage lights, but the mob of people seemed to pulse like a pumping heart in time with his chords. The buzz from Doh's joint had dulled his frustration with Marty and the loss of the kind of night he'd wanted. It was so easy to think of nothing, to connect with the eyes in the crowd without really looking, to grin without feeling. It was all just a farce, anyway. None of them really understood any of it, not in a million years.

About halfway through the show the pushing started; Joe noticed the rippling of bodies moving forward and back. Joe squinted but the stage lights made everything a blur. Between songs he asked the mob to save the slam dancing for the disco clubs.

"Are you really quitting?" someone shouted.

Joe's smile tightened. Ignoring the question, he turned back to Doh and Marsh and nodded. Marsh ticked one, two, three, and they opened fast and hard into *Double Down High*, to which the crowd cheered, the front row of girls hopping up and down, squealing, their foreheads glistening with sweat from the heat inside, the summer night, and the jostling, dancing, jumping. He transitioned into *Coal Mine*, noticing again the pushing, swaying, and the aggressive pushing back. The girls in the front row shouted something he couldn't hear, one of them shoving back, which sent a ripple into the dark, invisible crowd. Joe's lips and fingers continued on as the ripple came back harder, smashing the girls against the stage and into Joe's microphone stand, which crashed right into his mouth.

Joe's hands came up to his throbbing teeth, but Doh and Marsh kept playing. Did the mob even know he'd been hit? He had the strange sensation of blindness as his tongue felt along the inside of his teeth—nothing broken.

His strumming hand balled into a fist. "Jesus fuck, people!" he shouted. He looked back at the band and yelled at them to stop. They looked bewildered, as if he'd pulled them from a dream.

Joe turned back to the crowd, reached up to wiggle his front right tooth. Shit, was it loose? A metallic taste in his mouth told him he was bleeding. He felt the sudden urge to spit. The crowd's noise behind him faded as he strode off stage.

Doh met him in the alley. "Let me see it," he urged.

Joe pulled up his top lip and watched Doherty squint at his tooth in the darkness.

"You're fine, dude. They're all still there."

"I know, you asshole," Joe replied, but he was lisping, his front tooth hurt with each *s*.

Doh's eyes were resigned. "You wanna call it, then?"

Joe spit again. "No," he replied, as anger seethed up from his toes, filled his gut. *People should be good to each other* rang in his head. "Let's finish this."

The crowd seemed subdued when he returned but Joe kept a close eye on the mic. They played their last songs from the playlist, and then he told Doh and Marsh he wanted to do one on his own.

He focused on a place between the lights where the black blur didn't hurt his eyes, and strummed the opening, letting his fingers take over and his mind drift back to the time he liked to remember most. She was there, watching him with her stormy eyes, laughing with her mouth wide open, making love to him in the honeymoon *bure's* big bed. He wanted her to be here with him when the words left his lips. *Over the Falls* was the only way he knew how to tell her that he'd fallen for her and couldn't believe he'd been stupid enough to lose her.

What kind of fool was I?
You saw me comin' a mile away
You took my hand and told me to stay
Here I was thinkin' I'd be your savior
But you had me beat. I was the failure

Looking back, Joe knew he'd thought of being something of a savior figure to Lorna, with her dark secrets, the hidden feelings he could sense, and her inner struggle for peace. He thought he could help her. And how? First by judging her, and then by pushing her to confront her past. She had been right to walk away. Maybe the persisting pain he felt would keep him honest from now on. *People should be good to each other*, he thought.

> Over the falls for you
> Over the falls, my heart wide open
> Crushed by the weight
> And now it's too late
> Over the falls and I'm drowning, drowning

The crowd seemed unimpressed with the piece, but Joe didn't care, it hadn't been for them. The band picked it up again with the encore, and by the end Joe's throat felt sore and dry and his eyes stung from the cigarette smoke and his teeth throbbed from the mic slamming into it and he knew he was ready. His shoulders felt heavy, his diaphragm ached, and his back was tight. He knew he'd sleep like a log and wake up with a murkiness in his head that would persist for days.

Fuck 'em. He was not going to miss a single minute of it.

# TWENTY-FIVE

Río Limón, Mexico

Lorna woke to her watch's alarm at five a.m. and slipped out of the hotel, a borrowed board tucked beneath her arm. The nightlong rainfall had turned the sandy streets muddy, with ridges of sand piled up against the buildings, and water still flowing, thin and clear over the road. The cool, moist air sent a quick shiver over her skin as she sidestepped puddles and piles of deposited garbage on her way to the marina, but by the time she turned down the narrow road to the water, the back of her neck felt sticky with sweat.

Alex's boat bobbed silently, tied to an anchor. She had no choice but to paddle out to it. Once onboard, she pulled up the surfboard and sat down to wait. She found a towel beneath one of the benches and dried her face. With only the quiet lapping of waves against the hull and the tapping of halyards and thread of current swishing against the rocks to keep her company, she decided to lie down to look at the stars, vibrant between the patches of cloud.

Lorna had thought all night about Alex's condition. She doubted Carlos knew how to take care of her when things got worse. Lorna was supposed to be back at work in two days—an idea that seemed like it belonged to another world.

Soon the surfer's voices and the sound of their sandals scuffing the gravel road floated across the water. Lorna's insides twisted with nerves. She heard a splash then Alex appeared at the stern.

"How're your feet?" Lorna asked, sitting up.

Alex blinked at her. "What are you doing here?"

"Thought I'd go surfing today," Lorna said. "That okay?"

Alex's eyes darkened. "Little Lorna Kai's joining the game, huh?" she said evenly, moving to the bow to release the anchor.

"Who diagnosed you with diabetes?" Lorna fired back as Alex moved to the engine.

"What?" Alex replied, annoyed. "Who told you?"

"Nobody told me," Lorna replied.

"I did," Alex said dismissively. She started the engine and putted the boat toward the dock.

"Diabetes isn't the problem, Alex," Lorna blurted. In Alex's case, diabetes was secondary to the tumor. Sometimes diabetes could even be a misdiagnosis, an early warning sign. If only Alex had seen a doctor instead of Ask Jeeves, he or she might have seen the growth, maybe even stopped it.

Alex ignored her comment and the surfers jumped on, stowing their boards and gear quickly. "Lorna here's gonna tag along," Alex addressed the others as she idled the boat out of the bay. "Feel free to burn her, if you can," she said, her sideways grin aimed at the dark horizon.

Alex steered the boat north through the inky black water, exiting the harbor just as the sun's first blush appeared over the distant mountains. Lorna observed the surfers apply sunscreen, organize their gear, and watch the horizon with determined eyes. Most hadn't given her a second glance. She didn't care if they burned her. She was here to get her message across to Alex, whether she wanted to hear it or not.

After racing past shadowed cliffs and rocky points, the sea spray misting her cheeks, they passed a rounded point of land and entered a broad bay. Alex continued to the northern edge of the bay and idled the boat. In the dawn's calm stillness, all eyes watched the horizon for waves. When the first bump of a set rose from the black water, Lorna could feel the adrenaline, the hope, rippling through the crew. In the first rays of sunshine, the wave curled forward, the lip a line of white lace tumbling through space, its underbelly a smooth crescent. A deep rumble roared across the water like boulders rolling down a mountainside. One of the surfers looked back at Alex, a question in his eyes.

"Let's do it," Alex replied, putting the boat in gear to anchor it farther outside.

Meanwhile the surfers gathered their boards, attaching leashes, donning rash guards. One even took a leak off the back while Alex secured the bow anchor. Lorna watched them scurry from the boat, their muscular backs and shoulders pulling deep strokes through the water. Once satisfied with the anchor, Alex readied to join them, donning a sleeveless rashie and attaching her leash. Tiny waves tapped against the hull of the boat, a sound like confetti rattling inside a bag.

"So did the onion trick work or not?" Lorna asked.

Alex frowned.

Lorna wondered angrily if Carlos had ignored her advice.

"I thought that was some of Carlos's folk wisdom again," Alex said quietly, rummaging in her bag for a tube of sunscreen.

"I learned it from a boat captain in Greece," Lorna said, remembering the snorkeling trip she'd been on with the other AP Bio kids her junior year in Sicily. "This idiot kid tried to pick up a black urchin." Lorna shook her head. "Oh, that's right," she added, the bitterness like ice in her veins, "you'd dropped off the face of the earth by then."

Alex squeezed out a blob of sunscreen and smeared it across her cheeks. She seemed not to hear Lorna's comment.

"I've been wondering if the onions in Greece are special some- how?" she continued, enjoying the way Alex pretended not to hear her, and her sudden sense of control. She knew her voice was too loud, her words too forceful. "And, well, that was a long time ago, and I thought maybe it might be some fluke, you know?" Alex faced the waves but didn't seem to see them. "So tell me, did it work?" Lorna asked again.

"Yes!" Alex hissed, attaching her leash. "It worked. Now can we get on with our day here?" she added before slipping over the side with her board.

Lorna didn't even try to take waves; instead she watched Alex shepherd the team riders. Occasionally Alex paddled into a peak, but with each one she seemed less committed, something Lorna had never seen.

"Look, either surf or go back to the boat," Alex finally said to her on her way back to the lineup. "You're a distraction just sitting here."

Lorna paddled into the mix but it didn't feel right. She watched the team riders charge hard with their super-late drops and big airs. She was blown away by their stamina and daredevil antics, their in- tense competition, the way they took off on waves that were sure to close out, trapping them inside. The idea of trying to keep up with them only sapped her energy further.

Suddenly she didn't see Alex, and searched the water for her silver-blonde head. Finally she spotted her, almost to the boat. Lorna sprinted to catch her, the speech she'd prepared ringing in her head. But when she came to the boat, a noise from the other side slowed her movements. A noise like coughing, or was it splashing? Retching. Lorna followed the sound.

Alex was treading water and splashing at a swirl of bright yellow bile.

"You okay?" Lorna asked after she'd stopped coughing.

Alex kept her back to the boat. She tucked her board sideways beneath her like a log, then rinsed her face with a scoop of seawater. "There's a bottle of water," she said in a scratchy voice. "In the box under the seat."

Lorna climbed aboard and found the bottle. "Here," she said, handing down it to Alex.

"Thanks," Alex said, sipping slowly.

Lorna sat on one of the benches and watched the surfers tick off waves. "When I was in Fiji I cut my leg pretty bad," she said carefully, touching the still-tender scar. She squinted at the surfers trading waves in the distance.

"I was pretty scared. Nobody knew what to do." Lorna remembered how alone she'd felt, and how powerless. "I got sick in the jeep on the way to the hospital. I didn't know what was going to happen. I mean, would they try to amputate my leg? Would I bleed out before they could see me? Would I get AIDS from a dirty needle?" She picked at a section of peeling paint along the gunwale.

"After going through that, with strangers . . . " Her voice caught at the memory of how she had begged Joe to stay with her. She'd been so desperate to trust anyone then. How stupid she'd been, letting herself fall for Joe and his bullshit ideals. "If you want me to go, I'll go." Lorna watched Alex slowly tread water, her profiled face quiet.

"It's cancer, isn't it?" Alex asked softly.

Lorna sighed. "Yes," she said.

"Bad?"

"Yes."

Alex studied her board for a moment. "I used to be able to keep up with these guys," Alex said quietly. "I'd go out all day, and then Carlos and I would catch the evening glass, or go body boarding, or fishing. I'm lucky to be able to carry my board up to the apartment after a day like this."

"Are you depressed?" Lorna asked.

"I don't have time to be depressed! Christ, Lorna!" Alex barked, glaring at Lorna. She looked away with a huff. "How much time do I have?"

Lorna's brain tried frantically to weave the matrix together that would give her the answer.

"Years? Months?" Alex prompted, looking exasperated.

"Two months, maybe more," Lorna replied uneasily, knowing Alex would be lucky to make it to September. And now, if she was fighting a staph infection, it could be sooner.

Alex's tanned face visibly paled. She whispered something then turned away again.

A feeling of shame rose up in Lorna. After so much time of keeping this inside her, of wanting to release it, how could she just now wonder how Alex would feel hearing those words? With horror, Lorna thought of all the things happening in the future that Alex would miss: exploring new territory, surfing with Carlos, watching Sophie grow up. She thought of all the waves that would break without her there to discover them, master them, share them with friends or Carlos, maybe even Lorna if it wasn't already too late for that. Lorna closed her eyes. "I wish I could say something different," she said.

Alex was silent for a long time. "I thought it was just a bad stomach bug, that maybe with the diabetes . . . but nothing I tried made it get better." She gazed toward the shore, her expression hidden and her voice detached, strangely calm. "I came to Port Angeles to get the boat. We'd been working on it, retrofitting the galley, building bunks in the cabins."

Lorna was confused. What boat? But then Alex continued: "I thought I'd come see you. I guess I probably knew you could help, but I didn't think it was anything . . . " She took a breath and Lorna saw her thin shoulder blades poking outward, like bird wings.

Lorna completed the thought: *serious.* "My stuff that got stolen," she said, the humiliating image of grubby hands reaching into the Ziploc to read the labels then chucking some or all into the street when the names didn't make sense. "I had brought some things for you. For things like insomnia and pain. Until we get you to a hospital." She said this last bit trying not to use her doctor voice, which would have been impatient, clinical, her you-should-have-come-in-sooner voice.

"Not now," Alex said in a faraway voice. "Not yet, okay?" she said.

Lorna heard the soft paddle strokes of the surfers and turned to see the pack approaching the boat. Lorna struggled to control her sense of time running out, like stepping into quicksand—the more you struggled the quicker you sank. *This is real!* She wanted to scream. *We have no more time!* Lorna felt sick at the knowledge of what was to come—further weight loss, the pain, jaundice, the gruesome swelling. Alex needed to be somewhere with professionals and medications that could make her more comfortable. Lorna shuddered at the thought of staying in Río Limón, of Alex dying in pain and—worse yet—that she would be helpless to stop it.

"There still might be something they could do!" Lorna urged quietly. "There's treatments, drugs that can keep you from vomiting, give you more energy."

"No," Alex replied, her voice hard. "We do this my way."

# TWENTY-SIX

Santa Cruz, California

Joe pulled his Subaru up to the curb in front of the tiny duplex. He watched Francine for a reaction, but she only blinked.

The old engine stalled before he could shut it off, so he set the brake and stepped out of the car, reaching in the back for the bag of groceries. Francine lifted a large box of diapers from the trunk and followed him.

The tiny moonscape yard held one stumpy palm tree and a path lined with white rocks. Joe made a note to fix a cracked board in the sagging porch and opened the squeaky screen. Chris answered his knock, holding a jar of baby food in one hand and a tiny spoon in the other, and grinned when he saw Joe.

"I was just gonna feed her." He let them in and quickly returned to the cramped kitchen, where Carrie babbled at them from her high chair. Chris nodded toward the back of the house. "Em's getting ready."

Joe introduced Francine, who offered a meek hello, then placed the diapers in the hallway leading to the bedroom. He put the groceries in the kitchen.

"No, man, we're okay, I worked this week," Chris said, his face tight.

"I can still help, right?" Joe unloaded the groceries quickly and tucked the bag below the sink.

Chris spooned the mush from the jar into Carrie's tiny and obliging mouth. "Thanks," he said quietly, focusing on Carrie as she took in another spoonful.

"Let me do that. Grab Em and get outta here," Joe said.

Chris seemed to think about it for a moment then handed over the jar and spoon. "Keep this handy," he said of the washcloth strategically placed on the nearby counter before sidestepping out of the kitchen.

Joe pulled the stool toward him and dipped the spoon into the jar. By the time he had the spoon halfway to Carrie, her mouth gaped wide open. "Hungry, huh?" he asked her. She banged her fat palms on the tray and opened her little mouth again. He popped the second jar's lid.

He had been coming regularly to give his sister Emily and Chris a break. He was glad to do it for them, but really he came to see Carrie. He'd held her within the first hour of her life and had watched her grow, heard her laugh, seen her learn something new. Sure, he could be doing other things, but he knew that if he waited until she was older to get to know her, it would be too late. But bringing Francine was a huge gamble. Had she really changed? He'd overheard her say to a friend one time that she couldn't imagine having kids—too messy, too time-consuming, let alone what it would do to her body. Joe hadn't been able to get past that. Tonight would show him if things were different.

"Okay," Emily said, entering the kitchen. "I've got her jammies laid out on our bed." Em was dressed in jeans and flip flops, and her long hair was draped over her shoulder like a shiny cape. She reached in to quickly wipe Carrie's face. "I just pumped, so give this to her now, and tonight you can thaw one from the freezer," she said, handing Joe a warm bottle of breast milk. He felt Francine bristle. Joe let it go—breastfeeding was a little freaky but also totally normal. And it was free; a can of formula cost twenty-five bucks.

Emily acknowledged Francine with a nod then blinked at Joe, either dismissing Francine or not quite registering her. "You sure you're good?" she said, scrutinizing him with her eyes.

Joe grinned. "Go have fun."

Emily let out an anxious sigh. Chris grabbed her hand and tugged a little, but Emily broke away to kiss Carrie on the head. "Be a good girl for Uncle Joe, okay?" she whispered to her, stroking her fine hair.

"C'mon Em," Chris said from the doorway. "She'll be fine."

"I know, I know," Emily said, finally joining him.

After the door closed Carrie's lower lip trembled. "It's okay," Joe said in a soothing voice, hoping to avoid a full fit. "Mommy'll be back soon."

Carrie whimpered.

"Should we have some milk?" he asked, wagging the warm bottle in front of her. He scooped her from her high chair and moved to the couch, where he cradled Carrie and popped the bottle into her puckering mouth. Carrie's face calmed, and Joe smiled. "That's better, huh?" he asked. He looked at Francine. "You want to try?" he asked.

Francine shrugged her lips. "That's okay," she replied. But she sat close.

After, Joe moved to the floor, with Carrie next to him, and pulled out the box of wooden blocks. "You want to empty it?" he asked her.

Carrie waved her arms and hummed with excitement. Her eyes focused on a blue block inside the box, which she picked out and put in her mouth.

Joe looked up at Francine, still sitting on the couch. "Feel free to join us," he said.

She carefully slid to the floor. "So, when does she go to bed?"

Joe frowned at her. "Not soon," he said. Was he nuts for trying to share this with her? He watched Carrie gnaw on the corner of a different block, a long thread of drool dangling down her front.

"I didn't mean it like that," Francine sighed. "I just want to know the plan."

Joe lifted an eyebrow. "This"—he nodded to Carrie, who dropped the block and tried to grab it—"is the plan."

"Okay," Francine said, a little defensively.

Carrie toppled over, gouging her head on a few of the blocks. Her mouth turned down and she started wailing. Joe scooped her up, trying not to make a big deal out of it; she was fine. Carrie pushed back from him, howling.

"Want to go to for a walk?" Joe asked her.

"Isn't it going to get dark soon?" Francine said.

"We've got an hour," Joe replied, rubbing Carrie's back.

"You're gonna let her get dirty like that?" Francine said to Joe who was sitting at the edge of the swing set while Carrie patted the wood chips with her fingers.

Joe tried to be patient. He'd visited the home Francine grew up in—not a speck of dirt in sight, everything in its place. "That's what being a kid is all about. Plus we'll give her a bath."

"Just don't let her put her fingers in her mouth!" Francine said, horrified, as Carrie dropped a dirt clod on her own head.

Joe ignored this and poked Carrie in her soft middle. "You wanna swing?" he asked her as she giggled and tried to push his hand away.

Carrie hummed and kicked her feet.

"Why don't you push her?" Joe said to Francine and lifted Carrie into one of the baby swings.

Francine stood behind and gave the swing a small push.

"You can go higher," Joe said encouragingly.

Francine pushed a little harder. "Is she okay?" she asked.

Joe grinned. "She's fine."

Carrie squealed, her thin tuft of hair fluffing in the breeze.

"It won't make her sick, will it?" Francine asked as Carrie kicked her feet.

Joe shrugged.

Francine pushed her in silence for a while.

"You want to go down the slide?" Joe asked after Carrie got tired of swinging.

Carrie looked to where Joe was pointing, the breeze still fluffing her fine hair.

Joe stopped the swing and pulled Carrie out, then offered her to Francine. "You want to take her?" he said.

"Huh?" she said, accepting the baby as if she was made of porcelain.

"Just put her in your lap," Joe said.

Francine held Carrie facing out, her arms stiff, and walked towards the jungle gym steps.

Joe moved toward the bottom of the slide to catch them. Finally, they came down. Carrie shrieked. Francine handed Carrie over and yelped at the stain on her shorts.

"Oops," Joe said, suppressing a chuckle. He turned Carrie around and made a goofy face at her. He caught the whiff of sweet potato poop. "Somebody dropped a bomb."

Francine looked paralyzed. "Oh my God." She dashed off in the direction of the bathroom.

Joe grabbed Carrie's bag and followed. But there wasn't a changing table in the men's room.

"Hey, babe?" he yelled from outside the door, still holding Carrie at arm's length, the wipes and a diaper tucked under his arm, the clean set of clothes draped over his shoulder.

"This is disgusting!" Francine shrieked.

"Um, babe, I got a little favor to ask you," he said.

"I'm going to have to throw these shorts away!"

Joe couldn't wait any longer. "Hope no one is in here," he said, rushing in.

"What are you doing?" Francine asked, aghast.

Joe searched the stalls for a baby changer. "Little help, here?" he asked after finding one.

She walked to him, looking cross, the front of her shorts wet, with a yellow-brown blob staining the left cuff.

"Open it?" he said, nodding at the device.

She pulled down the table.

"Some paper towels, or something," he said. Carrie began to whimper. "It's okay," he cooed to her as Francine yanked paper towels from the dispenser.

Finally, Joe was able to put Carrie down. He whipped open the snaps on her pants.

"Oh God," Francine said, holding her nose. "I think I'm going to be sick."

"I'm not exactly in heaven over here either," he said as Francine disappeared. He finished changing Carrie, cleaned the changing table, wrapped up her soiled clothing, used a baby wipe to wash his hands, and found Francine outside with her arms crossed. Joe put Carrie in the stroller, and they walked home in silence.

# TWENTY-SEVEN

Río Limón, Mexico

Carlos's voice startled her from sleep. Lorna woke to him hovering over her in the cramped room, shaking her. "You must come," he said. "The fever."

Lorna leapt from the bed and pulled on her trunks, her feet finding her flip flops by feel. She followed Carlos into the dark night, barely noticing Seth standing outside, waiting to lock the exterior doors behind them. Carlos must have called him. Lorna hurried across the deserted beach with Carlos, her mind spinning. *The urchins*, she thought with dread. *An infection.* Lorna's worst fear came true: she had started the antibiotics too late.

Lorna raced up the apartment stairs behind Carlos who opened the door and led her to the bathroom.

Alex sat on the floor wearing a T-shirt and underwear, her hair wet. Her face was tight with pain and she was breathing in ragged gulps. The stifling room smelled of excrement and something sharp, oniony.

"What happened?" she said, kneeling down, fingering Alex's wrist for a pulse, realizing the oniony smell came from her breath.

"I'm cold," Alex said, her teeth chattering. "Carlos says I gotta take a cold shower, but I'm cold," she said again, shivering.

"You've got a high fever," Lorna replied. *And a rapid pulse*, she thought with increasing anxiety. "Did you give her any Tylenol? Motrin?" she asked Carlos.

"Yes, Tylenol."

"How much? When?"

Carlos's hands fluttered at his sides. "Um," he said, seemingly at a loss.

"Carlos!" Lorna barked. "Focus, okay?"

"Two pills, about two hours ago," Carlos said finally, looking scared.

One thousand milligrams. "Get me some Motrin, and let's get her to the bed." Not for the first time, Lorna agonized over the loss of her stolen meds. Alex needed a hospital. There they could do so much more.

Carlos returned, and they managed to get Alex to swallow the pills with some water.

"Where does it hurt?" Lorna asked, gently lifting one of her feet to look for signs of the infection. If only she could give her something stronger, like Clindamycin, or would such a powerful drug just burn a hole through Alex's already beat-up GI tract? Levofloxacin would squelch this bug in twenty-four hours, but they might as well drop a bomb on her liver.

Alex hissed in pain as Lorna palpated the sole of Alex's foot.

Lorna peered at the skin, which was pink and swollen. She checked for the pinkish line growing upwards from Alex's heel that would signify a staph infection. Bingo. Three inches long, at least.

"Get me a bucket," she ordered to Carlos. "Make sure it's clean. Then add hot water." She turned to Alex. "Got any salt?"

Alex nodded, said something to Carlos in Spanish.

"Go!" Lorna ordered.

Lorna checked the other foot, finding a similar result. "You need IV antibiotics and pain meds." Alex looked away. "We can't stay here," Lorna said.

Alex shivered. "I'm not leaving."

"But this infection," Lorna said. "Your body isn't able to fight it alone. There's too much"—Lorna stopped, searching for words that wouldn't trigger Alex's rejection—"going on right now."

Carols returned with a mop bucket mostly full of water and a box of salt. Lorna told him how much salt to add then slowly placed Alex's left foot in the bucket.

"Ow!" Alex protested. "That's hot!"

Lorna coaxed Alex's right foot in.

"What's the closest major hospital?" Lorna asked Carlos.

Carlos blinked and his mouth opened. "Acapulco," he stammered.

Lorna pressed the heels of her hands into her eyes and silently cursed. Should she force Alex to suffer through 300 kilometers of potholed, bumpy roads, or could her field-med tricks do the job? Alex could get worse.

Alex shivered again. The hot water would hopefully draw out the infection, but it would do nothing for the high fever. She had to hope the Motrin, coupled with the Tylenol already onboard, would work its magic soon.

"You need better drugs," Lorna said to Alex.

"Then get them," Alex said through chattering teeth. She took a deep breath. "You got the antibiotics, right?"

Lorna rubbed her face with her hands and sighed. "It's not that easy."

"But you're a doctor," Alex wheezed. "Can't you just tell them you're a doctor?"

"No!" Lorna said, crossing her arms.

Alex shivered again.

"Sometimes, people tell me they can get medications here," Carlos interrupted, his eyes flashing with urgency, as if he'd finally found a way to be useful. "That it is easier."

"Not the drugs we're looking for now," Lorna said, her voice edged with impatience.

"I don't want to leave," Alex sobbed suddenly. "Everything I have is here!" she cried, her frail body rocking back and forth. "They'll hook me up to tubes and wires and machines, and I'll be stuck there!" she managed between tight breaths. "I can't do it!" she shouted, her pained eyes flashing between Carlos and Lorna.

Lorna's heart ached. She should have forced Alex to leave the minute she'd found her. But Alex was right; once the doctors handled the infection, they'd move on to the cancer. They'd poke her and scan her and tell her about best-case scenarios. There would be doctors and nurses, all strangers, discussing her case during rounds as if she wasn't sitting right there in a shapeless gown, afraid, confused, alone. Lorna knew it all so well.

But keeping Alex in Río Limón would prove disastrous; it meant that Alex would experience more pain, more suffering.

Lorna thought of Río Limón's sandy beach, the sounds of the waves combing the shore, the rain pounding on the roof, the palm trees' blades shifting in the breezes, the smell of ocean salt and someone's cooking. Paradise. She knew why Alex wanted to stay. *But I'll be the one who lives with the consequences*, she thought.

Lorna stood on the balcony, watching the black sea's restless surface glisten beneath the moon's pale glow. Carlos was leaning against the railing, smoking a cigarette. The apartment's door stood slightly ajar, in case Alex woke.

"The group coming tomorrow," Carlos said, "is an older group. Lawyers from Los Angeles." He exhaled a stream of tobacco smoke. "They come same week every year."

Lorna rubbed her forehead, wishing Carlos smoked something besides cigarettes. "Can you run it?"

Carlos nodded. "This one is okay for me," he said.

"What about after that?"

"Alex will be better then. She just needs rest."

Lorna shook her head vigorously. "Noooo," she said, watching him smoke. Alex's health was taking a turn for the worse. She needed Carlos to understand this, and to get ready.

Lorna had witnessed the pride Alex experienced from her hard work. Alex had a reputation now, one she'd earned. Could Carlos carry on without her? Alex wouldn't want to lose it all, even if it meant letting someone else run the show. Would Carlos be a hindrance in this or an ally?

Her gut clenched at the thought of telling Becca and Seth. Lorna hadn't been able to find a way or a time to tell them what was ahead. They were all in this together—them, Carlos, and now Lorna. She wondered how they could they keep things from falling apart.

"You got a lead on getting drugs, then?" Lorna asked.

Carlos didn't look at her. "There are certain doctors who . . . "

"Find out how, okay?"

Carlos's dark look made it obvious that he resented her tone. But she only needed him to trust her; friendship wasn't important.

"I will try."

*You better do more than try*, Lorna thought, scrutinizing him with a long look.

"The boat is here," Carlos said, after putting out his cigarette against the concrete wall.

"Boat?" Lorna asked, confused.

Carlos gave her a sideways glance. "For new trips, longer trips. For clients." Carlos's eyes sparkled. "It is from a dive business. Twin screws. To access places we have found, waves too far for the panga."

"You bought a boat?" Lorna mumbled as it sunk in.

"She did not tell you?" Carlos said, blinking.

Lorna shook her head. Then she remembered Alex explaining the reason for their trip to Washington—to work on "the boat."

"We go to Port Angeles," said Carlos. "We work on the boat for six weeks, fixing the berths for bunks, refinishing the deck, tuning the engines. We pay to have it trailered down because we must return for the season."

"And it's here?" The pieces were coming together now, but Lorna knew there was no way they could manage a boat, let alone "new trips."

"No. In Manzanillo. The harbor in Limón cannot handle the size."

Lorna remembered Manzanillo from her first and last day as Alex's airport shuttle bunny. "Sell it," Lorna said quickly, keeping her voice down.

Carlos stiffened. "Why would I do such a thing?"

Lorna turned to him. "Because she's not going to get better. Can you run the day tours *and* a charter business? Dump the boat now, before you get buried."

Carlos sighed. "We must not talk this way, *Pajarito*," he said. "This boat is her dream. There are many places she desires to explore."

Lorna thought about the swelling she'd observed in Alex's midsection from fluids drawn in by the cancer cells. Her body's fluids would continue to collect there, and soon she wouldn't be capable of paddling a surfboard. How long would her kidneys hold out?

"I'm telling you, her searching days are done."

"You don't know her!" Carlos hissed, stabbing his stubby index finger at Lorna's chest. "She will die if I tell her I sell the boat!"

"Then take it offshore and sink it, tell her pirates stole it, claim the insurance money and be relieved it's gone."

Carlos's eyes grew wider as she talked. "For a person so smart, you are a slow learner," he said—his voice tight, not with anger, but disappointment. "She has a plan for this boat, a plan that includes you. Take it away and you take away her hope, her reason to fight. This," he paused to look around, "is all she has left. Take it away and you will lose her forever."

# TWENTY-EIGHT

## Santa Cruz, California

Joe's legs swirled over the kelp bed beneath him as he watched the tiny waves sweep past the cliff.

Marty slipped off his board and floated. "Man, this is dismal," he said with a sigh and then kicked back onto his board.

Joe shrugged. "Beats workin," he said.

"Aw, listen to you," Marty scoffed. "Last week you couldn't hardly sleep you were so fired up on this new job."

"That was before the architect turned into an asshole." Joe still knew he'd made the right choice: doing work he felt good about. He just wished it involved more actual building and less bickering, less whining. He'd berated the mason for taking a two-hour lunch break—one Joe knew he used to squeeze in a session here at Cowell's. "Hey, I'd love to check out for a few hours too, go catch some waves, but we're on a deadline here," he'd said, feeling the tension in his neck and temples. But the mason had been lazy and careless for the rest of the day, sulking by Joe when they passed.

"You wanna go see Death Cab on Saturday?" he asked Marty.

Marty's shoulders seemed to slump. "Can't," he said.

Joe raised his eyebrows.

"We gotta go to the city, see Jen's mom."

Joe didn't reply. Jen's mom wasn't one of Marty's favorite people.

"You know she's pushing Jen to remodel our kitchen?" Marty said. "We just moved in, for crying out loud!"

Joe knew Marty could have lived forever in the tiny apartment he rented before meeting Jen. "She wants Jen to be happy, that's all," Joe replied with a shrug.

"I think she just wants me shackled," Marty huffed. "A new kitchen would set me back ten grand."

Joe smirked. "Not if I did it."

Marty's eyes darkened. "I just want us to enjoy ourselves for a while, okay?"

"Don't let her stop you, then."

"Francine's parents back yet?" Marty asked.

Joe inhaled a pensive breath. "No," he replied. Francine's parents wouldn't return from Europe for another month, and Joe planned to savor the time. They always seemed to fill Francine's head with all kinds of psycho bullshit. She denied it, but her behavior always changed whenever they were around. It drove him nuts. "She came by the site the other day, brought me lunch."

Marty raised his eyebrows. What he didn't ask enveloped them like a dark fog. Could she stay faithful?

"You want this one?" Joe asked, eyeing an incoming set.

Marty spun and paddled alongside Joe, racing him. "Give it, man," he said between breaths. "I gotta survive a weekend eating bok choy and listening to Yanni, trying to keep a little shit dog from eating my shoes!"

Joe chopped the sweet peppers for the salad while Francine measured rice into the pot, her summer skirt flaring as she moved.

"It's going to be fine," Joe told Francine.

"But you never told me they don't like fish!" she replied, panicked.

"I didn't say that they didn't like fish," he replied, leaning against the counter. "My dad fished for twenty-five years. I think they'd just prefer to eat something else, is all."

"What am I going to do?" Francine yelled, eyeing the sleek salmon fillet laid out on the broiler pan.

Joe set his beer down and gently turned her shoulders to face him. "It will be fine," he said calmly. "They'll love it."

Francine's long lashes fluttered. "Promise?"

"I promise."

She relaxed in his hold.

"Want me to set the table?" he asked.

"Please," she said quickly, refocusing on the stove. "And pour me some wine, I'm so nervous I'm bound to spill something."

"Is the rice okay?" Francine asked, her face aghast.

"It's fine, dear," said Joe's mom.

"I should have added more chicken broth," Francine said after tasting a small bite, her brow creased with worry.

Joe squeezed her leg beneath the table. "Francine's applying for her real estate license," he told them.

"Your what?" his dad asked, looking confused.

"She's going to get a job selling houses," Joe said, not louder like his sister Annabelle always did, but more simply, with a little more space between the words.

"Oh," his dad replied, looking impressed.

"My uncle works in commercial sales, so I'm hoping he'll send me some referrals," Francine said with a knowing grin.

"Do you plan to work in the city or stay local?" his mom asked, separating the tiny fish bones from the flesh with her fork, a motion she could probably do in her sleep.

Joe tasted the salmon and held back his disappointment—she'd overcooked it.

Francine paused. "It depends," she said, eyeing Joe.

The city might hold greater opportunities, but if she stayed, she could become a part of the community, and with him in the construction business, their businesses could grow, together. It was the kind of divisive, philosophical standpoint that caused their worst fights. Francine wanted a Haight Street address with a nearby yoga studio, Moroccan food, and boutique dress shops; he wanted to drink Coors with his neighbors, surf the break down the street, ride his bike instead of drive.

"So, Mrs. Foss, can I ask you a gardening question?" Francine asked.

Joe was as surprised as his mom.

After helping his parents to their car—his mom's hip wasn't so stable anymore, and his dad might have forgotten where they parked altogether, Joe returned to the apartment to find Francine at the sink. He pressed his body to her backside and squeezed her shoulders. She leaned her head back and he kissed her neck. He'd been hungry for her since dessert, which didn't taste nearly as good as she would.

His hands caressed her warm belly beneath her shirt. She turned off the water and sighed. She kissed his cheek playfully.

"Was it okay?" she asked.

"Mmm," he replied, turning her around and kissing her lips. He caressed the skin under her shirt. It was more than okay. He let himself believe that she'd meant it, that she'd changed.

She kissed him back, her tongue teasing his, her hands pulling him closer. He unbuttoned her shirt and it fell to the floor. He stroked her breasts over the silky bra's fabric, feeling her nipples harden. She leaned back and he lowered his lips to tease her there; he found the bra's clasp and unhooked it. Her warm skin was so soft, smelling of her spicy perfume and a trace of garlic. His whole body ached for her. He moved to his knees, ducking under her skirt to tug the panties down. He followed her tan line to her inner thigh. She welcomed him, moaning, her hands weaving through his hair. He grasped her hips as she rocked with him, wanting to experience as much of her pleasure.

"Joe," she breathed, her hips curling backward. "We should, I need . . . "

Joe's head buzzed with desire, and he kissed his way back to her soft breasts. He removed his shorts and her skirt, his breathing labored, rushed. He kissed her, their naked bodies clinging to each other. In a swift move, he lifted her to the counter and slid inside her. Her warmth enveloped him and he groaned. Her legs wrapped around him, squeezing, pulling him closer. "Oh God, Joe," she breathed.

Her body arched and he bent his head to her breasts again. He thrust faster; the tingling of his climax quickened. Was she close? He couldn't always tell and she hated if he asked. He wanted to wait for her but began losing control—her perfect body, her full breasts, her sexy shoulders thrown back, with the dirty dishes in the sink and her panties on the floor. And just the way she had been looking at him lately, like she cared about him, really cared, about the real him, not the one she'd seen on the stage, like maybe she could commit to his ideal of the simple life, the one filled with love and hard work and friendship and compromises and joy and he wanted that, he wanted to believe that she wanted it too. But more than anything, he wanted to be done with looking and waiting, wanted to be done regretting what he'd lost.

He wanted to stop missing Lorna.

# TWENTY-NINE

Río Limón, Mexico

While Alex napped in what Lorna hoped was Percocet-induced comfort, Lorna scrubbed and cleaned the apartment. Alex had beaten the infection caused by the urchins but there was a new problem: her increasing pain. Carlos had connected Lorna to a doctor who—for a price—had prescribed exactly ten Percocet.

Lorna knew this need for stronger pain meds meant that Alex's working days were numbered; she might even begin to lose interest the things she still loved, like surfing or paddling her outrigger. Lorna knew she would need to obtain stronger meds before Alex's pain increased. Which it would.

When Alex groaned in her sleep, Lorna rushed to her side, but Alex's breathing returned to normal. Lorna returned to the kitchen countertop where a can of cleaner and a new sponge waited. During the week before, Carlos had handled the lawyer group without trouble, but he would need help with the incoming group of young pros. Would Alex be strong enough, or would she have to step in? Lorna also wondered about the boat moored in Manzanillo's harbor; she and Carlos had yet to decide its fate.

What about the plan for the boat Carlos had told her about? *A plan that includes you.* The idea of it was preposterous. What would she and Alex do with a boat? She imagined Alex at the helm, smiling with the wind in her hair while Lorna was on her knees, seasick in the tiny head. Lorna wanted nothing to do with it. She wasn't here to be Alex's sidekick.

Lorna moved on to the living room, dusting the coffee table, sliding the easy chair's cushion back into place. Waves crashed on the shore below, and Lorna paused in the doorway, taking in the beautiful bay and the ripples of swell, before straightening the pile of surfing magazines beneath the hammock. She noticed a new one and was shocked that it was July's issue. *What happened to June?* Lorna remembered calling her chief of residency at the end of her first week in Río Limón. She had begged for more time, and they'd agreed on a leave of absence, though Lorna didn't know what that meant for her future—besides angry coworkers.

She flipped through the magazine, but the mouth-watering photos of perfect waves and highly skilled surfers with their this-is-no-big-deal-I-could-do-this-in-my-sleep expressions only depressed her. She could not imagine their life of mindless freedom, their only worry the next contest or scoring with some girl at a party. Now, every thought in her head began with Alex, what she might need, what might happen next.

She was about to return the magazine to the stack when a picture caught her attention. She looked closer. *Could it be?* She recognized Bukuya, and the surfer tucked into the big, beautiful barrel was none other than Garth. She remembered his photographer vying for position on the inside the entire session. It was a great photo; they were both probably ecstatic. She scanned the caption:

Garth Towner of NSW tangling with rogue wave in Fiji, right before skipping out on his latest contest to ride big Teahupo'o. Apparently Billabong isn't worried about Towner's plan to quit the tour next year. Could big-wave surfing be his future?

She reread the caption thoughtfully, focusing on the last part: "quit the tour next year. Could big-wave surfing be his future?" She recalled a comment she'd overheard from one of the team riders weeks ago: *Rode that big wave in Fiji. Says he's gonna surf a fifty-footer.* Had they been talking about Garth?

A hissing noise from behind the screen pulled Lorna from her thoughts. The hiss turned into a long, mournful moan.

"Alex?" Lorna called out, and rushed to the bed.

Alex was sitting up in bed, her face twisted in pain. She gripped her stomach, but it seemed she couldn't speak.

"How bad is it?" Lorna asked. Could she already need another dose? "One to ten," she reminded, indicating the pain scale she used every day in the E.R. and that she had taught to Alex: one for no pain, ten for the worst pain you've ever felt in your life.

Alex gave a kind of whimpering cry, her expression twisted with anguish. She opened her mouth but another wave of pain hit her, and she looked up at Lorna, tears streaming down her cheeks.

"Okay," Lorna said, and rushed to the kitchen cabinet where she kept the drugs.

She tried another dose, and they waited a half hour, Lorna trying a cold pack on Alex's abdomen, massage of her shoulders, pinching pressure points on her hands. But Alex's body trembled from the pain, her torso tensing with each passing minute. Lorna tried to get her to breathe regularly, kneeling in front of her, holding her hands and keeping eye contact while they breathed together. "Imagine your pain is a color," she said, something she remembered an L&D nurse doing once. "What color is it?"

Alex didn't answer, just clenched her eyes shut.

"Okay, how about green," Lorna said, squeezing Alex's sweaty hands.

"I can't!" Alex cried, her entire upper body heaving up and down with each breath, so that they were loud and fast, too fast. "Please," she gasped. She moaned and her face twisted in pain.

Lorna rushed to the cupboard and slid another pill into her palm. This was it; she couldn't give her any more. "Here," she said, offering it to Alex, who quickly forced it between her lips, chased it down with a glug of water.

"Okay, let's breathe," Lorna said, grasping her hands again and focusing on her eyes.

With their eyes locked, breathing in tandem, the minutes crawled by. After ten minutes the agony surrounding her eyes lessened. At fifteen she breathed a little easier. "I have to . . . " Alex said, her eyes filling with panic.

Lorna knew that look and raced to the kitchen for the bucket but didn't make it in time. Alex retched on the floor, pulled to her knees by the force of it. Lorna fell beside her, rubbing her back as Alex sobbed. Lorna noticed that she'd soiled herself as well.

"Let's get you cleaned up," Lorna replied quietly, helping Alex to her feet.

Lorna held it together until Alex was clean and resting on fresh sheets, halfway back into sleep.

Lorna tiptoed to the balcony, where the emotion came tumbling out in choking, heaving sobs and fat tears that darkened the gray concrete at her feet.

Alex felt better in the morning, and refused to take a day off. Lorna and Carlos made a plan. They decided that Alex could work as long as it felt good to her and didn't cause her pain. In the mornings, Alex would take the group to Buzzard's or Locos Manos or

Pirate's. After that Seth and Becca would serve up a big lunch before siesta. Then Carlos would shuttle the surfers somewhere local in the afternoon. A few times they did surf El Boca, and Carlos lived up to his reputation, scoring longer and more rides than anyone else while making it look effortless. But Lorna could never watch them for long; she was too busy caring for Alex.

Every morning when Lorna woke she swore that today she'd force Alex to leave Río Limón for someplace bigger, with better care. But the day would pass in a blur and then Lorna would collapse at night, exhausted.

Lorna wondered how Alex was hanging on. Her GI system, already finicky, was tolerating less and less—most of what she ate didn't stay in her system for long. Sometimes Alex refused to eat before going surfing in the morning because she hoped it would keep her guts from exploding while they were at sea. The apartment stunk of loose stool. Lorna winced every time Alex disappeared into the bathroom. Afterwards, she would go in and clean up, barely keeping her own stomach settled in the process. To make matters worse, the hard rain of late made sewers overflow throughout the town, and the foul scent hovered like a fog. When Alex slept, Lorna cleaned, scrubbing the bathroom floor, the toilet, shower, sink, the kitchen counters. She didn't know what else to do with her pent-up energy.

Usually she accompanied Alex in the morning; a routine that began to feel like a job. But she was too worried about Alex—her pain level, her hydration, her liver capabilities, the state of her GI tract, and whether she had an appetite for a toasted bagel and cream cheese or cubes of sweet mango—to resent this. The mental tracking and anticipating of Alex's needs wore Lorna down, made her react rather than think; she became numb to her own emotions. Surfing El Boca on the mornings she didn't go with Alex restored her spirits somewhat, but there was always so much to do. Alex regularly sweated through her sheets, or sometimes soiled them; she owned only two towels and they needed constant washing, as did her clothes, which picked up her increasingly sour smell. The only laundromat in town was behind the Mini Super, and every other day Lorna would be there with her coins and her thoughts. Or, she was treating surfers: stitching up cuts, dosing out Pepto-Bismol, evaluating symptoms of what was most likely a case of *tourista* rather than SARS, and once even relocating a shoulder. She performed the urchin removal ceremony several times. The surfers called her "doc," and Carlos or Becca began introducing her that way, so it stuck.

She was surprised how it bored her, treating these privileged few. It made her miss the E.R.'s constant flux of problems, some complex, some simple, some a total waste of time, but at least the work and demographic varied. It kept her on her toes, kept her sharp. And she could always ask for help, whether from an anesthesiologist, a radiologist, or the attending physician; she never had to make decisions alone unless she felt confident. So the day she first noticed Alex's jaundice, all confidence simply evaporated. And there was no one to call.

It was in the whites of Alex's eyes—just a hint of yellow. Maybe it had been there before, but she just hadn't noticed. Nowadays, Alex was spending more time indoors, so she wasn't wearing her sunglasses. It was all happening too fast. That day Lorna looked at a calendar hanging in the office downstairs. She realized that she'd been in Río Limón for almost two months. Why had it seemed like so much less than that? She knew she needed to move Alex before it was too late.

# THIRTY

San Francisco, California

Joe paid the ten-dollar coat-check fee, silencing his inner voice that screamed at him to just stash their coats behind a booth somewhere. They had parked outside the city and hopped the BART to the Wharf, where they'd had a late dinner, Francine picking at her food nervously, or was it just eagerness?

The Star Room had great dance tunes on Saturday nights, and he wasn't disappointed. As he led Francine to the dance floor, Earth, Wind, and Fire grooved, "On and on and on and on . . . " The band was already setting up, and the energy from the glass-walled dance floor and the music and the other people rocking out gave his belly a quick rush. By the end of the night, he'd be sweaty and hungry and happy from cutting loose. Francine's cheeks would be rosy red, and her eyes would still be sparkling as she guzzled water, holding her thick hair off her moist neck. She'd retrieve her shoes from some corner of the dance floor and fall asleep on his shoulder while the BART whisked them away from the city.

Francine once told him that his music had gotten her attention, but his dancing had made him irresistible. Not that he possessed some repertoire of great moves, or style. He just loved it, wasn't afraid to go crazy. His sisters had probably set him up for this, with all their lip-synching and the way they'd sweep him up in their

Friday night disco dance parties. He remembered them dressing him up in wild costumes and performing for their parents. "Girls love a boy who can dance," his oldest sister Annabelle always told him. He hadn't needed much encouragement. His parents danced together all the time, ballroom style, swing, or even disco if he and his sisters begged. Joe loved seeing the glow on their faces, the shimmer and playfulness in their eyes. "Music is one of the greatest gifts there is," his mom told him. "Let it move you," she always used to say when they danced together, her body loose and lithe and full of energy.

Halfway into adolescence, Joe realized he loved the music—the melodies and chords—as much or more than dancing to it. He'd played violin and piano early, at home, and then in eighth grade he switched to guitar. He could play almost anything, including base, trumpet, mandolin. He just needed a little time to get to know the instrument. Whenever he tried something new, it was like re-connecting rather than beginning, as if he'd learned the instrument before and just needed to remind his fingers what to do. The closest he could find to the euphoria of making music was making love. But music could be shared with more people, and the high could last for days.

A slender black woman, dressed in sleek black pants and shimmery shirt, heels, and plenty of gold jewelry, adjusted the mic, her long black lashes fluttering like a doe's. The guitarist, a white guy with a beard, and the bassist, also white, twiddled and adjusted their sound, taped down cords: the usual drill. The drummer, an Asian man with a four-inch Fu Manchu, took a long drink from a glass then settled into his stool, looking calm. But the air had a firecracker buzz to it, and Joe's fingers twitched in anticipation. When their sound blasted, base pumping, voices rich and perfect, he grabbed Francine, who was perched along the edge of a booth sipping her drink, and yanked her toward the stage.

They bounded into the melee of swirling bodies. Joe gave a tipsy couple plenty of space. He figured they were celebrating something big because they were dressed in fancy eveningwear: the woman in a long, elegant red dress and high heels, and the man in an expensive suit. A group of older women danced in a tight circle; there were more couples than he could count. The jubilant mix pulsed with the music; grinning faces glistening with sweat, some a little too self-conscious. He loved them all for it—for the energy, for the sensation of being alive together, and for sharing the feeling that nothing else mattered except letting the music move you.

"We should take dance lessons together sometime," he shouted into Francine's ear.

She looked at him quizzically. "Why? I could teach you whatever you want to learn." She arched her eyebrow seductively and moved in close to him, her hips swaying, her arms reaching up, exposing the creamy, toned skin of her belly.

"You could dance for me all day long like that," he said into her ear again, running his hand along her waistline then reaching for her hand to spin her. Her long hair twirled out, wrapping seductively over her face when she came to an abrupt halt, her green eyes sultry as she sashayed back to him, their hips finding each other's, grinding to the beat as one until she broke away. "It'd be fun, that's all," he shouted over the music, thinking of his parents doing the jitterbug in the kitchen.

Joe was sure the club had maxed out the capacity. The dance floor was like a mosh pit of people gyrating and bouncing and stomping, singing the words at the top of their lungs to the Bee Gees, The Village People, Diana Ross, and the like. Maybe it was too crowded and hot, or maybe the woman in the red dress simply had downed one drink too many. She backed into Francine, her spiky heel gouging her ankle. Then, her date's champagne glass went flying into space and crashed to the floor. The glass shards were instantly pulverized beneath all the stomping feet. Joe scooped up Francine and rushed her to the carpet, much to her surprise. "What's going on?" she asked, confused.

"Glass," he said, setting her into a booth. He crouched at her bare feet—Francine always danced with her shoes off. "Did you get any?" He couldn't see in the dim light of the club.

"I don't think so," she replied, still looking puzzled. "Where did it come from?"

"They have a rule against glassware on the dance floor for a reason." The noise of the music drilled into his head. What if Francine had stepped on the glass? It could have happened so easily, so quickly. "How's your ankle?" he asked.

Francine inspected the reddish mark, the top layer of skin peeled back. "It'll be fine," she said. "Maybe I should get my shoes."

"I'll go," Joe said, rising. He pushed through the crowd, weaving toward the place he remembered her leaving the black sandals. After scooping them up, he spotted the owner of the champagne glass and moved toward him.

"Hey!" Joe shouted.

Startled, the man looked up, but his woozy, drunk face grinned as he said: "Sorry, I'm taken, bro," then laughed, eyeing the woman in the red dress to see if she would laugh, too. She only looked confused.

"You see that sign?" Joe said, pointing past the man's nose to the wall near the bottleneck entry to the dance floor where a sign read: NO GLASSWARE.

"Yeah?" the man said.

Joe pointed toward where Francine was sitting. "My girl nearly got cut by that glass you launched," he shouted over the booming music.

"Someone bumped me!" the man yelled back. Joe could see the people around them watching them nervously. The man's date seemed to have disappeared.

"This is a daaannce ffloooor!" Joe yelled, drawing out the letters. "That's what people do, asshole, they bump," he said, leaning in to the man's face. "Next time ask for plastic," he added, and spun away.

The blow came from behind, catching him in the side of the head. Joe spun, fists ready, but someone grabbed the man, whose eyes were ablaze, teeth bared like a wild horse. A large black man appeared out of thin air, separating them like a wall. He eyed Joe suspiciously then escorted the other man toward the door.

Joe returned to Francine, who was watching the bouncer lead the man away. "What happened?"

"Nothing," Joe said as the adrenaline ebbed from his veins. He exhaled, cheeks puffed, and handed Francine her shoes. "You hungry?" he sighed.

"Sure," she said quietly, not looking at him.

Joe got their coats and met Francine in the lobby. She pushed the elevator call button and stared up at the glowing numbers.

"I can't believe that guy," Joe said, still feeling jittery. He hadn't fought anyone since middle school, when a few blockhead-types called him queer for playing the violin. His sisters had not trained him well for that endeavor. Not that he hadn't learned how to hold his own, but he so rarely encountered a threat. Why tonight?

Francine exhaled heavily as they entered the elevator car. She still hadn't met his eyes. Was she embarrassed by him? Angry that the man had spoiled the rest of their night? She pressed the button and the doors closed.

"I mean, what if that glass had cut you? It probably exploded into smithereens. We would have been picking it out of your foot for the rest of the night. You wouldn't have been able to dance for weeks."

Suddenly Francine burst into tears.

Surprised, Joe pulled her to him, his hands wrapping around her shoulders. "Hey," he cooed. "What's up? Did I scare you?" He cursed himself for losing his cool. Why hadn't he just left it alone? "You want to go back? That guy is probably gone."

Francine cried quietly, her arms hugging herself inside his embrace.

"I just got scared that somebody might hurt you, baby. I just reacted, I guess." Joe closed his eyes and smelled the last hint of her perfume mixed with her moist skin. "I'm sorry," he sighed, rocking her.

"It's not that," Francine whispered, her sobs fading.

Joe smoothed back her long hair and lifted her cheeks so their eyes met.

"I'm pregnant," she whispered.

"You sure it's yours?" Marty asked, finishing his beer, crushing the can then punting it into the trash bin at the edge of the cliff. They'd intended to go surfing, but they'd made it only as far as the 7-Eleven then up to the cliffs, a spot they'd frequented since Marty got a car for his sixteenth birthday.

"Don't be an ass," Joe replied, running a hand through his hair. "Of course it's mine."

"You having memory failure or something? Don't you remember the Fourth of July?"

"That was last summer," Joe mumbled, downing his beer but not bothering to crush it before tossing it into the bin.

"What makes you think she's changed?" Marty asked, cracking open another Coors.

The memory of looking for a bathroom but finding Francine half-naked with someone Joe had never seen before instead flooded his mind. He'd stood there with his knees wobbling while Francine rolled her eyes. "Can we talk about this later?" she'd said. No remorse, no apology, no idea that she'd hurt him, again. "He was a talent scout," Francine said later.

"For what, hookers?" he'd shouted.

Francine's eyes turned cold. "We never said we wouldn't see other people," she had told him, her voice hard, her chest puffed with restrained hostility. "And if I'm gonna make it, I need to keep my options open."

Joe had never agreed to this theory. If you were good enough, people would notice you. But Francine didn't really know what she wanted. Sometimes it was performing on stage; sometimes it was modeling. For a while it had been PR. Now it was real estate.

Joe shrugged, realizing Marty was still waiting for his answer. He remembered the dinner she cooked for his folks, the worry lines creased on her forehead, the way her delicate fingers offered them bread, like a gift. "It just feels different." He remembered their lovemaking in the kitchen and sighed. He hadn't seen her in almost a week.

"So what are you gonna do?" Marty asked, squinting at him.

"Get married." Joe knew it was right. He wanted it to be right. Hell, hadn't he been waiting for this? He'd always pictured himself as a father, a husband, dedicated, hard-working, honest, fair. He just didn't know how Francine felt. Were her tears just a reaction to the hormones? Or was she as terrorized as she had appeared that night? Sure, he was scared, too, but there was a new little tingle inside him that hummed every time he thought of the baby. *His* baby. The tingle spread through him, and he smiled. How could he not?

"You ask her yet?" Marty tossed his latest empty at the bin.

"No," he replied, the tingle disappearing, his shoulders slumping, as if weighted. He needed to convince her that this would work.

"Good luck, man," Marty said, slapping him on the shoulder.

Joe glanced at his friend, whose expression told him he was going to need all the luck he could get.

# THIRTY-ONE

## Lazaro Cardenas, Mexico

Lorna sat in a plastic chair wondering how doctors' waiting areas looked the same around the world, save for the magazines: uncomfortable chairs, pastel prints on the walls, the occasional fish tank. Lorna bounced her crossed leg and waited.

At first the receptionist hadn't understood her. "I don't need much of his time," she'd said, louder than necessary, after denying having an appointment. "Just tell him my name," she said, writing it down. "*Solo cinco minutes*," she added, hoping Spanish had finally overtaken her half-forgotten Italian.

Lorna was dressed in flip flops, board shorts, a bikini top, and a T-shirt. She hadn't showered in several days, or slept well for nearly a week. She noticed her dirty toenails and a new sore on her big toe. Had she bumped into something while racing to Alex's bedside in the darkness? A few of the other patrons in the waiting area, all well-dressed, were badly hiding their interest. Lorna felt their curious eyes peering at her over their magazines.

"I'm here for my mother," she said to one particularly bold woman wearing tight brown pants and too much lipstick. "She needs drugs."

But the woman's gaze had already flicked away.

Lorna began chewing her nails, a new habit to add to her irrepressible jaw clenching. Would the thousand pesos stashed in a special slot she had created in the side of her bikini top be enough? She rubbed the lump to make sure it hadn't migrated.

The receptionist called the lipstick woman's name, and she disappeared quickly through the open door. Lorna watched her go, chewing her nails again, then realized she'd have to spit out the pieces on the waiting room carpet, so stopped. She shoved her hands beneath her thighs.

The pale yellow walls did not calm her, nor did the soft music. She grabbed a magazine and flipped through it, then tossed it back to the table, annoyed. Movie stars on vacation, models smiling on the arm of some multimillionaire, rock stars in ripped jeans and black T-shirts screaming into a microphone were not part of her world.

Lorna thought back to her conversation with Seth and Becca the day before:

"She's not getting better," Lorna had said, watching them to make sure they understood. "Her pain is worsening, and yesterday the pills didn't help."

"But you said last time that this . . . breakthrough pain," Becca said the words slowly, warily, as if they were an animal that might bite her, " . . . went away."

"Not this time," Lorna explained. She imagined Alex having another episode while driving the boat, or while surfing with her clients. "She can't work anymore."

Becca had offered to help with laundry; Seth promised to keep making Alex the smoothies she loved. Lorna had started keeping mangoes on hand; Alex craved them night and day. Lorna even took to wearing Alex's buck knife. Besides coming in handy on the boat, it made quick work of the mangoes' tough skin.

Lorna had also taken over Alex's role as lead surfing guide. At first, operating the boat and being in charge made her anxious, but her comfort had increased.

Lorna wondered where Carlos was surfing this afternoon—
Buzzard's? The swell had slowly died throughout the week. She
wondered if the ocean would turn flat tomorrow, like it had her first
day in Río Limón. They'd also received their first hurricane warning
of the season. It looked to be headed further south, but Carlos was
keeping an eye on it. She wondered if they should call the guests
scheduled for the coming week and cancel. She didn't have the
energy to shuttle around unhappy guests while Alex might need her.

Alex needed that Dilaudid. Some Lorazepam would be nice,
too. Should she ask about a paracentesis kit, so she could drain the
fluid in her abdomen? There was nothing she could do about the
jaundice, and if pruritus began, Lorna could hopefully keep it under
control with Benadryl. Alex still had good days, when her breathing
seemed easier and her eyes were clear, days where she went down to
the office or out for a swim. But those days were becoming less and
less frequent.

As soon as the receptionist left her alone with the doctor, Lorna
said, "She needs more."

The doctor gave her a thin smile but his eyes, the way they
watched her disdainfully, betrayed him. "Why not tell me who they
are really for?" he said quietly.

Lorna froze. "What?" she said, confused.

The doctor looked her up and down again. "I can get you
some help."

Of course. Her unwashed hair. Her attire. He thought she was
some kind of addict. "Jesus," she breathed. "My mother is dying,"
she said, the anger exploding in her head, making the back of her
eyeballs throb.

"So you say," the doctor replied.

Lorna tried to keep it together. "I have money," she said, slapping her wad of bills on the man's desk.

The doctor eyed the bills suspiciously. "Why morphine? For this kind of money, elsewhere you could get . . . "

Lorna's temper flared. After the nerve-racking drive, the long night of little sleep pacing with Alex, rubbing her back and trying ice and then heat, cold showers, codeine and more codeine and then finally the last Dilaudid, and now this accusation? The thought had already occurred to her—street drugs were everywhere, especially in a city like this. She thought of the crack addicts in Río Limón who'd undoubtedly made off with her life savings and her collection of meds. "Ooo, let's try this one next," she imagined one saying giddily to the other.

Lorna had reached her limit. "You think I'm going to give my mother heroine, or crack? No!" she cried, slamming her fist on his desk. The doctor recoiled, his eyes nervous.

Lorna imagined the addicts floating off to a recreational high while Alex sweated through another episode in agony. "I can't make her come here. She's too weak, now, anyways. She's so swollen she looks pregnant. She can barely eat. Her piss is so dark it's brown. Her scapulas look like bird wings. She is suffering," Lorna finished, breathing hard. "This is not about me," she added tersely, staring him down.

In the end she wasn't sure if he believed her. In the E.R., she'd listened to many an addict perform just such a speech, even better ones. Not that she cared. He wrote her the prescription, and that was all that mattered. "Do not come back here," he said, eyeing her with distaste.

But Lorna was halfway to the door. She knew she wouldn't need to come back.

∿∿∿

Lorna parked Alex's Ranger on the street and rushed toward the apartment, anxious to check on Alex. The soft crush of the surf grew louder as she leaped the steps two at a time. She heard voices: Alex's, and a man's. Not Carlos's—the cadence was different, yet familiar. Frowning, her heart beating fast, she barged into the apartment, the plastic bag from the *farmacia* clutched in her fist.

"G'day, doc," Garth said from Alex's couch.

Lorna's jaw dropped open. Her pulse slammed into her temples and she winced. She tried to breathe but her lungs seemed to have stopped working.

Alex stood in the kitchen in front of the hotplate. Was she *cooking*? Lorna scanned the rest of the apartment.

"Glad to see you made it," Garth said, his eyes sparkling.

An unexpected bubble of laughter erupted from Lorna's lips. She felt dizzy. "Er," she tried. The laughter came again, a nervous, fluttering bark. This time she clapped her free hand over her mouth to stop it.

"Lorna and I had some good waves in Fiji, didn't we?" Garth said, glancing at Alex, who was dressed in loose-fitting pants and a baggy sweatshirt despite the substantial humidity.

Lorna realized she was still rooted to the middle of the room, clutching the bag tight. "Um," she mumbled, knowing she needed to put away the pills. But something on the bulletin board had caught her attention.

"Why didn't you tell me you knew Garth?" Alex said in a tone she'd not heard her use before—shaming? Alarmed?

Lorna readjusted her grip on the bag. "Um," she tried again, trying to think of an answer.

Alex returned to the living area with a plain black mug, a tea bag's string hanging over the side. "I'm out of milk," she said apologetically. *Tea. She made him tea*, Lorna thought, watching Alex in disbelief. Alex hadn't had milk in her apartment in months. She would sometimes drink the almond milk Becca made from scratch. She liked the unsweetened hibiscus tea Becca brewed, too. But there were days she could barely hold down water.

"No worries," Garth said as Alex delivered the mug. The alarm bells clanged in Lorna's head—she could see the pain the movement caused her.

Lorna watched them chatter about Garth's latest conquest, the tour in general, and Alex's business. Still bewildered, Lorna made her way to a chair while her head throbbed. She remembered the *Surfer Magazine* article and his leaving the tour for big waves.

"So you have a boat now," he said to Alex.

Lorna watched Alex's eyes flash—she and Carlos hadn't told Alex about the boat yet. Secretly, Lorna hoped the boat would stay in Manzanillo for good. It would just have to be moved back in the off-season. *She has a plan for this boat, a plan that includes you,* Carlos had said. But so much had changed since he'd shared this with her. Lorna didn't have the patience to deal with whatever this "plan" was.

"Who told you that?" Alex said airily.

Garth dismissed the question with a wave of his hand and set his tea on the coffee table. "Have you been out there yet this season?" Garth said.

Alex gave Garth a scrutinizing look. "Like I would tell you if I had," she said in a cool voice.

Lorna felt like her synapses were firing at half-speed. "Out where?" she asked. But Alex and Garth continued to ignore her.

"Tell me where it is," Garth said to Alex. There was a yearning in his eyes. "I'll take good care of it, I promise," he said.

"What's this about?" Lorna blurted.

Garth lay back against the couch, spreading his wingspan over the back of the cushions. He eyed them both keenly, seeming to think about something for a minute before replying, "This is about the wave your mum found. It's called Las Muelas."

# THIRTY-TWO

"I don't know what you're talking about," Alex said in an even tone while her body, stiff and alerted, told another story.

Garth raised an eyebrow. "You can't take it with you," he said darkly, giving her body a quick scan. "Why not share it before it's too late?"

Lorna jumped out of her chair. *Bastard*, Lorna thought. He knew she was sick. "Get out!" Lorna growled, her fury growing.

"People are gonna find out about it soon enough," Garth said. He locked eyes with Lorna. "I just want one crack at it first. Is that too much to ask?"

"Get OUT!" Lorna said, rushing toward him.

"Okay, okay," he said, jumping up and dashing for the door, like a cat.

Breathing fast, Lorna watched him bounce down the steps. She remembered the peculiar question Alex had asked her that first day, after her underwhelming greeting. *Are you alone?* Had Alex been worried about somebody following her to Río Limón? Somebody like Garth?

Lorna returned to an empty room. "Alex?" she called out, alarmed. A muffled noise came from the bathroom.

Alex was on her knees at the toilet, wiping her mouth. "When he was here . . . before . . . " She sat back, grimacing. "One time he saw . . . " She paused, turned her face toward the ceiling, her mouth a tight o sucking in labored breaths. "The charts."

Lorna got a damp washcloth and dabbed Alex's neck and forehead.

Alex coughed, sucking in air between breaths. "I never should have taken that picture," she groaned.

Lorna realized what had bothered her about the bulletin board: the photo of Alex's wave was missing. Las Muelas.

Alex slumped against the wall, her knees pulled up tight. "You can never let him have it. He'll . . . "—she exhaled a heavy breath— "exploit it."

"Does Carlos know about it?" Lorna asked.

Alex moved to stand, breathing audibly. "He used to go with me."

"Not anymore?" Lorna helped her shuffle to the couch.

Alex shook her head.

Lorna remembered Garth's words: *People are gonna find out about it soon enough.* "Why is it such a secret?" she asked, confused.

Alex slid the missing photo from beneath one of the couch cushions, plus a worn black notebook, and gave them to Lorna. "Because I've been saving it," she said, the tension in her face easing. The wave of pain was ebbing.

"For what?" Lorna replied, staring first at the photo then at Alex.

"For you," Alex replied. "For us," she added.

A strange mix of emotions swirled inside her. She studied the photo of the menacing wave, a strong sense of foreboding taking hold in her gut. With dread, she realized that Alex had been planning all along to take her there.

"What do you want me to do?" she asked after a long moment, her voice shaky.

"Whatever it takes to keep it that way," Alex replied.

∿∿∿

Lorna waited until Alex was comfortable before heading down the stairs to look for Carlos.

"She's really sick, isn't she?" Garth's voice said behind her.

Lorna whirled around. "Like you care," she said. "Now please go away."

"I know this is . . . awkward," he said, not looking at her.

Lorna slapped him, hard. "Awkward?" she hissed.

Stunned, Garth rubbed his cheek. "Jesus," he said. "What the hell?"

"Leave us alone!"

"What's she got? AIDS?"

Lorna went to slap him again but he caught her wrist. "Ow!" she cried as he twisted it, making her skin burn.

He let go. "Just don't let her die with the secret, all right?"

A groan of anguish ripped through her. "I don't give a shit about her secret," she whispered.

He sighed. "I'm sorry. I didn't plan this."

Lorna swiped at her cheeks. Why did this have to happen now? Why couldn't Garth have come in a week or, better yet, after . . . Lorna couldn't finish the thought. "Why is this wave so important to you?" she asked.

His eyes lit up. "Because I think it's going be as good or better than all the rest—Cortes Banks, Jaws, Maverick's. Do you know what that means? I'll have at least a year or two to ride it before the word gets out." He locked eyes with her. "I need this, Lorna," he said.

"Las Muelas isn't mine to give away," Lorna said, surprised at her own conviction. Las Muelas was just a wave, right?

"Either you help me," he said, his eyes burning with the intensity she remembered from Fiji. "Or I take it. Either way I'm not leaving without it."

Lorna watched him wander toward Hotel Las Olas, and then she stepped into the office where Carlos was talking into the phone.

"Do you remember a former client named Garth?'" Lorna asked after he'd hung up. She dropped heavily into the office chair. "Aussie. He's a pro surfer."

Carlos stopped pecking at the computer keys to peer at Lorna. "Why?"

Lorna tapped the eraser end of a pencil against the desk. "He's here, hanging around," Lorna said, not looking at him.

"Not as a guest," Carlos said, frowning.

Lorna shook her head and looked out the window. "Do you remember him harassing Alex about something?"

Now Carlos sat upright, his eyes flashing. "No. Is this true?"

Lorna decided to downplay it, and shrugged. "Alex just didn't seem too happy to see him, that's all."

Carlos's shoulders relaxed. "Look at this," he said, handing her a shiny white page from the fax showing concentric, warped circles, each with an accompanying number. It was a swell forecast. Lorna studied it.

"How big?" she asked.

"Big." He made a towering arch with his arm over his head. "*Olas muy grandes*," he said.

"When?"

"Thursday, late in the day it will peak," he replied.

Lorna remembered a time when news of big waves would have sent a thrill of excitement through her veins. But now it only meant work.

"What about the hurricane?" she asked.

"It will get a little bumpy here, but will miss us."

She and Carlos had already established their plan. "Are you ready?" he asked her.

Lorna looked away, thinking of Garth. He'd likely sniffed out the wave during his last trip. When he met Lorna in Fiji, he'd figured out who she was. His invitation was all part of some plan to access Las Muelas.

She closed her eyes. What was she going to do?

Garth was right about one thing: if Alex had found some secret wave, it wouldn't stay hidden forever. Sooner or later, someone would find out. Lorna turned this over in her mind. Why not let Garth have it? Lorna didn't want to deal with a war between him and Alex. And the thought of surfing that wave: *Las Muelas*, whatever its name meant, was truly terrifying.

Lorna felt exhausted, like she could sleep for days. She didn't have time for Garth or this mystery wave and its protection. She needed to focus on Alex and on helping Carlos keep the business alive.

She vowed to hold Garth off for the time being—not that she had anything to tell him about Las Muelas, anyway.

"I'm ready," she said, thinking about the group of arriving surfers, who would be thrilled about the big swell, and how she would have to pretend to be excited, too.

That night, once inside her room, Lorna dug out Alex's black hardbound notebook. She smoothed the warped cover and fingered the water-stained pages that were fanned out and fat from use. There were secrets inside the pages; she could feel it.

With her eyes straining in the low light, she opened the book. The pages contained lists of strange numbers, scribbled notations in the margins, compass degrees, and what seemed like wind readings. There were sketches, too, of waves, sea life, and what looked like sections of reef, with wispy anemones, coral, and tendrils of kelp.

She leafed through the notebook, realizing that it was a journal from Alex's explorations of Las Muelas. Alex had recorded her time spent checking it, surfing it; she had documented its every mood. Lorna scanned one long entry, dated two years before: " . . . flat today but poked around the reef a bit. There's a fin-like ridge transecting its length, wonder if that's what cut me last time." Lorna flipped to an entry dated six months earlier: "Did I get some kind of bug from the water down here? Will drink only bottled from now on."

There were entries about the new boat, about her time in Port Angeles. Lorna didn't see anything about her visit to the E.R. or meeting Yoko. *And nothing about me.* A feeling of emptiness crashed over Lorna.

"Why?" she whispered into the dim, empty room.

She put the journal under her pillow and turned out the light. A part of her couldn't believe that Alex had been keeping Las Muelas for her. The other part, the one that was beginning to understand Alex, knew it made perfect sense. But did Alex think that bequeathing some grinding death wave could make up for the heartache of their past?

Las Muelas could be some kind of gift. Or a curse.

# THIRTY-THREE

## Sequoia National Park, California

Joe pumped his camp stove then primed it, managing to burn the hair off his thumb and index finger—a rite of passage he experienced every summer. He twiddled with the dial on the fuel can until a nice blue flame roared from the element, where he placed the pot of water to boil. Returning to the tent, he called out, "You decent?"

"Mmm," Francine replied sleepily.

Concerned, he unzipped the door and peered inside, where Francine, still in her hiking clothes, her long braid snaking down her back, lay curled inside a sleeping bag.

She turned to him, frowned. "I'm just so tired," she said. "I only meant to rest a little."

Joe had planned a short hike with one night out. Francine wasn't normally a hiker, and he was worried about her carrying a big pack, so he'd put most of the gear in his, leaving her with just her clothes and some food and a water bottle. He had been gone for less than half an hour to get water. "It's normal to be tired. You rest for as long as you need to," he said. "I'll be just outside, okay?" he added.

She nodded then turned away, settling back into the sleeping bag. Joe zipped the mesh door shut to keep out the bugs, hoping the fresh air would lift her spirits. Joe had read up on pregnancy—the fatigue, morning sickness, the importance of nutrition and moderate exercise. He had asked Francine if she was taking her prenatal vitamins, encouraged her to keep dancing, and told her they should schedule an appointment for her first ultrasound at about twelve weeks, which was approaching fast. He had also read that as many as one-third of pregnancies miscarried in the first trimester, a possibility that weighed on him.

They needed to talk about getting married, about where they would live, whether or not Francine still wanted to work, and what they would tell her parents. But he also didn't want to overwhelm her, so he focused on the first two: asking her to marry him and deciding where they would live. Her place was too small. His place was decent, but he didn't want to raise a family there—it was a run-down bachelor pad, a place he'd always considered temporary until he could build his own. He needed a few more years of solid employment to get a loan for such a project. So, should they buy a place? He could afford one of the smaller bungalows: nothing in town but maybe close enough to the surf for quick sessions. He could buy something now, and maybe in five years they could be ready for his project. They'd probably have another kid by then and would need more space.

Joe added the pasta to the water and stirred. That's what he would propose. Buy whatever they could afford now, build later. If she wanted to work, he would support that, as long as the baby wasn't in daycare too much. It was expensive, and he didn't want to pay for someone else to raise his kid. He knew his parents were getting too old to be much help. His sister Annabelle worked in a daycare, but it was attached to a Lutheran Church. He wasn't sure he was comfortable with the God thing. They might be able to afford a sitter if his business continued to grow.

He sliced up the cheese on the pot lid using his buck knife, remembering the salesman's quirky look when he had said he wasn't going to use the knife to skin animals. When the pasta was ready, he drained the water into the weeds and heated the fry pan, adding the generous pat of butter he'd packed in plastic wrap. He then added the cooked pasta and spices, letting it sizzle for a while.

He would propose to her at the waterfall later that night. It was a beautiful spot: the clear water cascaded over the granite, filling the air with mist that fed the tiny ferns and delicate moss campion. They could climb up a short cliff to the top, where he had already scouted a place to sit on the big flat rocks, a place with a view of the valley and the sound of the icy water rushing over the falls. He would tell her he loved her, that he wanted to spend his life with her and make her happy. They'd hike back tomorrow and tell their families.

Joe flipped the pasta, which had browned golden. Where would she want to get married? He hoped not a church, or worse, a country club. But he knew better than to expect she would choose the beach. After all, it was ultimately her day, and her parents would get what they wanted, so likely the country club. Just as long as it wasn't a church, he'd be okay with it.

He stirred the pasta one last time, layered the cheese over the top, and closed the lid so it would melt. He sipped from his water bottle, trying to ignore the way his fingers trembled. Why should he be nervous? They were doing the right thing. Everything would work out. It always did in the end, didn't it?

After the meal, Francine eating everything in her bowl, Joe cleaned up quickly and invited her to check out the sunset. He made sure to bring his down jacket and the extra foam pad he'd brought for them to sit on. Francine put on the wool hat he'd made her bring and the long johns. "Do I look crunchy?" she asked playfully as they headed up the trail, holding hands. He glanced at her. "You look beautiful," he said. It was true what they said about pregnant women. They had a certain . . . glow, and Francine was no exception. Especially when she smiled. Joe vowed to make her smile as much as possible. He wanted a lifetime of her smiles, of her laugh, of the light filling her green eyes.

Joe heard the tumbling hiss of the waterfall before they rounded the corner.

Francine uttered a tiny gasp. "Wow," she said.

He smiled at her. "We can climb to the top. There's a killer view," he said.

She smiled. "Okay."

He led her to the edge of the wooden bridge, the spray from the cascading water crisp and clean, cooling his skin.

Francine smiled. "It's gorgeous!" she said. The peppered granite, smoothed by centuries of pounding water, looked as shiny as silk.

Joe grinned. He climbed up the series of rocks, testing each one for its sturdiness. "Come on up," he said from a few feet above her. There were worn spots in certain places in the dirt where others before him had climbed. His sunset vista was not a new discovery.

They reached the top, Joe steadying her for the last few steps, and gazed at the view of the forested valley, the air cool and moist. The stunted trees, bent and gnarled from winter storms and the exposure to the constant wind, clustered at the edge of the precipice like dwarfs, their bristles thick and beard-like. The sun had already passed below the distant ridge, casting a yellow glow over the treetops and turning the lake at the bottom of the valley into a black mirror.

Joe spread the foam pad over a large flat rock; they sat close together. Francine shivered, and Joe draped his down coat over her shoulders. "Better?" he asked.

"Mmm," she replied, her gaze fixed on the fading orange of the horizon.

Joe's pulse thumped in his chest, seemed to echo off his ribs. He slipped off his gloves, which were moist from his sweat. A gust of warm wind, rising from the valley, carried a hint of meadow grass and pinesap. Should he take her hand? No, his fingers were shaking. A distant contrail grew across the sky, making a fat white slash against the glow.

"My dad explained to me why they do that," she said, watching the contrail, too. "Something about condensation and ice crystals, I can't remember now."

Joe nodded distractedly. "It's like when you breathe out on a cold day," he said, thinking of his own breaths, faster, and shaky. He suddenly wanted to get this over with.

"Then how come we aren't making them now?" she asked, turning to him with puzzlement in her eyes.

Joe sighed nervously. "Because there's probably not enough moisture in the air."

"But there is up there," she said, looking again at the fading contrail. "Doesn't that mean bad weather?"

Joe shrugged. "Not necessarily."

She seemed to accept this.

Joe wished he had brought his water bottle; he was suddenly thirsty. "Francine, I . . . " he started. He felt a sudden, penetrating unease. His head pounded, and he tried to breathe slowly, easily. He took her hand, looked at it, so slender, smooth, fragile. Could he keep her safe? Could he take care of her? "I wanted to share this with you . . . " he managed. Her eyes didn't smile when he looked into them—they were dark, and serious.

"I know things aren't perfect right now," he stammered then stopped. That wasn't what he'd wanted to say! "I want to be with you. I want to be together," he rushed. "I love you and I want to build a life together." There, that was closer. Why was this so hard?

He opened his mouth and forced the rest of the words, his heart pounding, his core fluttery, making him feel clammy, sick almost: "Will you marry me?"

"Yes," she replied, evenly, her eyes steady, calm.

They made their way back to camp by the light of Joe's head-lamp and prepared for bed. Joe's body felt tingly, amped, the way it used to before a big show, or surfing big waves. He hadn't planned to seduce her, knowing the lack of a hot shower afterwards would be distasteful to her. But that glow, and her smile, and the extra fullness of her breasts, did something to him. Or maybe it was the fresh air, the open sky above them, the feeling that they were truly alone. Or maybe it was her hormones at work again—she seemed as hungry for him as he was for her. He was careful to keep her warm in the loose coverings of their sleeping bags, with their awkward mummy shape and hoods, their slick nylon sliding easily over the air mattresses as they undressed. When they were finished, their skin hot and their breaths in tandem, he felt so exhausted he would have fallen asleep with her on his chest.

An hour into the drive home, Francine grabbed the door handle. "Pull over," she whispered, her face ashen.

"What's wrong?" Joe said, searching for a safe place to turn off the freeway.

"I . . . " she stammered.

Joe reached over her to roll down the window, but he bumped her square in the chest and she cried out. "Sorry!" he said, wincing, his eyes still searching for an exit, a pullout, something. Cars whizzed by his gutless Subaru, spraying him with road dust.

"Joe," Francine moaned. Her face looked sweaty.

Joe cut the wheel and edged as close off the road as he could. Francine opened the door and half stepped, half fell to her knees as the horrible retching sounds began. He raced to her side of the car, closing his eyes against the blast of a passing semi. Francine had regained her feet and was leaning over, one hand holding her hair back from the vomit pouring out of her mouth.

"Oh, baby," he said, going to her as the wave ebbed.

She spat a few times, her breaths still uneven, ragged.

He rubbed her back. Another spasm began; he could feel it beginning in her ribs. Just the sound of it tormented him, and he wasn't the one puking.

"Do you think it's something you ate?" he asked, racking his brain to figure out what it could be.

"No," she said, spitting. "It just came out of nowhere."

"Do you have a fever?" he asked, feeling her forehead. It felt normal.

"I feel fine, now," Francine said.

Joe realized that Francine was experiencing morning sickness, and for a moment, his heart leapt with excitement. This was from the baby! Then he remembered how awful she must feel.

She braced on her knees for a long time with him holding her hair, rubbing her shoulders. Once back in the car, she drank a little water.

"I've heard that ginger can help with nausea," he said.

"Take me home," she sighed, closing her eyes.

# THIRTY-FOUR

## Santa Cruz, California

Joe felt Carrie become heavy in his arms as he did laps back and forth down the hallway. Her little face, snuggled into his arm, had changed so much. She was crawling and into everything! Joe sighed, knowing he needed to put her down in her crib as Emily had asked him to do, but it was so tempting to hold her a little longer.

Francine said she was too sick to come with him, that the smell of poop or baby food would surely send her racing for the toilet. Joe tried not to worry. But they hadn't yet made the doctor's appointment. She hadn't told her parents. He had bought her a copy of the book the librarian had helped him find, one with details of each week's developmental phases as well as answers to questions about nutrition, exercise, and how to choose a good doctor. She had thanked him by pinching her eyes with her fingers. He tried to read the chapter about the second month, describing how the baby had fingernails and a beating heart, but she said it made her sick to listen.

Joe stood in front of Carrie's crib, looking at the colorful animal mobile hanging over it, at the quilt his mom had sewn, draped over the rocking chair. He eyed the small dresser and remembered the laundry he wanted to fold. Carrie's breaths moved deeply, her lids fluttered. Her warmth had spread to his body, and when he finally put her down, he felt chilled. He traced the edge of her hairline with the tip of his thumb and marveled at her perfect nose, her delicate eyelashes. What would his child look like? A shiver of joy jiggled that place deep in his belly again, spreading outward, weaving through his ribs and into his heart. Smiling, he left the door ajar and tiptoed into the living room where the laundry pile and a cold beer waited.

At the job site the next day, the radio DJ jabbered on while Joe stood reviewing the plans with the framer, who suggested moving the staircase entrance. It always came down to the builders; architects never could figure out dimensions. He and his crew were always adding space here, taking it away there, or making it more useable. When Joe first heard the song from the radio, it didn't stand out until it was almost over. He found himself losing his concentration, standing there with his tape measure extended. What the hell was that song doing on the radio?

Over the falls for you
Over the falls, my heart wide open
Crushed by the weight
And now it's too late
Over the falls and I'm drowning, drowning

He raced to the radio and turned it off, breathing hard.
"Hey!" someone called out from the second floor.
"I'm trying to think down here!" Joe called back.
"Fuckin-A!"
Joe looked back at the framer. "What was that distance again?" he asked.

The following Sunday, he took Francine to his parents' house for dinner. He had asked all of his siblings to come, so they knew something was up.

They were all in the backyard, some playing hoops, some in the sandbox with the littles, some standing around in flip flops holding beers when his mother called out, "Supper!"

Joe led Francine to the picnic table that earlier he had helped set with Kelly and her five-year old son, Mal. Francine had been parked in front of the kiddie pool with Maggie and her two kids, dipping her bare feet in and looking green. He knew Mags had talked her ear off, which was probably best, given Francine's stoic state lately. His fingers, moist with sweat, felt slippery in Francine's while they held hands beneath the table.

With so many people there, supper was more of a feeding frenzy than anything else, but at least these days they had enough food for all the mouths. He remembered as a kid his mother quietly reminding him of his two-glass limit of milk. He remembered casseroles, and in the summer, a concoction called "Garden Goulash," a mushy, tasteless mass made mostly of his mother's garden squash. He still couldn't eat squash. But tonight plates heaped high with steak and grilled chicken crowded the table with bowls of potato salad, corn on the cob, a basket of his mother's buttermilk rolls. They talked of music, about Joe's new project, about Kelly's husband Timmy, deployed since May, about Em's upcoming performance, and who'd been surfing and where. Joe could hardly wait until after the meal when they'd all play music together.

When the frenzy slowed and the noise level softened, kids having already left the table to play, Joe's fingers trembled with the excitement of his news. He grabbed his beer and raised it, tapped it with a fork.

Slowly, conversations ebbed and all eyes turned to him.

"Francine and I have an announcement to make," he said, barely able to hold back his grin. He glanced at Francine, whose eyes reflected his own hopes, his desire.

"We're getting married," he said calmly, still watching her, his pride swelling.

His family cheered, murmured questions about when, where. He put up his hand. "I'm not finished," he scolded, grinning fully now. He drank in this moment of their anticipation for a moment before shouting, "We're also having a baby!"

They ate it up, jumping to their feet, pulling Francine too, into hugs and kisses and more questions. He answered as best he could: only ten weeks, so no, they didn't know if it was a boy or a girl, but secretly he hoped for a girl; they weren't sure where they would live yet, but he had convinced Francine to look at a few houses; no, the wedding date wasn't set yet, but he hoped it would be soon, before winter. She still needed to tell her parents, who had just returned from Europe. When he had a moment to take a breath, he searched for Francine and caught just the flash of her skirt as she ran inside. Was she going to be sick again? "She's been really sick," he explained to Annabelle and his mom, who nodded sympathetically.

"Ginger ale sometimes works," his mom said.

Joe sighed, wondering if he had pushed Francine too hard. She hadn't even met half of these people before, and suddenly they were family. "I'll tell her. Thanks, Ma," Joe replied, knowing it was going to take a lot more than ginger ale to alleviate Francine's fear.

Joe pulled his Subaru away from the house they'd just toured. "Well?" he asked carefully.

"I don't know, Joe!" Francine groaned. "You're the one who knows about this stuff."

Joe turned the radio down. "Okay," he said gently, eyeing her, "but I want you to like it, too." The house was tiny, yes, but it had a fenced backyard and a decent kitchen. A garage, even. Sure, it needed work, like a new bathroom and a new roof, but he'd have that licked before they moved in.

"I can't do this," Francine said, closing her eyes.

Joe's heart jumped into his throat. "What do you mean?"

"I just . . . " She tapped her thumbnails together in her lap. "You decide, okay?"

Joe knew there were plenty of other houses they could look at, but this one offered the best location, and he was excited about doing the projects it came with. They could make it theirs. He wanted her to be excited about it, too. "You okay?" he asked, bracing himself for her answer as they idled at a stoplight. Since the dinner at his folks' place, she had been irritable, distant. They hadn't been out together; she sometimes didn't return his calls right away. She still hadn't seen the doctor.

She sighed. "It's just a lot to think about."

"It's just a house," he replied, taking her hand.

She glanced at him, her green eyes clear but neutral. "It feels like more than that," she replied.

"Is it the mortgage? Are you worried about the money?"

She shook her head.

"Your folks?" he asked, dreading their reaction. Francine wanted to tell them alone—much to his protest, this Friday.

"Yeah," she said. "I just . . . " she trailed off. "My parents aren't like yours, Joe," she added. "They both had careers. Working was always important to them."

"Working is important to my folks, too," he added, a little too defensively. Something was distracting him. Something from the radio. The light turned green and he accelerated.

"I know," Francine said. "I didn't mean it that way."

Joe shook his head.

"It's just so cliché," she sighed. "I get knocked up by my rock-star boyfriend," she said.

"I'm not a rock star," he countered. Where had he heard the song before, and why did it annoy him so much? "I have a job. A good job. I'm making money, I can support you."

"But that's just it," Francine said, tears springing from her eyes. "I don't want you to support me. My parents won't see it as support-ive. They'll see it as ruining my future, stealing my independence."

*Over the falls and I'm drowning, drowning*

"God damn it!" Joe slammed his fist at the radio button, silenc-ing it. Who the hell leaked that song to the station? Doherty? Some crazy fan? He'd have to find out and put a stop to it. Hearing it was like torture. He had moved on. He wanted that other life to end, wanted to stop dreaming about her, stop waking up wondering where she was. He wanted it to stop hurting.

Francine was looking at him funny.

He exhaled heavily. "However they react, we'll get through it together," Joe said quietly. "And I never asked you to give up your career if that's what you want," he added. "This isn't some kind of death sentence, you know." He regretted his words immediately.

Francine began to cry.

He pulled the car over and reached for her. "Shit, I'm sorry," he said, hugging her close. "That was a stupid thing to say." He kissed the top of her head. "I know it's scary, but we can do this together, okay?" he said as she sniffed into his sleeve.

# THIRTY-FIVE

## Río Limón, Mexico

"No!" Lorna said again. "I'm not doing it!"

"Look," Alex said. "I might not get another chance."

Lorna felt the words sink in. She closed her eyes, knowing Alex was right. By now she knew the journal by heart. This incoming swell, the one Carlos had shared with her, was perfect for Las Muelas. There might not be another like it for months, maybe longer. "You really think you're strong enough?" Lorna asked quietly.

Alex's mouth hardened into a tight line.

Lorna felt as if trapped in a powerful current. *No,* she wanted to say. *This isn't the end! Not yet!* "You don't have to do this," she said as tears welled up in her eyes.

"You know I do," Alex replied.

They sat in silence for a while, Alex bundled in a blanket, reclined on the couch, Lorna silently wiping her wet cheeks.

"We need the boat," Alex said.

Lorna had been afraid of this. "We can't take the panga?" she asked anyway.

Alex sighed. "No. And besides, Carlos will need it for the tours."

Anxiety coiled around Lorna's insides, laced her rib cage tight, like a vice.

"You have to get it," Alex said.

Lorna shook her head. "No, Carlos should. I can run the tours while he's gone."

Alex didn't reply but her look said it all.

Lorna jumped to her feet. "I don't know how to operate a boat like that!" The thought terrified her: the open ocean, navigating for hundreds of miles, alone on a big boat. What if something broke down? What if she ran into something? She'd heard horror stories about random shipping containers floating around silently, waiting to be crashed into in the middle of the night. *Oh God*, she thought. *Will I have to spend the night at sea?*

"You'll be fine," Alex replied. "The course is already charted. There's two GPS units, supplies . . . "

"You don't want him to know," Lorna said slowly, thinking of Carlos. "Do you?"

Alex broke from her speech.

"You're not going to tell him that we're going?" Lorna said. "You're just gonna hop on the boat and not say anything?"

"I'll talk to him," Alex said, looking tired. "He'll understand."

"Then why not ask him to get the boat?" Lorna tried again.

"Because he won't!" Alex hissed. "He won't leave me," she said.

"This is crazy," Lorna said, shaking her head.

When she left the apartment an hour later with Alex's plan swirling in her head, she was too preoccupied to notice the sound of footsteps descending the stairs below or see Garth's shadow slipping behind the corner.

Although her boat skills had improved since leading her own groups in the panga, she was no match for a huge powerboat with a $250,000 price tag. As she stepped onboard the *Pearl Shadow* that afternoon she wondered if the boat could sense her apprehension. Lorna unlocked the sliding rear door and stepped inside a small galley. She squinted down the narrow corridor, noting the doors to the cabins, to the main bridge. A set of stairs led down to the stateroom Alex had described.

After tucking the water bottles, snacks, and some store-bought pastries into the small refrigerator and tossing her borrowed back-pack onto the dining table, she climbed the wooden ladder to the flybridge. It was so quiet she could hear her breaths echoing inside the vinyl bubble. The dials and switches stared back at her—fuel gauge, battery level, GPS, engine temperature, radar, rpms, oil pressure. Overwhelmed, she sat on the cushy chair and forced a series of deep breaths into her lungs.

She wrapped her fingers around the solid ball tips of the twin throttle levers and practiced the clicking motion required to "lock" them together. With a sigh, she removed the list Carlos had made from her pocket and began checking off the "things to do before leaving the harbor" section:

Radar and radio: working.
Batteries: charged.
Fuel: full.

Carlos had taught her the math: the boat held 400 gallons of fuel, so if Lorna ran the boat at twelve to thirteen knots and had no major mishaps, she'd have twenty-four hours of fuel time, which was more than enough as long as she stayed on course, didn't battle major headwinds, or get lost.

Lorna fell asleep in one of the cabins rereading Alex's journal and woke to the thud it made hitting the floor. The gentle rocking of the boat unnerved rather than soothed her. She checked her watch: 5:08 a.m. She sighed and rolled over, trying to block out all the strange noises: thumps, creaks, city noises carrying across the water, engines drumming in the distance. A half-hour later, she couldn't stand it anymore, and got out of bed.

After washing her face and making a cup of instant coffee, Lorna grabbed the food bag and the journal and climbed to the flybridge. Just a hint of dawn was spreading across the sky. She took a deep breath and sat on the edge of the white vinyl seat. When she was ready, she turned the ignition, the twin engines' low rumble sending a spark through her heart. She did not feel ready for this.

After the engines warmed up, she raised the harbormaster on the radio, her voice shaky while she listed the details of her voyage and then untied and slowly navigated into the murky marina waters. But the big boat responded so differently than the panga, the throttle levers were frighteningly stiff, and the steering slow to respond. She crept slowly toward the exit, her eyes searching for obstacles in the near dark, anticipating her course so as not to over- or under-steer. Crashing the boat before leaving the harbor was not an option. Her heart beat staccato style against her ribs, and her jaw felt stiff from concentrating. Finally, she rounded the breakwater and breathed a sigh of relief. She eased the throttle up a little, sighting on the rocky silhouette of the point guarding the far edge of the bay, and headed out to sea.

Perched so high, fully enclosed in her clear bubble, with the sea spray splashing the hull and engine rumbling beneath her feet, she was overcome with emotion. She had not been alone in weeks, and the strain of keeping Alex comfortable had stolen her ability to think of anything else. She pictured Alex as she worked on this boat in Port Angeles, her brow furrowed, her neck beaded with sweat, all the while dreaming of the waves she would discover. The fact that Alex was not here cast a pall over what should have been a feeling of freedom, a release. Her eyes blurred with tears; in her wildest dreams, she would never have imagined this.

Keeping track of all the gauges, as well as her location on the GPS, then cross-checking with the nautical charts required her total focus. And there were obstacles ahead, marked in the course notes that Lorna affixed to the console just below the GPS unit: shoals, tide rips, river mouths; but there were those she couldn't see, such as other boats, or sudden storms. And there were plenty of things that could go wrong: electrical failure, an engine fire, something as easy as a bilge pump going out that she had no idea how to fix. Or things could go awry because of high seas. She could lose her way, hit something, or run out of fuel.

She avoided her first obstacle, a shallow shelf, and tried to relax her shoulders. She marked her progress with a pencil she kept threaded between her visor and the groove above her right ear. She talked to herself, mumbling "there it is" when she spotted an important landmark or "fix" as Carlos had called it.

Just before noon she idled near a cluster of crumbly rocks that were home to a family of large black birds, their white guano staining the tips of the black peaks. She listened to the swell crash against them and marked her progress while nibbling on Fritos. Her next fix was a lighthouse perched on a rocky headland known for its spectacular diving. With a stretch of straightforward navigating ahead, she tried out the autopilot and sat back in an attempt to enjoy the ride. If all continued to go well, she might make Río Limón by nightfall.

When she reached the craggy cliffs and the lighthouse, she allowed a moment of relief: two-thirds of her journey was complete. Her anxiety lessened further when she noticed the cluster of boats on the choppy surface, anchored above the diving destination Carlos had described. Somehow their presence comforted her. On one boat, a man fishing off the stern gave her a lazy wave; Lorna returned the wave, grinning.

The fat sun off her starboard seemed to accelerate as it approached the horizon, highlighting the edges of a strange type of cloud cover—like fish scales—that had grown from the west. She was down to a third of her fuel. How had she used so much? Was it the autopilot? Had she gone too fast? Her head pounded from the squinting, the concentrating, the worrying. She'd only managed to drink one liter of water and her stomach, after surviving on junk all day, felt like it might try to eat itself.

According to the GPS and charts, she was close to Río Limón's tiny harbor; all that remained was rounding a headland that seemed endless. *Come on already.* Finally the curve eased inland and she recognized Pirate's Point, the spray off the peeling waves like a thousand diamonds in the soft, pinkish light. The little peelers broke almost on shore. Lorna shook her head. The big swell Alex needed for Las Muelas was due to arrive but there was no sign of it. Maybe Carlos's predictions were off. The possibility filled her with anguish.

She entered Limon's protected waters, and Carlos was waiting to help her anchor, a difficult task in the near dark. After Carlos secured the big boat, the quiet washed over her like a sigh. Lorna made her way to the galley to store the journal and leftover food, the boat rocking gently beneath her. She knew that for hours after returning to land, her body would still toss and sway. She stepped to the stern, dreading doing it all again tomorrow.

"I think I'll swim in," Lorna said to Carlos. She threw her T-shirt into the panga.

Carlos eyed the shore, easily a half-mile away, and nodded, the strain evident in the tightness around his eyes, his jaw. "I will wait," he said, then turned the boat and glided away.

The silky black water beckoned, and Lorna stepped up to the stern gunwale and dove clear of the boat. The impact of the warm water awakened her skin and washed her clean of the stress and grime of her journey. She swam hard for the harbor, checking occasionally for the lights. The work felt good in her arms, her thighs, the tops of her feet. Had Alex had a good day? Carlos hadn't said anything, but they were beyond that now. There seemed to be new issues almost every day. Would Alex be asleep or awake, pacing, worrying herself into exhaustion about the boat?

Lorna had decided that after tomorrow, she would help Garth work with Carlos to find some way that they could coexist. If he promised to take good care of the crew in Río Limón, she would give Garth his shot at Las Muelas.

Lorna swam past the pangas carefully, trying not to think about all the oil slicks and rotten bait often thrown overboard. She waded onto shore and squeezed out a hank of her tangled curls. The sharp gravel pricked her feet like glass shards so she goose-stepped quickly to the road where Carlos waited in the van.

She would keep the journal though. It had been a gift from Alex and she didn't want to share it with anyone.

# THIRTY-SIX

## Santa Cruz, California

Although Joe told himself it was just a little thing, no big deal, he had the saleswoman wrap it. When she asked him if it was a girl or a boy, he said it was too early to know, so she wrapped it in yellow paper with a pale green ribbon. He put the present on the seat next to him in the car, ready for when he went over to Francine's later, hoping it would make her smile. He would remind her that after the first trimester she would feel better, get her energy back. To his relief she had finally scheduled her first appointment and they planned to go together. After they listened to the baby's heartbeat, the staff would do some tests to make sure everything was okay. A little zip of energy passed through him. Would they be able to see anything on the ultrasound? He got jittery just thinking about it. A tiny hand? Kicking feet?

The afternoon dragged on with an endless stream of problems, he swore that after this contract he would think twice before working for a greedy fat cat. Whoever heard of a home with three hot tubs? And trying to charge *him* when it had been the rich guy's own brother who had fucked up the ordering of the front door, again. When Joe finally finished for the day, his mind turning these problems over and over, he had forgotten about his evening plans until the present reminded him.

Grinning, he started the old engine and cruised to Francine's apartment. But when he went up to her place, she wasn't home; the windows were dark. He checked his watch again. He was a few minutes late. Had she gone out? He knocked again. Could she be asleep? But after five minutes, he could sense the emptiness inside her place. She wasn't there.

Confused, he tucked the present under his arm and walked back to his car where he slumped into his seat. A funny, nervous kind of feeling spread through his gut. He didn't like it. Something was wrong. Could something have happened? Was she hurt? He knew she had finished work an hour ago and planned to be home studying for her upcoming test. Had she simply lost track of the time?

His recently acquired cell phone—a device he still wasn't so sure he wanted, or needed—had a dead battery, so he decided to go home and wait for her call. He placed the present next to him and put the car in gear.

His home phone had a few voicemail messages, but none from Francine. He called her place and left a message asking her to call, trying not to sound worried. She would probably call any minute and accuse him of freaking out.

He grabbed his guitar and shuffled to the back porch, keeping the door open so he could hear the phone. The music came to him and he let his mind loosen as his muscles took over, his lungs filling with the summer-sweet air, his bare foot keeping time on the cool concrete patio. But a part of him couldn't quite release his fear that something was wrong.

After an hour he gave up playing. He called her work but of course they were closed. He called directory assistance for her friend

Mallory, who answered on the fourth ring, surprised to hear his voice. No, she hadn't seen Francine in a few days. Was she with her parents? Could something have happened to them? No, she would have called him or come by the site to tell him such news. He thought about calling her parents, but realized he'd just worry them—or start an argument.

Where the hell was she?

Francine finally called that night, after Joe had fallen asleep on the couch.

"Are you okay? What happened?" Joe asked, relief and anger flooding his thoughts.

"I went into the city," she said quietly.

"I thought you were going to study for your test?" he asked.

The line buzzed with her silence for a long minute. "I auditioned today."

"Auditioned?" Joe asked, confused. "Auditioned for what?"

"*Fiddler on the Roof.* Performances start in December."

Joe rubbed the side of his head. "Do they have parts for pregnant women or something?" He tried to imagine Francine with a round belly spinning like a top or leaping across the stage.

"No," she sighed, sounding distant. He waited through another long pause.

"It was just for fun," she finally said.

Joe sighed. "Oh," he said. "What if you get a part?"

"Then I guess I'll have to tell them I changed my mind," she said bitterly.

"What's wrong, baby?" Joe asked quietly.

Francine sighed. "Nothing. I just needed to get away for a day, that's all."

"Can I come over?" He looked at his watch. Almost eleven o'clock.

"I'm tired, Joe."

"How about tomorrow? I could take you to breakfast?"

"I gotta work early," she replied. "Look, I'll call you, okay?"

Joe felt that same nervousness in his gut. "Okay," he said. "I love you," he added. But she had already ended the call.

Their conversation haunted Joe into the early hours of the morning. He couldn't sleep. Why had she gone all the way to the city and auditioned for something she couldn't participate in? Why hadn't she used the afternoon to study? Joe finally ripped back the covers at just after 5:00 a.m. If he hurried he could catch her before she left her apartment. He told himself he just wanted to see her, make sure she was okay.

But she was not home. Her apartment seemed as lifeless as the previous afternoon, the shades drawn and the windows dark. He checked his watch. Sometimes she went to the gym before going to work. Could that be why she was gone? But she hadn't been to the gym in weeks, not since the morning sickness had started. Joe decided to go to the café where she worked and wait for her to appear.

But at a quarter past seven he still did not see her car enter the parking lot, nor did he see her enter the building. He went in and greeted the other barista, a girl with dreadlocks swirled into a fat bun on the top of her head. "Francine coming in today?" he asked her. Just then another café employee emerged from the back carrying a crate packed with milk cartons.

Dreadlock Girl made a face. "Called in sick. Otherwise I'd still be in bed."

Joe's temples throbbed. "Sick?" he asked again.

"She ain't been herself for weeks though, man, I just hope I don't get it," Dreadlock Girl added.

Joe mumbled his thanks and stalked out the door, his head aching, as if some giant was pinching it, like a pea. Francine wasn't home and she wasn't at work. A rush of fear overcame him and he balled his fists. What was going on?

She called the next morning, her voice somber.

"Where the hell have you been?" Joe half-shouted into the phone. He'd paced every floorboard in his place, wondering where she might be, or whom she might be with.

He hadn't slept a wink.

Francine only sighed. "I need you to come over," she said.

"We made a commitment, Francine!" he shouted. "You came to me, remember? You wanted this too!"

Francine's hard-edged voice cut him off. "I'm not sleeping around, okay?"

Joe sighed, exasperated. Hadn't Marty warned him? What else could it be? "I'm on my way," he growled and hung up the phone.

Joe gunned his engine down the quiet street, rolling the stop sign and accelerating past the cafés and the bookstore, the tire shop. He ran his hand through his hair, his mind racing through the possibilities. What had she done? Where had she been? Or was he blowing this all out of proportion? Maybe she'd been with her parents, or maybe she really had been sick. So then why hadn't she called him?

He parked next to the curb and peered up at her door where the windows shone with light from inside; she'd opened the blinds. The present Joe had bought two days ago rested on the seat next to him, and he debated whether to follow through with giving it to her. He closed his eyes, his fingers gripping the wheel. "Fuck!" he barked to the dashboard.

In the end, he brought the present. They were in this together. She had said yes; everything would work out. He knocked and heard her call out for him to come in. When he entered, she was sitting on the couch, her eyes not meeting his.

He closed the door. He was aware of the present in his hands, but somehow he knew now was not the time to offer it. He put it on the coffee table and joined her on the couch. A flash of pain tightened her face as he did so. Had something happened to her? An accident? She looked so . . . frail. Joe's heart began to pound into his throat. He ignored the sudden sickening dread growing inside him.

"I just want to know if you're okay," he said, his voice sounding garbled, like someone else's.

She nodded. "Yeah, I'm okay."

"Whatever it is," he said, reaching for her hand. "We'll get through it."

Francine averted his eyes. "It's gone," she said.

Joe squinted at her, confused. "What do you mean? What's gone?" Had she been robbed? Her car stolen?

"The . . . " She hung her head, and Joe realized her other arm was wrapped loosely around her abdomen.

"Did something happen?" Joe asked. Had there been something the matter with the baby? His head throbbed. If she had been bleeding, it could be the beginnings of a miscarriage. There were still things they could do to stop it! They should be leaving for the hospital right now! Had her audition started something? Had she pushed herself too hard? He grabbed her hand and tried to pull her up. "We need to get to the doctor!" he said.

But Francine resisted. "Nothing happened," she said.

He looked at her, dropped her hand. What was she saying? A sob escaped his lips as he realized what he was missing.

"I . . . had it done," she said with difficulty.

Joe's heart stopped, his mind went blank. "No-no-no-no," he moaned. He lunged for Francine's shoulders. "What did you do?" he cried.

Her eyes filled with tears. "I couldn't go through with it, Joe," she said.

Joe released her, feeling the room spin. He gripped the edge of the couch. Francine was saying something, but he didn't hear it. She had ended it. She'd done it without him, without asking him, without wondering what he might think. He had asked her to marry him for God's sake! He had told his parents! He had made an offer on a house! They were a week away from hearing the heartbeat. He had seen it all in his mind: the sleepless nights, the sweet baby smell, rocking her to sleep, and teaching her to walk and ride a bike and love music. And Francine had taken all of that away.

"I'm sorry," she whispered.

"How could you?" he howled, pressing the heels of his hands into his eyes. "Oh God," he managed, stumbling through the door.

# THIRTY-SEVEN

Río Limón, Mexico

With the help of her watch alarm, Lorna met Carlos and Alex at the van before dawn. Carlos's face was tight with worry.

"What's wrong?" Lorna whispered to him as they loaded their gear into the back.

"He's just worried about the storm," Alex said.

"What storm?" Lorna asked. She remembered the strangely shaped clouds the previous day, but the morning's conditions were mild—there was barely a whisper of wind.

Carlos shook his head. He spoke something to Alex in Spanish. He sounded angry, frustrated. Alex replied, her hands on her hips. Lorna knew that stance—the "I'm doing it anyway" stance.

"Let's go," Alex said, shuffling to the passenger seat.

Carlos looked at Lorna and sighed.

At the harbor, they loaded the boards and gear carefully into the panga, and Lorna clambered in with a plastic grocery sack containing mangoes and fresh tortillas for Alex and some sandwiches for herself. Carlos steered towards the hulking silhouette of the *Pearl Shadow*. Alex held the side of the big boat as Lorna climbed onboard, then he took the surfboards and supplies from Carlos's outstretched hands. He did not look at her.

When it was time, Carlos and Alex embraced, and Lorna was taken aback at how small Alex looked in his arms, like a child. He spoke softly to her in Spanish as he held her, stroking her hair. When they kissed, Lorna looked away.

Onboard the boat, Alex seemed to regain some of her spark, her eyes bright as she took it all in. She breathed deep and nodded at Lorna. "Time to go," she said. Dressed in limp board shorts, a baggy sweatshirt, flip flops, and a visor, Alex could have been her old self if it wasn't for the way the trunks sagged off her frame and her hair looked dull and flat.

Lorna stowed their bags inside one of the cabins. She placed Alex's mangoes and tortillas in the fridge below her own grocery bag from the day before. The boards remained facedown on the stern deck. While Alex climbed the ladder to the flybridge, Lorna took one last look at the shore. Moments later, the engines rumbled to life. Lorna untied the bow from the buoy and they were underway.

The black ocean showed no sign of the advancing swell, but by the time the sun rose, the rolling beneath the hull had increased. Alex insisted they wear scopolamine patches to ward off seasickness and Lorna was thankful. Soon she could see undulations of swell on the horizon. She was amazed that so much swell could arrive so suddenly and with so little wind. It felt like magic.

Lorna used Alex's buck knife to slice up a mango, but it was no easy task as the boat's rocking increased. Alex had already switched to navigating from the main bridge. Bracing her hip against the tiny counter space, Lorna sliced off the wide side of the mango, scored the flesh, and inverted the skin to reveal small yellow cubes standing upright—mango Hawaiian style. She took it to Alex, sliding one hand along the wall for balance.

"Thanks," Alex said when Lorna put a cubed wedge into her hands.

Satisfied when Alex nibbled it clean, Lorna returned to the galley. She had just cleaned her hands and the sticky knife when Alex called her back.

"Can you take over?" Alex said when Lorna rushed in.

"What's wrong?" she asked. Lorna had the Dilaudid on standby. Could she need one? Lorna took the helm as Alex shuffled away, her eyes droopy.

"Tired," Alex murmured, then disappeared like a shadow.

Lorna checked the GPS, knowing it had been preset for their destination. She should be tired from the previous day and several nights with not enough sleep, but her awareness felt sharp, heightened. Her back was sore, however, and she did a few quick twists in an attempt to loosen her muscles.

Lorna swallowed the knot of nerves tightening her throat and checked her watch. Would Alex revive by the time they arrived? "Okay," she said to the empty pilothouse. Perched on the edge of the captain's chair, Lorna remembered Carlos's comment: *She is also my friend.* He was loyal, and kind, and though it was obvious he disapproved of this trip, he'd helped her prepare; he'd not stood in her way. Lorna wondered what he received in return.

The *Pearl Shadow* crested a wide band of swell and Lorna instinctively pulled back on the throttle: the trough behind dropped away steeply and Lorna had a sudden fear that she'd bury the bow, which landed hard, making Lorna's knees buckle. Something crashed.

"Alex?" she hollered down the hallway, keeping her eyes on the horizon.

After a long silence, Lorna hollered again, louder.

Finally, Alex's sleepy voice replied, "Fridge popped open."

Lorna sighed. "Everything okay?" She slowed the boat even more as *Pearl Shadow* ascended another hulking ripple.

"We're good," Alex replied. "Full steam ahead."

Lorna's mind buzzed with the steady increase in adrenaline dumping into her bloodstream. If the swells were big enough to rock this huge boat, what would they do to a shallow, open-sea shelf?

She recalled the highlights skimmed from the journal: where to wait for waves, what to watch out for, how the tides affected the ocean currents and the wave's behavior. She remembered surfing Pipeline. *Is that what I'm heading into?* Lorna remembered being ignored the minute she reached the lineup, huffing and so nervous her limbs felt shaky, like leaves quivering in the wind. So when Alex had turned to her and said, "This one's yours," Lorna had paddled for all she was worth, hoping that if she showed no fear, no hesitation, Alex would notice. Later Lorna realized how out of position she had been on that wave. Lorna had always wondered if Alex had been challenging her to try to pull it off anyway—an impossible task at a place like Pipe. After Lorna washed ashore, practically kissing the ground, Alex remained in the lineup, her back to the beach. Dripping a trail of orange-red blood from her reef cuts, Lorna made her way home. Hours later, when Alex returned, she only had words for her own stories.

But it was possible that Alex had given Lorna the journal as a way to make up for that mistake. Back then, Alex surfed Pipe regularly, she knew its moods, its many faces, but had never shared such knowledge with Lorna. Since then Lorna had begun to think of it as purposeful. It was as if Alex's power fed off her need for control and to be the very best. Alex had probably taken Lorna out there as a way to prove that once and for all.

Possibly, this whole ceremony surrounding Las Muelas was Alex's way of making it right, a show of forgiveness. Or, she was bringing Lorna out here for one last showdown—Alex proving she was still the best. Lorna didn't want to compete with Alex anymore.

She grimaced at the rows upon rows of rolling swell marching to meet her, and wondered: how had she agreed to this?

According to Alex's notes, the underwater shelf beneath Las Muelas created an ocean oasis for fish, sharks, and seals that relied on its dense kelp beds for food and shelter. Her marine biology self would have loved it, but her surfer self, the one about to be immersed in such a dense population of sea life was downright spooked.

But when the dark lines of swell on the horizon became fluffy mounds and the boat was bucking over the broad backs of swell, Lorna forgot all about sharks and giant squid. Gooseflesh pimpled her legs and her throat went dry. She checked her watch: just after 9:00 a.m. The air seemed to thicken and hum with an increasing energy, flooding her body with nerves. The wispy horsetail clouds that had been tinged with pink and shiny gold at dawn had turned into a dirty white scrim of hazy clouds, casting the water with a green-black gloss. She wondered if this was the edge of the storm that Carlos had been so worried about.

"Alex?" Lorna called out to the hallway. A light chop ruffled the sea's undulating surface. She could see where the wave—a left— broke because of the frothy, turbulent foam piles stacked the length of several football fields. It amazed her that such a violent explosion of water could then morph back into smooth black-blue ridges, marching towards the coast like some robotic convoy. Lorna could easily determine the deep channel, but worried about anchoring. Not on the rock shelf: it was too dangerous. Somewhere sandy and with the right depth.

"Alex!" Lorna called again. Had something happened? In her already heightened state of anxiety, the thought of trying to handle the anchoring alone sent her into a mild panic. *This is crazy*, she thought.

Then Alex croaked: "Lorna."

Lorna risked a look behind her and caught a glimpse of Alex on all fours outside of the head.

Fear like a cool snake slid down Lorna's spine. She glanced back at the horizon and the dark ridges—more like mountains really—of swell. "What's wrong?" she called to her.

"I forgot . . . " Alex said. Lorna had to strain to hear the words. She could see Alex's thin sides expanding and contracting with rapid breaths as she struggled to finish her sentence. " . . . how this is."

Lorna couldn't idle and drift, the boat could end up broadside to one of the swells. She could try to anchor—something she had only done in the panga and never with complete confidence. "Hold on," she said, setting a westerly course with the GPS and turning on the autopilot.

"Why didn't you say something?" Lorna cried as she helped Alex to the stateroom. "We could have turned back!" Alex couldn't remember how many times she'd vomited. How dehydrated had she become? Her pulse felt fast but not weak, which was encouraging.

Alex shook her head. Her pale skin shone with a sickly dampness. "We are doing this," she croaked.

"No way. We're turning around. You can barely stand!"

Alex grimaced. "The GPS will take you to the anchor," she said after breathing heavily for a long moment. "Just give me some drugs," Alex said, her sunken eyes meeting Lorna's. "I can do this."

"No," Lorna sighed. She should have known better, as much as she wanted to give this to Alex, she should have known it was impossible.

"Don't you want to know what it's like?" Alex said, a slight glimmer in her gaze.

Lorna let her hands fall against her thighs, feeling that old sense of helplessness, of knowing Alex would find a way to get what she wanted. "Not really."

Alex grinned, showing a glint of white teeth. "Liar."

"I read the journal. I get it, okay?" Lorna needed to return to the bridge, she didn't trust the autopilot in these big swells. And she was tired. She'd been behind the wheel of this boat for almost eighteen of the last thirty-six hours, with many more remaining before she could call it quits. "I'm just saying that maybe this isn't the day."

Alex's face quieted. "Then when?" Her eyes didn't flinch. "This is it for me, Lorna."

"Don't say that," Lorna breathed, her fingers shaking. Deep inside, she knew it was true, but still she pressed on. "We'll get another swell."

"When? Next week? Next month?"

Lorna braced herself against the wall as the boat rocked over another swell. She knew what Alex was implying: that she wouldn't be able to climb into the boat in a week. One month from now . . . Lorna pushed the thought away.

"Okay," Lorna said.

# THIRTY-EIGHT

Pacific Ocean

After Lorna shut off the engines, the sound of the wave exploding literally loosened her bowels and she had to race to the bathroom. Then, on shaky legs, she moved to the stern where she slid into the three-millimeter wetsuit Alex had loaned her. Even though the air temperature hovered in the eighties, Alex had insisted they bring the wetsuits for the cooler water and protection from the wind, plus they offered extra buoyancy. Lorna was glad of it as she paddled away from the boat, feeling chilled to her core.

Maybe it was the cocktail of meds onboard or maybe the roar of the distant wave heightened the anticipation, but Alex seemed to have improved. She had supervised the anchoring and pulled on her wetsuit unaided. Soon into their paddle, however, her pace lagged. Lorna looked back as she crested a massive mound of swell that lifted her high above Alex and the boat before they both blinked out of sight in the following trough. A rumble like an avalanche seemed to shake the air molecules around her. Her intestines clenched in spasm. A large seal popped up nearby, exhaling a startling "Pffffft!" Lorna cried out and froze in terror. The seal gave her a quick appraisal with his downturned eyes then submerged, seemingly swallowed by the sea and leaving barely a ripple.

Lorna drifted over another swell and sat up to watch Alex toil away, her forehead resting on her board, her arms dragging through the water with each stroke. Lorna spun around and paddled toward her, cursing herself for allowing this, for coming here, for agreeing to this doomed mission. Alex didn't have the strength for this.

"We're going back," Lorna said, half-shouting over the sound of the booming surf and stiff chop slapping their boards.

"I just need to rest . . . " Alex laid her cheek against her board.

"You're not strong enough," Lorna insisted, grabbing the rail of Alex's board to keep her close. They rose over another swell and Lorna glanced behind her, toward the acres of whitewater churning the sea into frothy foam. She swallowed. The bulldozing wall was at least six feet high, or higher. She tried not to think about how that would translate into the size of the actual wave.

Alex breathed hard, her low eyelids shading eyes that seemed to be focusing on something far away.

"Let's get back to the boat," Lorna said, wondering if she would have to tow her there.

"No," Alex breathed, her eyes clenched shut.

"Alex, you can't do this! I'm not going any farther!"

"Go without me," Alex said, her shoulders curling around her tiny frame.

Lorna didn't understand. "We're going back to the boat!" she said over the noisy sea rumbling and hissing and slapping at them.

Alex exhaled a long, shallow breath. "I thought I could." She shook her head. "But you can."

"What are you saying? We'll go back together! I'm not leaving you!"

Whatever pain episode Alex was fighting seemed to ebb, and she began to breathe easier. "I've wanted this for so long," she said. "Go."

Lorna tried to look Alex in the eyes. "I'm not doing this without you."

"You don't need me," Alex replied, a rueful smile twisting her lips. "I only got in your way." She swallowed with difficulty. "Now go. It's what you came for."

"I came to help you," Lorna pleaded. *Don't make me do this alone.*

"And you have," Alex replied stoically.

Their eyes finally connected, and Lorna felt something shift inside her. The feeling created space, let in air, lightness.

Alex pushed away from Lorna's grip.

The rumble of the wave pounded into Lorna's ears as Alex's strokes pulled her toward the boat. Lorna slipped into a wave trough; Alex and the boat blinked from sight.

Lorna hugged herself, shivering. Her inner voice instructed her to follow Alex. *She might need me.* She swiveled to face the wave but could only see whitewater and a cluster of birds rising up like a swarm of bees. The rumbling of the waves prevented her from hearing their cries. But there was another voice, telling her that Alex wouldn't accept her help now. *Don't you want to know what it's like?* she had said. Lorna realized that if she looked deep enough inside herself, she did. Of course she did.

She remembered Alex's notes in bits and pieces. *The takeoff into the bowl always feels late. Shoot straight through the Pit and if the backspray doesn't blow you off your feet then you've made it to the Race Track and the ride of your life.*

She also remembered the warnings. *Do not get caught inside, you'll drown before the whitewater lets you go. Commit yourself at the takeoff, going over the falls there will get you up close to the rocks.* Lorna shuddered. A head injury out here would certainly mean death. *Saw a shark take a seal today, came from below and ripped its head off. Scary shit.*

A moment later, another seal, this one with whiskers and a huge head poked his nose out of the water with a loud *spffft!* Instinctively, Lorna yanked her feet up. Wobbling, she gripped her rails to prevent falling off her board. The seal slipped his head back beneath the sea.

Another ridge of swell lifted her up, and she watched Alex's progress. *I've wanted this for so long,* she had said. *It's what you came for.* Lorna looked away, shivering, wondering if Alex was right.

Lorna thought back to that day at Pipe and tried to imagine what it would have been like if Alex had watched from the beach. If Alex had given her the same kind of information as she had about Las Muelas. Would Lorna still have chosen that fateful wave? She might not have chosen a wave at all—instead coming in with her tail between her legs, scared out of her mind. She could have triumphed, and enjoyed her mother's proud smile from the shore. Would Lorna have stopped trying to compete with Alex then? Would she have stopped mourning for the mother she wished for and begun accepting Alex as she was?

That day, Alex had intended to give her a kick in the ass. Even though it was far from what Lorna wanted, maybe it was what she'd needed. So what did that mean for Las Muelas? *The only thing to fear is the unknown,* Alex had once told her, quoting some famous big-wave pioneer.

There was a reason for that—sometimes the unknown could kill you.

But Lorna knew that she couldn't turn back. The feeling of cowardice—that sickening self-defeat that sat in her gut like tar after she'd bailed on a session—would haunt her forever. Every time she had packed up and driven away from a wave she had deemed too heavy or too frightening, her conviction would fade the more she reviewed her performance, and in the end she raced to the highway, believing it would melt her shame away faster. But it never did.

She would be at work, or cruising the aisles of the grocery store, or stuck in traffic, and the realization that she had chickened out would weigh on her, make her feel ashamed, unworthy.

Here, there would be no next time, no way to make up for the loss of what she knew was a one-time deal, a final chance to put it all right, to walk away with a new perspective about all that had been before, a way to cleanse the wounds. She imagined her future self remembering this day. Would she emerge as a coward or a conqueror?

Better to go forward and risk it all than to return empty-handed. Alex might be watching, but Lorna knew this journey was for herself, to push beyond the unknown, to leave this menacing, ugly place knowing she had no regrets, that she had given everything.

So she paddled across the wind-scuffed water, each swell she climbed bringing her closer to that unknown. The constant, sickening roar became distinct, individual waves exploding, a sound like a battlefield. Lorna began to count the explosions in order to measure the sets, but she would lose the sound in the troughs. So, three waves to a set? Five? She caught glimpses of unbroken waves, shining beneath the hazy sun. They could be ten feet or thirty—guessing would be fruitless. She put her head down and continued paddling, her clenched jaw aching.

Finally she came to within sight of the takeoff, the fine mist from expunging waves dusting her cheeks. What she saw through a thin haze of sea fog terrified her: a thick lip creating a square-shaped barrel, just moments after cresting; ugly boils at what she assumed was the drop that extended down the face. When the wave curled shut; a stream of forceful spit shot from its underbelly like a geyser. She smoothed the deck of the board Alex had insisted upon, hoping that it would serve her well in such terrorizing speed and stabilize her in the brutal surface chop Alex's notes had warned of. The extra length would provide the necessary velocity to launch into these giants, and the long, straight rocker would supposedly give her better control, better momentum.

The water beneath her had changed: bits of pulverized seaweed and mounds of tan-colored foam were piled like soap scum, rising air pockets made rings of white as the oxygen rejoined the atmosphere. A deepening fear gripped her spine like a vice, turning it into an immovable rod, making her feel stiff and tense. But still she pressed on. She would trace the hand of her mother's memories. She would push into this unknown. There was no alternative.

Lorna didn't pause before entering the take-off zone; her mind was focused. Sets steamed in regularly and broke with bone-breaking force two hundred yards from her position. She steered carefully, thinking only of one stroke, then the next, and of the hints and warnings from Alex's notes: *stay forward on the board, use the rail as your rocker—position your feet inside the stringer, stay low, open your shoulders and keep your body falling with the board. Be ready for the chandeliers inside the tube and the exploding mist hitting you in the back.* She was aware of the sound of her own breaths, of the big board cutting through the busy, chattering surface chop, of the pounding, relentless sound of the wave, like bombs dropping out of the sky.

Lorna could see no landmarks to use for lining up. The distant boat rocked in the deep water; somewhere below her the submerged rock shelf waited. A strong current sucked her towards the deep water, forcing her to paddle almost constantly to stay in one place. She had drifted too far inside when a new set of black ridges appeared on the horizon. They seemed to gain speed as they felt the steeply rising seabed.

The first wave stood up outside of her, and it was at least ten feet bigger than what Lorna had expected. Lorna pulled hard through the water for the outside, feeling every fiber and sinew acting to propel her in perfect synchronicity. When she reached the crest, paddling over a wave of such size created a new feeling in the pit of her stomach. What would it be like to ride something so massive, so raw and potent, so wild? And what would happen if she got caught inside? She paddled over two more waves, each one cresting with an eerie, banshee-like *whooosh* as she scratched over the frothy, thick lip, a sound like high-pitched wind, the kind you hear on a mountain top in a windstorm. She could feel each wave's explosion in her teeth, its eruption shooting icy shards of mist into her flesh.

Breathless but undeterred, she sat up and wiped her eyes clear. She was ready.

She seemed to wait a long time for another set, during which she stayed busy paddling and popping up to scan the horizon, her gut turning itself inside out. She began to wonder if the swell could be already fading when a distant blue-black line lifted itself off the ocean, as if it were being pulled from the heavens by some great hand. Although she could not see other ripples behind it, she knew they were there.

The line spread, thickened, seemed to race forward. Lorna checked the ocean all around her, searching for some form of assurance that she was in the right place, but there was only the foam and the hiss of fizzing bubbles escaping, the roar of spent waves progressing, the crumbled wall of foam fading back into the depths, and the wind.

*Not this one*, she told herself as she paddled for the outside. The thinning ridge of sapphire-blue water lifted higher still, drawing Lorna's eyes upward. She stroked hard over the meaty lip, sneaking a glance at the long drop she was leaving behind. As she cleared the crest and shook the mist clear of her eyes, the next wave already loomed, thick and fast and still building, the face of it rippled with wind, its lip a lacey blue-white. She knew it in her bones. This was the one. She turned and stroked hard, grabbing the thick, swift-moving water. The wave began to lift her, up, up; the wind cooled her face as she fought with every stroke to gain entry. She saw the distant boat and the acres of bright-white, churned-up foam. Her board began to pick up speed. *Now.*

Everything seemed to happen slowly, her arms pushing against the board, her spine tucking beneath her, and her feet connecting to the deck just inside of the stringer, her hips squaring to the line her eyes had locked onto, her fingers gripping the outside rail. She heard as much as felt the lip collapse behind her, the explosion blasting her ears. As she flew straight down, she dared not look back.

Her board chattered over the bumps and boils as the wave began to arch over her. Her legs began to burn from holding the tight line until finally the water smoothed. She executed a careful turn, her heart pounding against her chest, and then she was flying, gliding, racing forward, as if she were somehow soaring on air. She thought of the flying fish in the tropics bursting from the water with fairylike wings, seeming almost to hover as much as fly, their golden scales flashing in the sun before diving beneath surface again. The image of herself as some kind of flying creature took hold, and she began to relax, opening her shoulders, steadying her breathing as the tunnel closed in around her. She knew there was nothing in the world like this feeling of freedom and letting go. She risked looking up and was shocked to see the roof arching so high above her. Daggers of water peeled off to spear her head and shoulders as the tube spun like a centrifuge. The colors swirled over her, and the thunderous crush of cascading water lost their terror. In that release of her fear, she felt the elation, the joy, of what was happening.

The ceiling pulled back, and she shot from the tube into brightness, the spray from the wave's imploding innards blasting her like a fire hose. Blinded, she aimed high and flew over the top where her momentum sent her skimming across the choppy surface on the back of the wave. She flipped to her belly and paddled like mad to clear the impact zone.

As she skirted the following wave, stroking hard over its quickly peaking shoulder, she looked into the spinning tube and was shocked to see the depth of its cavern. And then it was gone and behind her, spewing and thundering, leaving her with a sense of wonder, disbelief, and shaky with the realization of her triumph.

# THIRTY-NINE

Pacific Ocean

Lorna pulled tired strokes towards the boat. Every muscle felt spent, but her heart felt light and free. The clouds had morphed into thick bumpy mounds, like a shaken jar of oil and water. It was beautiful, but in a way that made her uneasy. She was glad to be leaving.

Her mind returned to the waves she had ridden. The image of her board shooting down the wave's dark tunnel was like a stamp on her retina that she never wanted to forget. Her body felt alive and her mind clear. As the buzz faded, she was left with a sense of calm, and relief. She had done it.

If only Alex had experienced it, too. Seeing her ride Las Muelas would be incredible. But Lorna knew that would never happen. As she neared the boat, she pushed the sadness away. They had been here together; it was enough. Lorna pulled up to the ladder at the stern and climbed aboard.

"Alex?" she called out. She felt giddy, as if buzzing from some fantastic drug. "Mom?" The boat was quiet. She realized that Alex was probably resting. Shivering in the brisk wind, Lorna quickly shed her wetsuit and poured a jug of fresh water over her head, rinsing her face and hand-combing the salt from her hair. A roll of swell lifted the boat, unsettling her balance for a moment. In a hurry, she scrubbed herself dry with a towel, pulled on her board shorts and a sweatshirt, and stepped through the sliding glass door. Once inside, she froze.

Something was terribly wrong.

"Alex?" she cried out in panic. The inside of the boat looked like it had been hit by a tornado. Had a rogue wave jostled it? She moved to the galley where everything that had once been in a drawer or shelf was on the floor. A chill ran down her spine. "Alex?" she said, but it came out as a whisper.

"She's dead," a voice said from above.

Garth appeared, dressed in a black wetsuit. He was holding the binoculars and Alex's journal.

Lorna's mind raced. Alex? Dead? *No, no, no!* As if a switch was flipped, Lorna's shock turned to rage and she raced at him. "What did you do to her?" she cried, unleashing her fury, swinging her fists at him, punching, scratching.

"I didn't do anything!" he huffed, dodging her blows, grabbing her wrists, twisting.

She cried out as they struggled. She kicked him and as they toppled sideways, Lorna's head smashed into the wall. A hot pain erupted in her left ear, followed by a wave of nausea. Lorna forced her eyes to focus through the pain as she attacked him again. Garth wrapped her in a bear hug, and she struggled to escape but her tired muscles failed her. They were both breathing hard.

"She barely made it onto the boat!" he said. "I got her to the bed."

Slowly, Lorna stopped resisting. Her brain struggled to grasp what was happening.

"I could have gone out a lot sooner, but I waited," he said.

A part of her brain understood what Garth was telling her, but it was so hard to make sense of it through her throbbing head. *Alex,* she thought.

"I'm sorry, love," he said, loosening his hold on her. His voice sounded funny coming through only one ear.

"No," she sobbed into his chest. Garth held her in his strong arms as the boat rolled with the swells.

"I didn't want it to be this way, either," he said as she cried.

A long moment passed before he broke away. "Give me an hour, okay?"

She stared at him, confused.

"I have to do this," he said. His eyes shone with excitement. "You of all people should understand that."

As if in a dream, Lorna watched Garth walk to the back of the boat. He was leaving? He slid a board from behind a storage box, the tip of which was mounted with a camera. And then he was gone.

Lorna blinked, and he was gone from her thoughts as well.

Alex.

Lorna hurried to the stateroom. She wasn't dead. *Please no.* Outside Alex's door, she paused and tried to control her breaths. Why did they sound so loud? With trembling fingers she gripped the doorknob, but her fingers wouldn't turn it. A surge of sadness welled up inside her, and a sob burst from her lungs. She leaned her forehead on the door as the tears rolled off her cheeks. Finally, she opened the door.

Alex lay on the bed, her eyes closed. "Alex?" Lorna said softly. Alex's eyelids were a soft shade of lavender, like petals. Lorna smoothed the hair on Alex's forehead. Lorna had seen death so many times. It wasn't like it was in the movies, peaceful and with soft lighting. It was cold, and ugly. Lorna climbed into the bed beside Alex. The sound of her own blood rushing in her ears pulled the walls inward, made her want to scream. She put her arm around Alex's chest and stroked her cheek. She was still warm.

Later, when she would relive it, she would blame her vocation. She would say it was instinct; that her fingers had acted on their own accord when they slipped into the groove beneath Alex's jawline.

The first tap of Alex's pulse was so slight Lorna wondered if she'd imagined it. She adjusted the pressure slightly and waited again. "Alex," she urged, her heart bounding. "Can you hear me?" A feeling of hope shot through her. "Mom?" she tried again, ignoring the strange ringing in her ear. She sat up and shook Alex's shoulder. "Alex!" she said, louder. "Open your eyes!" Alex did not respond. "Can you squeeze my hand?" she said. Nothing. Lorna pinched the back of Alex's arm.

Alex moaned.

Lorna's heart leapt. Alex was alive.

Lorna's mind raced—there were no tools onboard to help Alex. *She needs oxygen, IV meds.* Lorna had to get her to a hospital. There were things they could do for her; she could still open her eyes. *Just one last time.* Once they returned to Río Limón, Lorna wondered if the pasture near the highway could double as a landing pad for a chopper. She raced to the main bridge to start the engines.

The acres of whitewater exploding on the horizon stared back at her, and she remembered: Garth was still out there.

# FORTY

Pacific Ocean

Lorna sighted through the binoculars again, telling herself to scan more slowly. She started at where the wave broke and moved toward the takeoff. The waves were closing out in massive explosions of whitewater, and the ocean was a deep blue-black.

"Where are you?" she whispered, her fingers gripping the barrels. She looked up and searched with her naked eye, squinting for a black dot. Ridges of wind chop stippled the dark water, and the strange clouds now had dark gray bellies slashed by blue stripes of vapor. The altered light made it appear much later than midday.

"Come on!" she said, her voice shaky as she raised the lenses again. She scanned the inside section's angry froth of whitewater. No sign of Garth there. Where the hell was he? She abandoned the binoculars on the bridge and slid down the ladder. In the stateroom, Alex's eyes were still closed.

"Alex?" Lorna said. She felt her pulse: still weak. "Alex!" Lorna said. "Open your eyes!" Lorna placed her cheek near Alex's face until she felt the puff of her breath. Lorna needed to leave, now.

*I need to do this*, Garth had said.

Again the cold ladder rungs were in her hands and cutting into her tired feet. She lifted the pair of heavy binoculars to her eyes again. How much longer could she stay out here? Lorna hadn't marked the time, but Garth's hour was certainly up. Alex couldn't wait any longer. "Where are you?" she begged, her words echoing inside the bridge. She completed a grid search of each wave trough as it reared up to break, starting at the takeoff and moving down the drop to the broken wave ahead of it, then back to the crest. She worked the sequence until she had covered the entire area. Then she did it again and again. He still wasn't there. She squeezed her eyes shut, and let her arms rest against the side of the bridge. She was shaking.

*Again*, she thought. She pulled the lenses up to her eyes and this time searched outside of the take-off zone, willing Garth's body to appear. Maybe he was outside, taking a breather, or waiting for a big set. Her eyes watered from the strain, and she paused to wipe them with the cuff of her sweatshirt. If only she could get closer! She willed every inch of her eyes—the corners and edges, every single nerve cell to find him. She decided to focus on the inside section, in case he was caught there, and counted out loud. How long could a person stay under? "One . . . two . . . three . . . four . . . " Sixty seconds? Ninety? "Eleven . . . twelve . . . " *Come on, Garth*, she thought. "Twenty . . . twenty-one . . . "

Lorna remembered getting caught inside at Bukuya. She remembered the sucking wave pulling her toward itself, like a hungry lion reeling in its wounded prey. Garth had dropped in on that wave outside of her, perfectly positioned. *I just can't see him—I'm missing him somehow.* Garth was here. He was born for this.

But Las Muelas was a different beast. A fall or bad positioning here would be much different.

Lorna remembered the look of determination on his face inside Alex's apartment. *I just want a crack at it.* Then, later: *I'm not leaving here without it.*

But then he had helped Alex. He had waited patiently for her to return, for her story to play out. Lorna realized how agonizing that must have been for someone like Garth.

As she scanned the inside section slowly, she murmured, "One hundred." The counting was reassuring. "One hundred and one . . . " Lorna remembered overhearing the pro surfers in Río Limón talking about Garth's big-wave obsession, and the *Surfer* story about his plan to quit the tour to surf big waves. *I need to do this*, he'd said. Not *I want to do this.*

*I need to. s*

"One hundred forty, one hundred forty-one." Lorna had planned to give him the GPS coordinates after this trip, but Garth couldn't wait. He had stowed away on the boat in order to satisfy his need. Las Muelas would break again—in a month or maybe not for a year, but it would have been his, for a time. But he couldn't wait. He saw his opportunity and grabbed it.

*I need to do this.*

"One hundred eighty-six, one hundred eighty-seven."

Lorna lowered the binoculars. Her mind refused the thought that was shoving its way in: nobody could hold a breath for that long. She looked for him between the wave and the boat, thinking that maybe he was paddling back. Garth wasn't there. He wasn't anywhere.

Lorna slid down the ladder and entered the Alex's room. Alex's breath rattled inside her thin chest; she grimaced when Lorna pinched the back of her hand. Lorna knelt at the bedside and laid her head on Alex's chest. "Tell me what to do," she whispered.

After a long moment, Lorna wondered if she could move the boat closer. *Maybe a different view would help.* Garth would have a shorter distance to paddle. *Yes*, she thought.

Lorna hurried to the flybridge and started the engines. Her shaking fingers flipped the anchor switch. *There's no going back now,* she thought as the windlass's motor whirred. She would never be able to anchor the boat on her own in these seas. When the anchor was stowed, she drove the boat slowly towards the horizon, which was edged with a strange, dark band. While bracing her feet and body firmly in place, she stole quick glances through the binoculars at the rising and sinking jaws of Las Muelas, searching for Garth.

When the bucking swells tossed the big boat, Lorna had to abandon the binoculars, so she could hold on and steer around the edge of a huge set. Lorna's stomach felt queasy. She wondered if the scopolamine patch was wearing off. She decided to move the boat farther outside and look back at the wave.

Outside the breaker zone, Lorna idled the boat and peered through the binoculars again, scanning left to right, seeing nothing but water. The boat jacked up violently. Lorna was thrown backwards, smacking her head then rolling forward as the boat crashed down the back of the swell. Lorna knew the main bridge was more stable. But the visibility up top was better.

Lorna crawled back to the wheel, her left ear ringing. She looked at the clouds that were blackening and billowing, like something out of a doomsday painting. She watched the now-strong wind churn the ocean's surface. Her teeth chattered. She remembered Carlos's concern about the storm, and a new feeling zipped through her. *Something is wrong, and I'm scared.*

She scanned the ocean again, counting, meticulously inspecting every corner of the wave's territory, willing Garth's black form to appear. But there was only ocean. *He's not there*, a voice inside her head said.

He'd asked for an hour, and she'd given him much more than that. She'd searched and searched, but he wasn't there. She watched a frothy wave rise up and pitch. Its boom and rumble hit her ears. *Something's happened to him. He fell, he was caught inside, he got sucked over the falls, and he's . . . gone.* But the thought of leaving made her cry out in anguish. How could she leave him out here?

The weather was changing. Alex was dying. She had to go.

*I need to do this,* Garth had said.

"So do I," Lorna said out loud as a gust of wind slammed into her vinyl bubble. Her cold fingers gripped the wheel as she turned the boat around.

# FORTY-ONE

Lorna pointed the bow towards Río Limón and focused on the GPS, the horizon, and the promise of land. Anything but what she was leaving behind. Feeling scattered, she tried Carlos on the radio but there was no answer. She tried again, but still no answer. "Shit!" she said. Was the *Pearl* too far out? She rehearsed the message she would send, though she doubted it would do much good. After all, there was nothing anyone could do for her now.

Lorna checked the GPS, gas gauges, and the horizon obsessively. With the following seas threatening to break over the stern and the powerful wind roughing up the peaks and sending spray in every direction, she found driving the boat much harder. She sometimes had to pull back on the throttle in order to keep the bow from burying into a trough, and sometimes she surfed her way down the broad backs of the massive swells. She was terrified of one of them breaking on the stern or catching them broadside. At some point it began to rain.

Using the autopilot at regular intervals, Lorna checked on Alex, but her condition didn't change. Lorna craved the E.R. with its bright lights and diagnostic tools, the IV fluids, meds and specialists standing by. How hard could she push the boat in these swells?

Her tired body couldn't keep up with the boat's rolling, and there was definitely something wrong with her balance. She fell every time she left the helm: bouncing off the narrow corridor walls or knocking her head on the stateroom doorway.

Looking out at the raging dark sea, she thought of Garth dropping into Las Muelas and imagined his body getting swallowed by the blue-black maelstrom.

She began to feel detached from it all, as if she was watching herself from above. "You're fucked," she told herself. *You're going to be fucked for a long time.*

Finally, Lorna saw the first glimpse of land: a distant, dark line in the distance.

Exhausted, Lorna cried out in relief.

She planned out her next steps once they reached shore. She tried Carlos again but heard only static. Where was he? She couldn't anchor the boat safely or get Alex ashore without him.

She squinted towards the land, trying to recognize details. The rain dimpled the stormy sea's surface and streaked the windshield in jagged spears. Lorna looked behind them, taking in the charcoal gray horizon and thick black clouds. Lorna shuddered at the idea of waiting any longer to leave Las Muelas. This was no average storm. Slowly, the land began to take shape, its rolling hills and soft, distant peaks emerging before her eyes. She engaged the autopilot and hurried to check on Alex.

"We did it, Alex!" she said, stroking Alex's forehead. "We're almost home!"

A whispery moan escaped Alex's lips.

Lorna's heart jumped into her throat. "Alex?" she cried. "Alex, can you hear me?" she said. She put her hand in Alex's. "Squeeze my hand!" she shouted.

Lorna felt the slightest pressure on her fingers.

"Alex?" Lorna said.

Alex's eyelids fluttered.

"That's it!" Lorna cried as a surge of hope filled her.

"Stop," Alex moaned, her voice barely audible above the thrumming engines.

Lorna's exploding optimism faltered. "Stop? But we're almost there," she said, caressing Alex's hand. "Carlos and I will get you to some help, okay?"

Alex's body was so still. "The boat," she whispered. "Stop."

"What?" Lorna asked, her voice panicky.

Alex squeezed her hand.

Lorna tried to resist the feeling of dread. She knew what was happening, but she resisted. Lorna waited but Alex didn't continue. Her mind seemed to split into two: there was the side that needed to keep going, to follow through with her plan to get Alex to shore and on to advanced care; and there was the other side that feared that Alex was slipping away.

Lorna sat for a long moment while her heart and mind struggled to work together.

"Please," Alex mumbled.

With tears streaming down her cheeks, Lorna returned to the bridge. Through the rain she could make out the brown ridge separating the harbor from Río Limón's tiny town. They were so close.

Her fingers trembled on the ignition key. *A wave could catch us broadside. We could drift off-course, smash against the cliffs.* Lorna shut down the engines and the silence settled over her. The rain tapped and slid down the windows. Waves rocked and pushed them silently in their pulse towards shore. Lorna's limbs felt tight and coiled, stiff.

Lorna crawled into bed with Alex and held her hand. "I'm here," she said. She wondered if Alex could hear the rain and the waves against the boat. Lorna's muscles welcomed the calm, but her mind still worried about the storm, and waves breaking over them. The boat dipped forward into a wave trough.

"Mom," Lorna began, but couldn't finish. Her shoulders clenched with a series of sobs. If only she had left Las Muelas sooner!

Alex squeezed her hand.

It was too much and Lorna began to sob. She saw herself waiting for waves at Las Muelas while white spray exploded behind her. "Please," Lorna begged, kissing Alex's temple. "Don't go. Not yet," she whispered. Alex's body was so shrunken, her childlike bones rattled and clanked inside her like dry sticks. Lorna placed her cheek against Alex's, her tears blurring her vision.

Lorna wasn't sure how long she held Alex there, the boat adrift and tossing, or when Alex stopped breathing. There was the sound of an engine, then voices in Spanish. Someone tried to pull Alex from her but she resisted. There was movement, bodies over her, more voices, the sound of the *Pearl's* big engines, the feel of Alex's cool, papery flesh against hers, the smell of land.

Lorna carried Alex into a waiting panga, and they were whisked to shore, her skin instantly soaked through from the cold rain and the sea spray. Waves thundered upon the beach, and darkness seemed to creep from the edges of the sky like spilled ink. To her surprise, the boat raced right to the shore and rode a swell up high onto the beach. Men appeared from the shadows to pull the boat up farther, bantering to each other in rapid Spanish; one of them helped Lorna, still carrying Alex, to a waiting jeep. The driver drove quickly through the village and Lorna blinked in surprise at the boarded-up windows and empty streets. From the front seat, the driver shot her a nervous look, but did not say anything.

Lorna saw a stout figure running toward them and her anxiety doubled: Carlos. He threw open the door, his eyes quickly turning from relief to confusion when he saw the bundle in her arms. Lorna could only watch.

The driver spoke sharply to Carlos. Carlos didn't reply, his face blank. His eyes met Lorna's.

"It's all my fault," Lorna said, her lip quavering.

Carlos stood in front of her and watched Alex's face for a long time, his fingertips sweeping across her hairline.

"She . . . " Lorna began but stopped.

Carlos leaned forward and embraced Lorna, their cheeks touching. He kissed her forehead then lifted Alex into his arms.

Lorna wanted to protest, to tell him so many things. Carlos took Alex's lifeless body from Lorna and walked away. The driver rolled the passenger window down and yelled something after him.

Carlos gave a sharp toss of his head in the direction of the highway. "*Váyanse!*" he barked.

Lorna knew that tone. It was an order. But to do what, Lorna didn't know. *Take her to jail? Leave without me?* As rain drummed on the roof, the driver paused and then glared at Lorna with bloodshot eyes. He muttered something and put the jeep in gear. They sped up the hill, and Lorna turned to watch Carlos disappear with Alex into the rain.

# FORTY-TWO

October 2004

Santa Cruz, California

Joe pretended to inspect the rack of surfboards propped against the back wall while Marty finished up at the register.

"When's he going to play again?" he heard the kid behind the counter quietly ask Marty.

Joe rolled his eyes and moved away from them. When were people going to fucking get it? The gig at the Garage had been his last. He strolled past the racks of T-shirts and hoodies and stopped cold in front of a table stacked with green trucker hats.

Joe heard the cash register close, and soon Marty was at his side holding his new leash. "Thanks, man," he said. "We can go . . . "

But Marty stopped mid-sentence when his gaze caught on what Joe was fingering. A hat printed with the message "Help Find Garth."

"What the . . . ?" Marty said, picking one up. "Garth Towner?" He looked at Joe. "Since when did he get lost?"

Joe walked to the counter with one of the hats. "What's this all about?" he asked the skinny kid.

"Dude, it's like, some kind of scandal or something," the kid sputtered, sounding nervous, or maybe he was tweaking or something, Joe wasn't sure. "His fiancée and his family are trying to raise some cash for a detective."

Joe raised an eyebrow at Marty. "Fiancée?" he mouthed.

"Scandal?" Marty mouthed back with a sarcastic twitch in his lips.

"So where was he last?" Joe asked the kid.

"Mex, man," the kid replied. "I think the hurricane got him."

"What hurricane?" Marty and Joe said in unison.

"That one that made the news last month," the kid stammered. "Heavy."

Joe hadn't watched the news in years. Where had Garth said he was going after Fiji? Joe only remembered him gloating about being on a podium. "Where in Mexico?" he asked, his thoughts stirring.

"Uh, south of Nexpa somewhere. You can look it up. They've got a website." The kid pointed to the small print on the back of the hat: www.helpfindGarth.org.

"I thought we were going surfing!" Marty protested as they pulled out of the parking lot.

"We will," Joe replied, speeding towards Marty's house.

Joe pecked in the website address, and the page loaded, showing a photo of Garth inside a massive barrel. A bunch of text followed.

Joe scanned it, waiting for the pieces to fall into place. Garth disappeared in Mexico . . . how? *People don't disappear.* The kid had said "south of Nexpa." Rio Nexpa was a well-known surf spot on the Michoacán coast.

. . . rumored to have visited the region where the storm destroyed a section of coastline in Michoacán, Mexico on August 16th.

Marty scrolled down to a map with arrows indicating the region.

. . . the storm also claimed the lives of seven residents, destroyed homes, caused severe flooding, and was responsible for over millions of dollars in damages.

"I remember that hurricane now," said Marty. "It was headed for Puerto but then beelined for Baja and thrashed everything on its way."

Joe was thinking back to that day in Fiji when they had all surfed Bukuya. Garth had nailed that big set, timing it perfectly. That shot had made it into the mag: he and Marty had seen it. So had Garth gone to this remote section of coastline to surf big waves? He remembered Garth telling Lorna about Alex's surf tours business. Michoacán sounded familiar, but that didn't mean much. He could have read about it in a magazine or heard about it in passing.

"I wonder . . . " he said, lost in thought.

"Huh?" Marty said.

"Nothing," Joe mumbled, scanning the rest of the story alongside Marty.

They reached the end. "It's been two months since anyone's seen him?" Marty huffed. "He's dead." Marty stood. "Let's go surfing."

Joe leaned against the upper deck railing of the half-built beach house, listening to the distant waves tumble onto the sand. The rest of the crew had left for the day. He was proud of the work he had put into the place. The extra details and design would make it a home of distinction, but he wondered if anyone would notice or care. Since the break with Francine, his work hadn't felt as satisfying. He wondered if that easy joy would return, or if this was just one more thing she had taken from him. He had been toying with the idea of quitting the construction business altogether, at least for a while. Maybe he would join the Peace Corps. Maybe he would go back to Fiji and record the music he had fallen in love with. That day in the Fijian village was never far from his thoughts. Those people had so little, yet they were filled with such joy and generosity. Why couldn't the rest of the world live that way? Maybe he would go build houses in places like that. Marty suggested he start his own Habitat for Humanity. Whatever it was, he wanted to do something worthwhile. Something other than helping rich people get richer.

Garth's disappearance was fading from the headlines. It spooked him, having surfed with a guy only a few months ago who was now probably dead. His backstory had been splayed across the latest issue of *Surfer*; he had dropped out of the tour to explore the coast of Michoacán. No one had seen or heard from him since the hurricane.

An idea had echoed inside his head for weeks. Lorna had said that Garth and Alex had surfed together in Mexico. Hadn't Lorna said it was in Michoacán somewhere? He wondered if he should try to contact Alex's surf tours company. *Forget it*, he thought. *It's none of my business.*

But he couldn't help wondering about Lorna—had she gone to Mexico after all? He tried to imagine her there with her sick mother, and Garth stirring things up. He couldn't shake the feeling that something had happened. Something bad.

*If only I knew she was okay.*

# FORTY-THREE

November 2004

Quezon Province, Philippines

Lorna felt Garth's arms around her; she could smell the neoprene and the sweat on his neck. They breathed together, and slowly she gave in to the strength of his embrace. "I have to do this," he said. In slow motion, Lorna watched Garth turn away and walk to the back of the boat.

Lorna woke to someone nudging her and blinked across the tiny plane at Simon, her Global Relief Corps coworker.

"You were screaming again," he said over the plane's whine.

Lorna looked out the window at the falling dusk and pushed away the last of the dream.

Simon settled back into his music-induced coma against the window, his headphones no doubt blaring reggae, or Beastie Boys, or something he called "downbeat lounge."

Lorna hugged her pack, the one stolen from her in Río Limón and returned by Becca at the makeshift shelter—the church in some little town she never learned the name of—during the hurricane.

"I only had time to get a few things," Becca had said while cradling a sleeping Sophie. Seth had shepherded the surf guests out of the country and would be stuck at the airport until the roads stopped flooding.

Inside the backpack, Lorna had found the clothes Becca loaned her as well as her Lonely Planet guidebook. The drugs and her clothing were still missing, but the hidden pocket along the back panel still held the emergency cash she had stowed and her passport. There was something else inside: the picture of Alex holding baby Fie. She removed the picture and gazed at it. Alex looked so . . . content. She wanted to keep it but knew she couldn't.

Lorna thrust the picture at Becca. "You should keep this," she said, swatting away a tear.

Becca had laid Sophie down on a cot, and Lorna noticed the dirty soles of her feet, as if she had been plucked from a sunny playground mid-stride.

"Why?" Becca asked, looking puzzled.

Lorna looked at the picture again and allowed herself to see what she hadn't before. *It's me.* Her breath caught in her throat. Of course, she thought. Alex looked too young for it to be a recent picture, and something about the style of her shirt seemed dated. The happiness on Alex's face as she gazed at the baby, *her* baby, gave Lorna goose bumps.

Alex had been in her arms only hours ago. Where had Carlos taken her? Lorna was suddenly afraid he would join them at the church. He would want answers—ones she couldn't give. A sob burst from her lips; Lorna slapped her hand over her mouth.

"Did something happen?" Becca said, her eyes wide and compassionate.

Lorna tried to take a deep breath but it lodged in her throat. How would she survive this?

Then Sophie woke up, frightened, and Becca lay down with her, speaking in hushed tones and rubbing her back. Lorna left them, afraid she would upset Sophie further.

More people streamed into the shelter, some badly wounded. Lorna couldn't stop herself from doing what came naturally. It happened without her even thinking about it. Supplies were limited, but Lorna knew how to make do. The work came as a welcome distraction. She had something to offer, and it kept her from thinking too much. The next morning, Lorna had been in the midst of creating a makeshift sling, when Dr. Kim Zeigler from Global Relief Corps and her team of six entered the church and took control. Dr. Zeigler took one look at Lorna's work and offered her a job.

*Yes*, Lorna had thought. *Take me away from this.*

The plane touched down with a jolt and decelerated hard. Lorna glanced through the tiny window at the few buildings flanking the runway and the empty, dark land beyond. There were no signs of the destroyed houses, suffering, and mayhem awaiting them just a bus ride away.

After months of dropping into disaster zones by plane, bus, and once a limousine, Lorna had grown used to the drill: establish (or create) a facility, set up supplies, open the doors, and start the triage process. Now they would start from ground zero again, staying until reinforcements arrived, sleeping on bare floors, working into exhaustion, exposing themselves to countless diseases and horrors, eating whatever was offered. In another time, Lorna might have loved it. The work was challenging and rewarding, yet there were times when she felt like she was losing her mind. She couldn't sleep, despite feeling perpetually exhausted; she couldn't eat. Her left eardrum, though better, still buzzed at times, causing her to miss instructions. Her fingers trembled at strange moments; she had nightmares when she was wide-awake. She once miscalculated a dose of medication for a child, and had she not realized her mistake at the last minute, she would have killed him. Another time she drew a complete blank in the middle of suturing a woman's foot.

And she couldn't stop looking over her shoulder.

When would they come for her?

# FORTY-FOUR

January 2005
Santa Cruz, California

At first, Joe didn't hear the phone ringing because he was playing guitar on his back porch. Since Francine, his music had an edge to it, and sometimes led him down dark roads where everything around him disappeared, sometimes for hours at a time. He had not talked to her and didn't want to. He would probably get around to forgiving her someday, but he wasn't there yet. There was a hole in his life now, and he felt different. He certainly had less tolerance for bullshit, so when the stranger on the other line identified himself as Roger Bowker, he replied, "I don't want any" and hung up.

The phone rang again. Joe stared at the phone. "Hello?" he sighed into the phone.

"I'm not selling anything," Roger Bowker's voice said, his tone neutral, not unpleasant.

"Okay," Joe said. He looked around his tiny cottage, remembering that he hadn't eaten dinner. He opened the fridge and leaned in, inspecting the bare contents.

"I'm investigating Garth Townsend's disappearance. Could you answer a few questions?"

The cool air from the fridge prickled his skin. He closed it. "Sure," he said, noting the quaver in his voice.

"You know he's been missing since last August."

Joe remembered the boat rides, the partying, and the way Garth had hogged his share of waves. "Yeah, I was sorry to hear about that," Joe replied, realizing that he meant it.

"I understand you were in Fiji at the same time as Garth."

"That's right," Joe said. He thought suddenly of Lorna. Had Roger Bowker called her, too?

"Did he say anything to you about his plans?"

"Not really," Joe stammered. "I mean, he bragged about winning his next contest, or something like that."

Roger Bowker paused, and Joe wondered if he was writing something down. "Did he talk about going to Mexico?"

Joe didn't know if he should say what Lorna had told him—that Garth knew where Alex was. "No," Joe answered, because it was true. Garth hadn't told him anything about Mexico. "He and I didn't really . . . talk," Joe added. He wanted to say that Garth had been sort of a prick at times, and cocky, but it didn't feel right.

"I'm also looking for another surfer who was there, Lorna Jacobs."

Joe's gut did an elevator drop to his knees.

"I understand you two had a relationship."

Joe's skin flushed with heat. "Uh," he stammered. *I'm not talking about this with you*, he wanted to say.

"She was in Río Limón at the same time as Garth, staying at the same hotel."

Joe froze.

"Her mother has a surf tour business there," Roger Bowker added.

In a flash, it all came together. He remembered Lorna telling him about Río Limón in Fiji. So Garth *had* gone back, and Lorna had been there, too. "Right," he managed to say.

"Do you know how I can reach her?" Roger Bowker asked. His voice was casual, but Joe could hear the strain behind it. As if Roger Bowker was hiding his eagerness.

"No."

"When did she last contact you?"

His heart pounded against his rib cage. "She hasn't," he said, which was hard to hear with the blood slamming into his ears.

Roger Bowker paused. "If she does, will you please ask her to get in touch with me? Here's my one-eight hundred number."

Joe copied down the number on an unpaid bill envelope and hung up.

Reeling, Joe stumbled outside. He blinked at the tiny houses, the people walking to the cliff to check the surf, the cars rolling by, and finally came to rest on his front stoop.

Something *had* happened in Río Limón during the hurricane, and Lorna was in trouble.

It was time to get in the game.

# FORTY-FIVE

February 2005

Sumatra, Indonesia

Lorna woke to the piercing cry of a rooster and the smell of rotting fish wafting through her window. She blinked at the dimly lit room and listened to her roommates' snoring. She had been dreaming about the boat again, about Garth.

She wiped sweat off her forehead with her T-shirt and pushed aside the mosquito net tent draped over her cot. After shaking out her boots to remove any unwelcome guests, she dry-brushed her teeth, slapped on a layer of mosquito repellent, and made her way slowly down the dark street.

The road grew muddier and increasingly blocked with debris: boats, bent metal, shredded plywood, bricks, snagged clothing crusted with dried mud. She passed three men digging in a field next to a pile of stiff and bloated bodies. She wondered if they were burying any of the patients she had failed to save. Near a pile of garbage, a sickly-looking cat chewed on some unidentified scrap of sinew.

As she approached the hotel that had become their triage center, the cries and moans of the wounded, waiting to be seen, drifted over the piles of wreckage and ravaged streets. The stench of death and rot filled her nostrils, and she began to breathe through her mouth. After suiting up and filling her pockets with gloves, she moved to the far side of the building and prepped for her day of death. When breakfast arrived, Lorna ate standing up in the storage room, rolling her neck from side to side while she chewed the rice and mystery meat mixed with spice, then burned her tongue on her tea as she tried to force it down with the food. After a long glug of chlorinated water from her water bottle, she returned to her station and greeted her first patient. Since the Indian Ocean tsunami had hit, the wave of patients had been constant, draining the last of Global Relief Corps' funding. Soon, Global Relief Corps would disperse. Zeeg would return to the States where she would pull per-diem shifts in her small town's E.R. by day and pursue grant money and donations by night. The rest of the crew would return to their jobs or resume their retired lives, until Global Relief Corp could start up again.

Lorna did not know where she would go. Back to her residency? The idea seemed foreign, like it belonged to another person.

During her residency in the E.R., patients had died all the time—in the first five minutes, after an hour-long struggle, in surgery, or in ICU. Death was just part of the job that she had grown to accept. But here, where entire families who had seen so much suffering waited just outside, accepting death didn't come easy. *I should be able to save them*, she thought. *To give some small bit of hope.* But she was failing. *Just like I failed Garth and Alex.*

When she was really sleep deprived, she saw Garth drowning, calling for help. And then there was Alex, who was waiting for her every time she closed her eyes. Sometimes Lorna would remember what Alex had said to her in the water that last day, but it didn't diminish the nightmares. She still woke up screaming. The picture of Alex holding Lorna as a baby went with her everywhere, but the connection she had felt at Las Muelas was fading every day.

She remembered the moment aboard the *Pearl Shadow* when she had watched herself from above: *You're going to be fucked for a long time.* Nothing had changed. Nothing *would* change. She would go on failing to save the people she loved.

The room became a blur and she found herself sobbing. There was a hand on her shoulder, but she pushed it away and stumbled out of the room.

Zeeg found Lorna in a crumpled heap next to the army jeep that had been out of gas for days.

"Everyone has hard days," Zeeg said. "Go get some sleep."

Lorna shook her head. "I can't."

"Maybe it's time you had a break."

Lorna gave a little laugh, which caught in her throat. She wiped her eyes.

"Some people use this job as an escape," Zeeg said. "But things have a way of catching up to you. Even here," she gestured to the ravaged landscape.

Lorna wondered if Zeeg knew about Garth or Alex. She let out a long, shaky breath.

"Both of my parents died in the Northridge earthquake," Zeeg said. Lorna looked into Zeeg's soft, sad eyes. "Don't make the same mistake I did and think you can outrun it."

Zeeg turned to go when Lorna stopped her. "How did you survive it?" she asked in a shaky voice.

Zeeg paused. "I had to grieve, to experience the pain. It's hard, but it'll kill you if you don't."

Lorna knew right away what Zeeg meant, and it terrified her.

She needed to return to Río Limón.

# FORTY-SIX

April 2005
Río Limón, Mexico

Lorna paused at the top of the gravel road, watching the two horses graze. She could smell the sea on the onshore breeze. The foal was bigger than the last time she had walked down this road, and he no longer clung to his mother's side. Lorna urged her feet to continue down the hill to Río Limón, but they refused. A wave of fear rumbled through her.

Finally, Lorna left the pasture and continued down the hill, feeling out of place while the chickens pecked at the dirt and women in faded aprons swept their sidewalks. Marks of the hurricane were everywhere. Water lines stained the sides of the buildings, and golden sand had been deposited in ridges along the curb and in thin sheets over the flattened weeds. The Mini Super's roof looked like it had partly caved in or been torn off. Two workers were pounding away at a replacement as she snuck past, while avoiding eye contact with a wrinkled woman in plastic shower shoes.

Ricardo's restaurant was simply gone: only coarse sand and the concrete kitchen island remained. Lorna remembered Ricardo's joyful singing, his fresh tortillas, and the café con leche she had grown to love. Likewise, the surf tours office building was gutted; the doors missing, windows smashed, the inside filled with sand and debris. Lorna took a deep breath and stepped onto the beach. The cerulean bay sparkled in the sunshine. In a flash, Lorna pictured Alex heading down for a swim. Her strength faltered, and Lorna felt another wave of pain building. Lorna saw herself with Alex that first day, surfing in the rain. She closed her eyes, but the tears came, burning her eyes. She crumpled into the soft sand and cried, gasping for breath as the hurt behind her eyes thudded against her skull. She gripped the hot sand, and the grains bit into her skin, crowded into her nails. Her body heaved and shuddered; it seemed the tears would never stop.

She was not sure how long she stayed there in the shade of the palm tree, but the wind had faded, filling the air with the scent of honey blossoms. The thud of hammers hitting wood seemed to sound from several places in town. She could hear the workers on the roof of the Mini Super chatter and laugh. Occasionally she heard other voices, broken by the grind of a saw.

Outside the Hotel Las Olas entrance, a pile of bent rebar and chunks of concrete, palm fronds, the wheel from a car body, its tire flat and cracked, a rusted metal bed frame, and two stained mattresses were piled precariously. Lorna took a shaky breath and stepped over the threshold, the metal gate squeaking on its hinges. She remembered the nights Carlos had come for her here, the two of them rushing across the sand in the dark.

Lorna stepped inside the hotel's shaded entrance. "Hello?" she whispered into the darkness. A thin layer of sand scraped noisily beneath her sneakers. She passed the office, which was bare. No desk, no bookshelf, no paintings on the walls. The tiny courtyard held only a large mound of sand piled in the center. Something was different about the outdoor shower though. It was lined with hand-painted colorful tiles, the kind she had seen in shop windows in bigger cities. This proof that they were staying filled Lorna with relief.

Voices drifted down from above. Lorna shrank into the shadows, her pulse racing. She looked up, relieved to see the roof intact. The doors on the rooms were open. Suddenly a figure moved down the walkway, pushing something. A broom. Then the air filled with golden sand, falling into Lorna's mouth, her hair, her nose. She ran down the corridor, sputtering.

The sand stung her eyes and she blinked and coughed. She ran for the exit, but a hand on her arm stopped her.

"Lorna?" Joe's bewildered voice muttered as she turned to face him.

She stared at him, a rush of emotions crowding into her brain. "What are you doing here?" she finally asked, unable to check her aggressive tone.

Joe's face looked pinched. "I'm sorry, I . . . "

Lorna released a shaky breath, and sized him up, slower this time. His eyes were still the same sparkly blue, but there was something different in them—a sharpness. It knocked something loose in her, a restless, bold feeling that she didn't recognize.

"I wanted to see if you were okay," Joe said, sighing. He was still staring at her in that intense way.

"Oh," Lorna said, crossing her arms. He came all this way, to Río Limón, to see if she was okay? Now he cares? Now he shows up?

"I was a jerk, before," he said in a rush, his jaw a hard line. "I never meant . . . it was just hard for me. . . "

*And it was a real cakewalk for me*, Lorna thought as the heartache came rushing back, her pulse thronging into her temples. Another wave of the restless feeling shivered through her.

Joe sighed. "I never thought you'd come back, or anything. I just came because . . . "

"Is that you, Lorna?" another voice called from the depths of the hotel.

Lorna watched Seth approach, wearing a tool belt. He stowed a large hammer in one of the loops and scooped up Lorna in a tight, long hug.

Seth's embrace caught her by surprise. Zeeg had been the only person to hug her for a long time, and that had only been when they had said goodbye. Lorna hadn't known how she would be received in Río Limón. In her mind, she was to blame for everything, even the storm.

"Who's that?" another voice called out from the entryway.

Lorna turned to see Fie running toward them, followed by Becca who was loaded down with bags and a large box.

Fie ran into Seth's arms, and Joe took Becca's load and disappeared into the back of the hotel.

"Lorna!" Becca cried, and again Lorna found herself squeezed in a warm, long embrace. "I'm so glad you're here!" Her eyes sparkled with such genuine appreciation that Lorna had to look away.

"I've brought lunch," Becca said.

"Mama made cookies," Fie said as Seth carried her towards the kitchen.

The kitchen was partly rebuilt. As Becca assembled the lunch, Joe and Seth were talking about the project. Had Joe been here, helping Seth? It made her feel disoriented. While she was running away from her problems, Joe was here, helping her friends rebuild their lives? Why?

"Nobody knew where you went after the storm," Becca said as they sat down. "One minute you were bandaging someone up and the next you were gone. We wondered if you'd gone back to the States."

Fie was sitting on Seth's lap, munching a green bell pepper whole, like an apple, from one hand, and wielding a chunk of cheese in the other. "But we never heard from you," he said, not looking at her.

Lorna lowered her head in shame. "I'm sorry," she said quickly. "It all sort of happened so fast."

"I'm sorry about Alex," Becca said, covering Lorna's hand with hers.

Lorna took a long breath. She hadn't talked about what happened with anyone. Now that she was here, all of her memories, of watching over Alex, of working with Becca and Seth to run the business, of surfing with the guests, fetching the boat from Morelia, were refocusing in her mind with a sharpness that took her breath away. "Thank you," she said in what sounded like a gasp. Lorna snuck a glance at Joe, who was watching her. How much did he know?

"So you're rebuilding," Lorna said, refocusing on her food, which was a crispy lettuce salad with chicken and beans and peppers and pumpkin seeds. The dressing was citrusy and tangy and the flavors were exploding in her mouth—she hadn't eaten anything this good in months.

Becca grinned. "This is home." She eyed Joe. "And we've had some great help."

Joe gave a little nod.

Lorna let her eyes linger on him a little longer. "So . . . how long have you been here?"

"A few weeks," he replied.

"We'd only just returned when he showed up," Becca added. "Usually, we're closed from about mid-October to April anyways, so after the hurricane, we salvaged what we could and left for Costa Rica."

"Costa Rica?" Lorna asked, confused.

"We have a resort-management gig there every winter," Seth said. "There's not enough business here to keep us going year-round. We go home, too, visit our families, all that."

Lorna nodded and then polished off the last of her meal. She had forgotten that food could taste so good.

"I'm so glad you've come back," Becca said. "You'll always have a home here, you know," she said, her eyes filling with warmth.

Lorna felt the tears well up in her eyes, and she had the urge to push back from the table and run—run away from the feelings of fear and restlessness churning inside her gut.

"Shall we get back to work?" Seth asked after a long glug of water from a Gatorade bottle. He lifted Fie from his lap and set her gently on her feet.

Joe pushed back from the table. "I'll cut those tiles," he said to Seth, who nodded.

Lorna stood up. "Uh, I can . . . " She looked at Becca.

"Help me clean up, and unload the other boxes."

Relieved to be put to work, Lorna cleared the dishes as Joe and Seth climbed up the spiral staircase. A moment later, the loud buzz of a saw came from the upstairs.

Becca eyed her. "I never would have thought someone like that would drop out of the sky and help us."

It took Lorna a moment to realize that "someone like that" meant "someone famous." She shook her head. It was all so weird. "He's . . . " She wanted to give some sort of value statement, like "he's great" or "he's a good friend" but she couldn't. She didn't really know him. She had thought she did, and then he had walked out on her. *But he's here now.* Her head began to ache.

"Are you okay?" Becca asked, watching Lorna rub her forehead.

*No, I'm pretty much not okay.* "I'm just tired," Lorna said.

"So where *have* you been?" Becca said as she rinsed the plates and silverware.

"Sort of everywhere. Remember that crew that came to the shelter?"

Becca nodded.

"I went to work for them."

"As a doctor," Becca murmured.

"Yeah, sort of. I mean, I'm not really a doctor yet, but Dr. Zeigler, that's my boss, was able to let me practice under her supervision." Lorna had paid for it, of course. She had been surprised to find out that the other doctors who volunteered with Global Relief Corps paid for their experience, too. Most of them were retired and used their experience with GRC to keep certified.

Lorna still wasn't sure where she would go to complete her final year of residency. Returning to the U.W. seemed like a step in the wrong direction. Disaster medicine, or "International Medicine" *was* a specialty. Zeeg had told her that it was possible for Lorna's relief work to be applied toward such a program. Lorna could re-route her career to mirror Zeeg's. But that didn't feel right, either.

"That sounds dangerous," Becca said. They finished with the dishes, and Lorna followed Becca, who scooped up Fie from her coloring project on the floor, and they headed outside.

They passed under the open atrium, where they could hear Joe and Seth working.

"Joe had this amazing idea for a tiled walkway up there," Becca said. "I can't wait to see it."

Joe again. Why was he here? How long was he planning on staying?

"Are there guests signed up?" Lorna asked, thinking of the summer south swells that would bring the clusters of young, wave-hogging pros. "And is Carlos still running the tour business?" Lorna could barely get out the last bit, as it brought up an image of Carlos sitting behind his computer, or snatching the van keys on his way out to make yet another airport pickup. She stopped before she got to the image of him lifting Alex from her arms.

"Yes, he's staying. And yes, the same development teams are coming in July. But there's a new group—just four guys. They're coming for a whole month."

"Huh," Lorna said, though she was not really listening. They were walking around the building, about to head to the street, when Lorna thought she saw something winking at her from the sea. She turned her head to see it more clearly, but there was only the flat, sparkling ocean, extending to the end of the world. She couldn't shake the thought that she had seen Alex, her white blonde head shining in the sun as she waited for a wave.

"Apparently, they're convinced there's a big wave here somewhere."

Lorna's breath caught in her throat. "Really?" she squeaked.

"Remember that pro, Garth? The one who went missing?" Becca looked back at Lorna, who was trying to screw her face into an expression that didn't resemble terror.

"Oh, right, you probably didn't hear about that," Becca said. "You were in Sri Lanka or Columbia or wherever."

Lorna swallowed.

"I guess there's a big wave he was looking for, offshore somewhere. Anyways, after the storm, he just disappeared."

Lorna felt like her throat was stuffed with cotton.

"It's just terrible what happened," Becca was saying, her expression grim as she opened the tailgate of a dusty blue truck. Just inside the bed was a small bicycle, with rusted handlebars and no pedals, and a helmet. She buckled the helmet onto Sophie's head and placed the bike next to her. Sophie swung a leg over the frame and was about to scoot off when Becca gave instructions in Spanish, using her finger to point at various landmarks.

"One time, she rode all the way to the harbor," Becca said, shaking her head.

Lorna wasn't sure letting a small child ride a bike in the street unsupervised was such a good idea, but accepted the box from Becca, and when they both had their load, headed back towards the hotel. "She's fine," Becca said, as if she were able to read Lorna's thoughts. "She has about seventeen surrogate aunties and uncles in this town."

Lorna rounded the corner to the sand, where she could hear small waves combing the shore. It was so peaceful and quiet, and even though the town was broken and so much had changed, it felt okay. As if it didn't matter that the storm had come. People would rebuild and start again. The sky and the ocean and the sand and the palm trees were still there. The feeling of the place—not just Alex's place, but hers, too—was still there. She realized that it did indeed feel like home.

But all of that would change once Las Muelas got discovered.

# FORTY-SEVEN

Río Limón, Mexico

Lorna worked all afternoon, either alongside Becca or taking care of Sophie, which meant reading to her in the hammock or going to the beach to look for shells. She found the little girl's company a refreshing change from the adults, who seemed to alternate between watching her and asking questions. Joe had kept to himself, and as she read to Fie or walked the tide line with her, Lorna's mind wheeled through all the things she should say or not say to him, and all the questions.

Now that he could see that she was "okay," would he leave?

Did she want him to?

They passed each other during their various duties. Each time, Lorna felt that same strange restless urge, but for what she didn't know.

"I called Carlos," Becca said as they finished scrubbing the walls and floors of the last downstairs room. They had hung new doors and curtains, rehung artwork, and washed and folded stacks of linens. Becca had insisted that Lorna stay in one of the hotel rooms for the night. Joe was staying in a rented room two blocks from the beach. Becca, Seth, and Fie would return to their apartment.

"Oh," Lorna said.

"He's in Lazaro Cardenas," Becca added. "But he'll be back in a few days. He's excited to see you."

*I'm not sure about that,* she thought, both dreading and anticipating their reunion. Would be blame her for Alex's death?

They all went for a swim in the ocean at the end of the work day,
and the feel of the cool water on her sweaty skin made her groan
with delight.

"You're welcome to come to our place for dinner," Becca said.

Lorna quickly declined. She was exhausted, and felt as if she had
imposed on the couple enough for one day. There were a few energy
bars and bananas in her backpack, and a full bottle of water.

Joe declined the dinner invitation as well, and soon the two of
them were alone in the water.

"There's good *carne asada* up the street," Joe said.

Lorna hesitated. But the scent of delicious cooking had wafted
down to the beach all afternoon, working her appetite into a frenzy.

"C'mon, I'll buy," he said, and she noticed that he was nervous, too.

They dried off and changed, and walked up the street. After
fumbling through ordering, the waiter quickly returned to their
sidewalk table with two sweating bottles of beer. Away from the
beach, the humidity plus the heat from the nearby cooking fire
was making sweat trickle down between her breasts and pool at her
lower back. She shifted in her seat, cooling her forehead with the
beer bottle.

In the diffuse light, she studied Joe's face. His cheeks had a fine
layer of stubble, but his jawline was as handsome as ever; his hair
had that casual shagginess that wasn't quite ready for a cut.

He caught her looking. "It's really good to see you, Lorna."

Lorna swallowed a nervous lump in her throat. Yes, it was . .
. good . . . to see him, too, but also . . . weird. "I still can't believe
you're here," she said in a shaky voice. "I . . . didn't think I would
see you . . . again."

"I didn't either." His eyes had changed. They were pleading with her. Like that moment he came to her door in Fiji. He had looked so relieved and completely focused. It was a wonderful, warm feeling to be looked at like that, she realized.

"Tell me about your travels," he said.

So she did, though sparingly. It felt strange to talk about it. She didn't have perspective, not yet. She told him a few stories—about being in charge of their camp's water purification in the Philippines using chlorine tablets that if handled incorrectly would have made chlorine gas and killed them all, dealing with a local hustler named Kibs in Sumatra in order to get back their delivery of antibiotics, and treating patients in Chile while the ground shook from powerful aftershocks.

"You should write a book," Joe said, listening in awe. "It sounds exciting, and meaningful."

Their food arrived: five tiny tacos piled with meat, onions, cilantro, and slices of avocado. The waiter also added a tray of several small jars of salsa and hot sauce. Lorna and Joe both tucked in.

"Did you quit the band?" she asked.

Joe had a mouthful of taco, and nodded. "Marty's still not over it."

Lorna smiled, thinking about Joe's friend. "How is Marty? Did his foot ever heal?"

Joe grinned. "Yep. He's good." He swallowed, took a sip of his beer. "He got married."

"Married?" Lorna paused to think about this.

"Yep. I tried to warn her, but she wouldn't listen." He winked at her.

Lorna focused on her food for a while. "It looks like you're pretty handy with a saw," she said. "Becca and Seth are lucky to have your help."

"I work in construction," he said with a shrug. "But they're the ones who've helped me," Joe said.

Lorna ate a bite of taco, its spicy heat burning her gums. "What do you mean?"

Joe sat back, wiped his lips. "There's a lot of money in Southern California, but the people are so into their image I can't even talk to them." A puff of heat from the barbeque enveloped their table. "Being here and helping your friends has reminded me that not all people are like that."

*Your friends*, Lorna repeated to herself, feeling a welcome twinge of belonging.

Joe sipped his beer again, draining it. "I quit the band and started building because, well, I thought I needed to get on with my life. But things didn't turn out the way I thought." He seemed to get lost in a memory, and Lorna waited, nibbling on another taco, and sipping her quickly warming beer.

"I should never have left you like that in Fiji," he said, looking at her with serious eyes.

Lorna felt a sudden warmth whoosh through her body. They had been so good together. She realized how much it still hurt and how much she still missed what they had started. "How did you even know I was here?"

"I didn't. I wanted to find you."

"Why?"

"Because I haven't been able to forget you."

Lorna let those words sink in.

"In Fiji, I didn't mean for it to be goodbye. I just couldn't understand why . . . I mean, my family is everything to me. It's taken me a while to realize that not everyone has a family like mine. That I'm lucky. My sisters and I and my parents, we're tight. There's nothing I wouldn't do for any of them."

Lorna struggled to stay in the warm glow he was creating for her, but she realized that what he was saying made it clear how different they were. There was no one in Lorna's life like that. Nobody to call when she needed help, no one to rely on.

"So when you said you weren't going to help your mom, I just, well, it just caught me off guard. But I had no right to judge you like that." He shook his head sharply, shuffling his feet as if he could stamp out his remorse. "I'm sorry."

Lorna tried to work out her feelings, but it was all so new. "I guess I shouldn't have left so fast either," she said, although she wasn't sure this was true.

"I should have offered to come here with you," he said, "but I was just too chicken." His eyes met hers briefly before looking away.

Lorna felt something shift inside her. But so much had happened since then, so much had changed. And it still hurt. *I wish things had been different, too*, she wanted to say, but the words wouldn't come. "So you just packed up and came here to wait for me?" she asked.

His face darkened.

Lorna's grin faded. "What?"

He looked at her, and she understood the expression that she hadn't been able to place before. Fear.

"What's wrong?" Lorna instinctively looked around them, at the lamp-lit street, the adjacent apartment building, at a passing car, its base thumping.

"A few months ago I got a phone call from a detective."

Lorna's skin prickled.

"He's trying to find Garth." Joe put down his taco, wiped his mouth. "He knew Garth and I had met in Fiji, and he knew you had, too. He somehow knew you and I had . . . " Joe seemed flustered. " . . . been together."

"He asked about me?"

Joe nodded. "He gave me his number. Asked me to pass it on to you if you contacted me."

The humidity felt like it was increasing by the minute. "Oh," was all she could think to say. Meanwhile her whole body felt like it was roasting on a stick.

Joe shook his head. "Seth tells me the detective was here after the hurricane."

Lorna pushed her food away. Her appetite had vanished. "I've wondered when it would happen. Or how. I've been waiting for it to happen, really. Everywhere I go I think about it."

Joe frowned. "Think about what?"

The tears spilled over her lids. "About what happened to Garth," she said.

Joe leaned forward, his eyes earnest. "You don't need to call this guy, okay? Everyone knows he's dead."

"But I know what happened. I was there," she said in a shaky voice. The film loop that played in her head started up again, but she couldn't find the words that went with it.

Joe sighed, seeming to struggle with something for a moment. "You don't owe him anything."

"But what about his family? If this detective is still looking for me, it means they still want answers. If it was my kid I'd want to know what happened."

Joe's expression hardened. "Sometimes the truth is more difficult to bear."

Lorna looked away, wiping her tears with the heel of her hand. Being here, in this village, with these memories made everything so sharp. She had been able to run away from it, push it to the back of her mind so that it was a diffuse, hazy sort of thing. But now, knowing there was someone searching, digging for the exact information that only she could provide renewed Garth's power over her. Her heart, which had seemed to open and fill with something other than pain and terror and hardship, snapped its doors shut once again.

Joe looked carefully at her, a question in his eyes. "Let his family keep their version of what happened to him. Your story won't help them," he said, reaching for her hand. "And it won't help you," he added.

After paying their tab, they walked slowly down the street. Joe stopped at the entrance to a brick building.

"Well, this is me," he said.

Lorna didn't want him to go. The restless, tingly engine purring in her belly didn't want him to go. "Do you want to sit on the beach for a little bit?" she asked.

Joe's eyes shot her a questioning—hopeful?—look. "Sure," he said.

Joe and Lorna walked to the slope of sand that led down to the water. The beach was dark, except for a shaft of light spilling from the streetlights through the gap between Ricardo's and the surf tours office.

Lorna thought the waves sounded louder than in the daylight. "It's steeper now," she said, paralleling the water's edge. An ocean wind cooled her face and arms.

"But the sand will get reworked, and it'll even out again. I mean, this place has seen storms before, and it's recovered. It just takes time."

Lorna nodded.

"Seth and I surfed this one place a few days ago. He called it *Punto de Cabra*. It was tiny but super fun. We were the only people there."

Lorna didn't know Punto de Cabra but figured it was a winter spot. A pang of longing stirred in her gut as she clicked through all the breaks she knew by heart. She wondered what it would feel like to surf again, after Las Muelas.

The waves broke and combed back along the coarse, storm-deposited sand. The rhythm was always there, washing in and out, and would always be there. She realized that the sound was mixed with her memories of Alex. *Whenever I need her*, she thought, *I can just listen.* A sensation of pain squeezed her chest, and she felt like she couldn't take a breath. Lorna realized that it was grief. *It's hard, but it'll kill you if you don't.*

"I thought I saw her today," Lorna said after the ache finally ebbed.

"Alex?"

Lorna nodded.

"I heard about how you took care of her."

Lorna thought of the sleepless nights, of the visits to the doctor's office to beg for meds. "It wasn't how I wanted it to be," she said. She pictured the moments on the boat. The two of them had been a team, heading out on their grand adventure. Their last. No matter what had happened after, Lorna knew that being able to give that to Alex had meant something. *To her and to me*, she thought.

"Things just got crazy," she said in a quaky voice. "I ended up running the business with Carlos and taking care of Alex, and she got sicker and sicker until . . . "

"I'm sorry she passed away." He peered at her. "It was brave of you to come. I mean, I know it must have been hard."

Lorna listened to the waves for a while, digging her toes into the cool sand.

"At least you got to say goodbye. A lot of people don't get that chance."

Lorna breathed in the salt and the clean air. The tingly, urging sensation had reached a full throb, and her heart seemed to be quickening. She wondered briefly if she might be having a panic attack, or some kind of heart palpitation.

Joe reached out to steady her. "You okay?" he asked.

Lorna stopped fighting the feeling that had been building inside her all day and looked into his eyes. They were serene and strong and hungry. He leaned close, and she kissed him. His lips were soft and tasted of spice. He kissed her back, a long and delicious kiss that reminded her of swinging in a hammock on a warm, sunny day. The humming engine in her belly was reaching a roar, and her blood was whooshing fast against her ears. He kissed her again, filling her with one burning purpose.

He pulled away, breathing hard. "I don't want you to think . . . "

She kissed him again, and it took him a long time to break away. Her skin felt electrified by desire. It was like she'd had an unending thirst that could finally be quenched.

" . . . that I came here because I wanted this."

"But you do want it, don't you?" she asked, fearing for a moment that she had mistook his kisses for something else.

"Yes," he said, kissing her lightly. "But I want it to be right."

Lorna kissed him, longer this time.

"I just want you to be sure," he said, his breaths fast.

She pulled out the key to the hotel. "I'm sure," she said.

# FORTY-EIGHT

Río Limón, Mexico

They made love again in the early morning, their hushed sounds mixing with the birdcalls and the soft waves lapping the shore. When Seth and Becca arrived at the hotel, the four of them tackled the tasks of the day: Lorna helped paint several rooms with Becca while Joe and Seth finished the roof. Between jobs Joe and Lorna found moments to be together—either a stolen kiss on the stairway or holding hands on their way to the kitchen, or meeting up in Lorna's room, or on the rooftop, which had been refurnished with two big, soft outdoor couches and chairs and a giant umbrella. By the end of the fifth day, Joe had moved into Lorna's room, and a rhythm to their days developed, the four them working side by side, and Joe and Lorna sneaking off together when they could. Sometimes they went out in the panga to surf or to look for deserted beaches, or to take a walk along the shore. Sometimes they watched Fie while Becca and Seth fetched supplies from the city. At the end of most every day, as the sun dropped low on the horizon, they all met up for a swim.

"Carlos called," Becca said one afternoon when they were all bobbing in the surf. Fie was wearing her alligator inner tube and big floppy sunhat. "He's going to come by in the morning."

"Okay," Lorna breathed.

That night, Lorna lay awake wondering what Carlos had in store for her.

"You want me to come along?" Joe asked, propping himself up on one elbow.

She stared at the ceiling for a moment. "I think it's better if I go alone."

"You're not scared of him, are you?" he said, caressing her bare hip.

"No," Lorna lied, the sensation of his touch stirring that same something inside her, that feeling of getting lost, of forgetting. She rolled to him and kissed her way down his neck, his chest, until he pulled her close and they were rocking together with the sea breeze cooling their skin and the cicadas buzzing in the trees, and she was crying out in release, in joy, and it wiped away thoughts of Carlos, Alex, and Garth, making them seem small, inconsequential, at least for a while.

The next morning, Lorna met Carlos on the curb in front of Ricardo's. He jumped out of the van to hug her, catching her by surprise. When he released her, his sharp black eyes gave her a long look.

*I've missed you*, she thought but could not say.

"Come," he said simply.

Lorna got into the van, and Carlos drove away from the town, turning a few times until they ascended a winding road. Between them a cup holder held two white paper cups and a clear plastic bag with pastries.

"Please," Carlos said, gesturing for her to eat.

Lorna a tentative sip of the hot coffee. *God, how I've missed good coffee*, she thought.

"I'm so glad you have come back."

"I'm sorry about—" she began.

Carlos waved her off.

"Where are we going?" she asked.

"You will see," he said with a twinkle in his eye.

They drove in silence for a while. "Becca tells me you'll carry on with the surf tours," she said.

Carlos nodded.

"I didn't hear about what happened to the boat," she said.

"It was lost," he replied.

Lorna imagined all the time and energy Carlos and Alex put into the *Pearl Shadow* only to have it play a part in her death.

"It was Alejandra's," Carlos replied easily. "I would not want to use it without her."

"But at least you could have sold it, or something," Lorna said.

"I don't think so," Carlos replied quickly, shaking his head. "Besides, there will be another boat. But this time we will keep it in Lazaro Cardenas."

Lorna blinked at him. "You mean, you're going back out there?" she asked.

"I cannot think as to why not," he said. "People have been calling. Asking. It is always how Alejandra thought it would go. This time it is better. Lazaro Cardenas has a big, deeper harbor. Lots of boats. We can keep it separate from Río."

Lorna thought about this. "Who's 'we'?"

"You, of course."

Lorna shook her head. "No," she said. "Find someone else."

"You are sure?" He snuck a glance in her direction.

"Yes," she said, and exhaled a shaky breath. She never wanted to see Las Muelas again—or Lazaro Cardenas, either, for that matter.

She remembered the shady doctor who had accused her of being an addict.

Carlos stopped in front of a grassy area surrounded by a tall metal fence—a cemetery.

"It is good you are here," Carlos said. "Alex will be happy."

The hairs on the back of Lorna's neck stood up. "Wait," she whispered. "Is this . . . " she trailed off. The cemetery was so silent and still. Carlos had opened the door and offered her a hand, but her body felt glued to the seat.

"I can't . . . " she said, her fingers trembling. She couldn't breathe.

"It is okay to be afraid," he said.

Finally, Lorna took his hand, and Carlos led her through an arched entryway and past tight rows of what looked like tiny houses topped with elaborate crosses. Each altar sat atop a long cement box several feet high. Some were covered with elaborate tiles and small planter boxes bursting with flowers. Glass candles and bouquets littered the sites, as if families made frequent visits. The pale dirt grounds were immaculate. Finally, they stopped in front of a white altar bathed in the early sun's pale glow. A pair of tiny birds chattered in the grass.

"With the sunrise," Carlos said, his pain clearly visible through his smile. "It is the best time of day." With that, he left her alone.

She panicked. "No!" she whimpered, wanting him to stay. The pain in her chest swelled, and she felt like she would burst. A wailing sound rushed from her lips, and she felt heavy. Her eyes stung with tears as she remembered paddling out next to Alex, her eyes alive and crackling with life. Lorna sunk to her knees and sobbed.

After a long time, Lorna returned to Carlos's truck, and he drove her back to Río Limón. He parked the truck and came around to say goodbye with a long, gentle hug.

"Go in peace, *Pajarito*," he said. "Alex died doing what she loved, with you. It is okay."

Time passed slowly, easily. Their days were filled with projects at the hotel, and in-between, when they weren't together, Joe played his guitar or met up with the kids who came down to the shore to play in the waves after school; sometimes Lorna went for long beach runs, sometimes a local would come seeking medical care—once, Lorna even delivered a baby. But Garth was always in her thoughts. Sometimes the nightmares would wake her, and she would be in Joe's arms, shaking. He would tell her that it was all right, that everything was okay.

But it wasn't. She would never be able to be free until she confessed to what she had done.

Each day, Becca, Seth, and Fie returned to their apartment for siesta, as if they could sense Joe and Lorna's desire to escape to the rooftop or their room. Once Becca had unexpectedly walked in on them—she had returned to the hotel and raced up the stairs where Joe and Lorna were enjoying one of the guest rooms.

"Are we weird?" Lorna asked Joe one such afternoon as they lay on the rooftop couch, naked and spent, watching the clouds pass above.

"Maybe," Joe answered. "Does it matter?"

They had talked about their lives, shared their dreams. Lorna wanted to finish her residency. Joe wanted to do something helpful, though he wasn't sure exactly what yet. Even though there were still so many holes in their plans, Joe was confident that everything would work out.

"The tours start up in two weeks," Lorna said. Becca had been on her computer all morning, having had Internet connection restored finally, in order to finalize the reservations.

"We could stay," Joe said. "There're jobs with Seth and Becca, and you said Carlos needs help."

Lorna shook her head. "I'll always want to come back," she said, thinking of the little altar at Alex's grave. "But I don't want to be here when the surfers come."

"Then maybe it's time we leave," he said, looking serious.

Lorna knew she was ready. "Where should we go?"

"How about Peru?" he joked.

Lorna couldn't hold it in any longer. "What about Garth?"

"What about him?"

They hadn't talked about Garth or the detective since that first night. It had been so easy to ignore the idea with Joe by her side. But Garth's family was waiting in agony, wondering. She was torturing them by not coming clean about what had happened. "There's just something I have to do," she said, as he began kissing her collarbone.

"Mmm," he said. "Me too." He made a trail of kisses down to her breasts.

Lorna's skin tingled. She wanted to tell him about what had happened at Las Muelas, but every time she did, she lost her nerve—either because she feared his rejection, or he said something important, or touched her in a way that made her unable to think straight.

Joe's fingers stroked her inner thigh. Then he was kissing her there, and her hips, already so eager for his touch, moved with him, arching in time with his caresses until the pleasure became almost unbearable, and she cried out from the joy and sweetness of what he was able to give her—hope and love and passion.

But then the tears came.

"What's wrong?" he said, his eyes full of compassion and worry.

Lorna listened to the waves lap the shore, trying to memorize the sound. Their time in Río Limón would stay with her forever, but she had to face the truth. "I called the detective," she said, closing her eyes tight so she wouldn't have to see his reaction.

"What?" he breathed.

"He's expecting me in two days. Garth's father will be there, too." In a shaky voice, Lorna told him about the café in the Acapulco mall.

Joe's eyes filled with worry. "Then I'll go with you," he said.

"No," Lorna wanted him to come, but she couldn't bear the thought of what it might do to him. "I need to go alone."

Joe sat up. "Why?"

"Because they might . . . take me away."

"Whoa. What in the world are you talking about? No one is going to take you away."

"It's my fault that he's . . . gone."

"How? Lorna, c'mon, you're scaring me."

"Because I left him out there," she said, remembering the loud surface chop chattering beneath Alex's surfboard, the gulls squawking above her, and the wave thundering in the distance.

"Out where?"

"Las Muelas."

Joe sighed. "Am I missing something here? None of this is making sense."

So Lorna told him about that day, about the wave and Alex and the boat and Garth. Joe listened, his eyes growing wide. When she was done, he held her for a long time. His skin smelled perfect, like river rocks drying in the sun. She tried to imprint the scent of him, so that it would stay in her heart forever.

"Lorna, you didn't cause this," he said, shifting to look at her. "He made the choice to go out there."

"But I left him!" she said. Why hadn't Garth taken the keys or tampered with the anchor? Something to keep her from abandoning him. *Because he trusted me*, she thought as her gut turned inside out. "What if he was there all along, and I just didn't see him?" Lorna said, swatting away tears. "The water was so dark. It was so hard to see!" her voice caught. She was losing control. Her lips felt rubbery, her blood pounded against her temples. She imagined Garth in the lineup watching her leave, his face contorting as he opened his mouth to yell NO!

"I should have refused to go out there," Lorna said, shaking her head, even though she never would have been able to deny Alex's last wish. And surfing Las Muelas had changed her. "I should have paddled back out to look for him," Lorna said.

"Then you'd be dead, too," Joe said in a hard voice. "You can let this go."

Lorna took a steadying breath. "I've tried to run from this. From him," she said, staring at the sky. All the worrying—looking over her shoulder, wondering when they would come for her—would never go away. "I can't run anymore."

And so Lorna found herself once again on a bus, but this time she wasn't alone. Joe refused to stay behind.

They found a hotel room in a sleazy tourist district close to the mall. The closest restaurant was Thai, so they ate there. That night, they huddled under their blankets in the air-conditioned room. As Lorna lay awake, listening to Joe's deep breathing, she sorted through her memories of the day at Las Muelas, rehearsing, she supposed, for the following morning. Alex was there in her mind, watching.

Lorna rose before dawn and silently gathered her things: passport, money, phone numbers, and slipped out the door. She remembered what Joe had said: *at least you got to say goodbye. A lot of people don't get that chance.*

She turned back to the door as her eyes filled with tears. "Goodbye," she whispered.

The mall was lit up so bright it hurt Lorna's eyes. The items for sale in the glass cases seemed foreign and completely superfluous. The metal hinges on the doors glistened with polish. The saleswomen wore silk shirts, lipstick, and were busy folding, tidying. The trashcans were shiny and empty, and there wasn't a speck of litter in sight. There was even a Starbucks, which made the sensation of being in the glitzy mall that much more unnerving.

Lorna found the café and had no trouble identifying Garth's father, who had white-blonde hair and jowly, red cheeks. He was wearing a yellow polo shirt, khaki pants, and boat shoes with no socks. His pale blue eyes were the same as his son's, and they bore into her when she approached the small metal table and cluster of ornately detailed metal chairs.

"Are you Lorna?" the man next to him said. His brown hair was edged with gray at the temples, and he was wearing a blue button-down shirt and dark slacks: the detective, Roger Bowker. Lorna eyed the three policemen clustered near the wall, each with a pistol on his hip. They were watching her carefully.

Lorna slid into one of the hard, cold chairs. "Yes," she said.

Roger Bowker introduced Garth's father, who did not offer to shake her hand.

"You said on the phone that you wanted to confess," Roger Bowker said.

Lorna took a deep, steadying breath and told them the story, doing her best to avoid crying, or begging, while Roger Bowker took notes, not interrupting once. When Lorna was done, her brain was buzzing and her mouth was dry. *It's relief,* she realized. *It's over.*

"I can't tell his fiancée this," Garth's father growled.

*Fiancée?* Lorna blinked at the thought of Garth committing to anything but the waves. "But it's the truth," Lorna said.

Garth's father gave her a sideways glance. "Did you love him?" he asked.

"What?" Lorna stammered. "No, I . . . " She stared at him in disbelief. She suddenly understood how his family would see her story. "We shared a connection," she said, stumbling with the words. "But it wasn't romantic." She realized that she did have feelings for Garth, but not in the way anyone else would understand. Lorna had spent plenty of time with someone just like him: Alex. Riding big waves was their calling; they were helpless to resist it. The two of them—Lorna too—had all been compelled to surf Las Muelas. She knew no one outside of that circle would understand why.

"I don't know what happened to him out there," Lorna said, "but he didn't come back."

Garth's father looked at her sharply. "And you think comin' here, tellin' me is going to help you feel better about it?" He rubbed his chapped hands together, making a sound like dry leaves rustling. "I'm not God," he said, standing.

Roger Bowker made eye contact with the police officers, who in three steps had boxed her in.

Lorna's look of alarm wasn't lost on the detective, who said, "Because you're an American, and the crime was committed in international waters—"

"Crime?" Lorna interrupted. Alarm bells were blaring somewhere in her mind.

Garth's father looked down on her with contempt. "Stay away from us," he said, and strode off.

"You'll need to go with the officers," Roger Bowker said, packing away his notebook and standing up to follow Garth's father. "The Towners plan to press charges. This is involuntary manslaughter. And there'll be a suit for wrongful death."

Lorna looked up at the officer standing by her side. "Manslaughter?" she said in a whisper as her palms began to sweat.

Lorna stood, and the officer wrapped his large hand around her bicep. The other officers filed in. *Crime. American. Wrongful death.*

Hearing a noise behind her, a kind of yelp, she turned, thinking Roger Bowker was yelling, but it was someone else.

The officers turned as well, and Lorna would remember later how smoothly they moved, how in control of the situation they appeared. Joe was sprinting toward them while looking at Lorna. He was speaking to her, but she couldn't hear him. It was like her ears had stopped being able to comprehend what he was saying. The police were pushing him back, and he was resisting, and there were tears in his eyes as he stared at her with that wounded, terrified look, and she tried to speak, tried to tell him that it was all right, that she had known this was how it would be. She wrestled against the officer and tried to get closer to him, so she could tell him that it was okay. She would do what they asked, and it would be all right. But there was a gun in the officer's hand, and someone was shouting, and people were staring. Then, her arm was wrenched behind her, and she was slammed down to the ground, her shoulder hitting something hard on the way. Lorna heard a sickening *pop* followed by a hot, white pain, and then nothing.

# FORTY-NINE

October 2008
Agate Beach, Oregon

Lorna finished stitching the filleted hand of a 300-pound Native American named Pickle. "Keep it clean and come back if you see any of the redness or pus we talked about, okay?" she instructed him.

Pickle nodded. "Thanks, doc," he said in an unusually high voice for someone so large. She knew he would return the next day with a freshly caught salmon. After running the community clinic for the past six months, she had a freezer full of salmon.

An hour later she closed the tiny hospital, a government-style building furry with green moss. She pedaled her bike towards the cabin, reviewing the day's patients in her mind. It had rained earlier in the day and the wet alder leaves shimmered like coins in the afternoon light. She stopped at her lookout and peered down at the tiny cove she sometimes surfed, watching a few sets roll in and crumble onto the rocky beach. Quickly she finished her ride home, stoked the woodstove, then suited up for a surf.

The police officer's aggressive takedown had posteriorly dislocated her left shoulder, and she had spent two days in agony waiting for medical attention, then surgery followed by two months in Mexico, first under guard in the hospital, then in physical therapy, all while trying to figure out the legal jaws that had closed around her. Joe had stayed by her side throughout the ordeal, researching her legal rights while she slept, and had become a drill sergeant in the rehabbing of her shoulder, which would never truly heal. Marty's father had a friend who specialized in international law. He had managed to get the legal charges against Lorna dropped. Joe and Lorna had been allowed to return to the States, but the wrongful death suit dragged on for almost two years. Because Lorna was a physician, the consequences had been dire. The Towner family demanded payment for the expenses they had incurred searching for Garth, plus damages. Her lawyer wanted to haggle over every penny, but Lorna gave in easily. If money could make them happy, she told him, let them have it.

She had denied the interview *Surfer Magazine* had hounded her for, but soon after, a smooth-talking woman representing an undisclosed client made her an offer for the location of Las Muelas. It had been a relief to tell the woman that she truly couldn't help her, no matter how much money they proposed. Everything had been in the journal, which the storm had taken. Carlos was the only one who had any true knowledge regarding Las Muelas, but she didn't tell the woman that. It would be up to him to decide how or if to publicize it.

Lorna had arranged to finish her residency at OHSU in Portland, even though switching states meant that she had to redo portions of her program. Joe had found a program in nonprofit management at Portland State. Oregon was still close enough to Joe's family and Marty and to her beloved Washington coast. Plus, there was no shortage of beautiful, wild beaches, forested mountains, and great waves.

Lorna picked her way carefully through the trees. It was dark inside the forest, but she knew the path by heart and descended steadily over roots and past ferns to the shore. On the beach, she built a new cairn for Garth next to the others. It hurt, but in a good way.

The waves in the cove were small but clean and the easy-gliding longboard rode them beautifully. She never tired of being in this water—whether the waves were two feet high or ten. Her shoulder's limited mobility meant that her shortboarding days were over, but she had grown to love the long, smooth glide of her longboard. Sometimes she heard Alex's voice inside her head, coaching her or poking fun. Now and then, Lorna thought she saw her sitting in the lineup, her white-blonde hair shining like silver, but it was just the light playing tricks. Lorna's heart always jumped—six months with the tribe had taught her a few things about ghosts—but in the end, she smiled. Maybe that was Alex's heaven, if there was such a thing: waiting for waves in a beautiful place, a safe place, knowing the next wave was yours to enjoy, to ride forever.

Lorna caught a wave and watched it rise up like a silken slope, its sheen turned pink by the fading sun. With the whitewater crowding her peripheral vision, she tucked low and sped forward until the wave collapsed in a cloud of whitewater.

A figure emerged from the forest dressed in a hooded black wet-suit. Lorna felt her heart fill with a deep, fluttery warmth as she watched the figure wade into the surf and paddle out.

"I'll never figure out why I agreed to this," Joe teased her as they met in the lineup, his eyes saying, "*Hi, I missed you,*" and hers replying, "*I missed you, too.*" He put his hands into his armpits and shivered. "I thought you didn't like cold?"

Lorna circled her legs in the chilly ocean. "Sometimes you have to let something go to find out what's important," she said. Every now and then she heard him play that song, about going over the falls, but there were new songs now, about crossing oceans and not having to say goodbye, and a love that can take you to the end of the world.

Joe looked at her, and the warmth that had begun when she first saw him spread to all the corners of her body. "You want this one?" he asked, eyeing a set.

"Yes!" she cried, swinging her board around with her good arm. Joe pivoted as well, and they raced each other, the wave drawing up behind them, its smooth blue face tipping, beginning to break. She dropped in just behind him, and he raced ahead, looking back in surprise to see that she was still there. They wove in and out of each other, laughing and tagging each other until the wave collapsed in a thump, knocking them both into the water.

Lorna came up sputtering, and looked for Joe who was standing in the shallows nearby holding his board, grinning at her. Another set wave feathered and broke, and the line of whitewater tumbled toward them. Just like it had for ages; just like it would forever.

Joe leaned over for a quick, cold-water kiss, his sparkly eyes alight with mischief, then lay prone on his board and paddled out, cresting the broken wave without breaking his stride. Lorna hopped onto her board, and followed.

# ACKNOWLEDGMENTS

So many people have helped make this book a reality. What began as a small idea became a concept that I couldn't forget, even though I tried many times. Thank you to my husband, Kurt, for supporting me from the very first moment the story formed in Fiji and for introducing me to surfing, which I love so much. Thank you to my parents. Even though I'm grown up, your support still means the world to me. For all things boat-related, a big thank you to Lt. Commander Jason Clodfelter, U.S. Navy. Thank you to Josh Henke, Flight RN, Dr. Leah Kiviat, and Dr. Jessie Knight for fine-tuning my medical knowledge; for the oncology details thank you, Dr. Ellen Chirichella. To Lillie Peery, many thanks for correcting my Spanish. For offering essential critiques of early drafts, I would like to thank Kari Hock, Janna Cawrse Esarey, Megan Chance, and Jeff Shelby. A heartfelt thanks goes out to my incredibly talented editor, Melanie Austin. And thank you to my daughters; for without you, the inspiration to tell this story wouldn't exist.

# ABOUT THE AUTHOR

AMY WAESCHLE is an author, professional editor, and wilderness medicine instructor for the Wilderness Medicine Institute. She is the author of *Going Over the Falls*, and *Chasing Waves, A Surfer's Tale of Obsessive Wandering*. Her stories have appeared in surfing and women's health magazines and publications such as *The Seattle Times*, *Sierra*, and *International Living*. When not writing, she works as an acquisition editor, fine-tuning manuscripts for publication. Amy graduated with a B.S. in Geology from the University of Washington, has a Masters in Teaching from Seattle University, and is a former National Outdoor Leadership School Field Instructor. She likes to surf, run mountain trails, travel, and spend time with her family. Amy and her husband live in Poulsbo, Washington with their two daughters. Contact her at amywaeschle.com and goingoverthefalls.com.